The House at Greenacres

DARCIE BOLEYN

The House at Greenacres

CANELO

First published in the United Kingdom in 2019 by Canelo

This edition published in the United Kingdom in 2020 by

Canelo Digital Publishing Limited
Third Floor, 20 Mortimer Street
London W1T 3JW
United Kingdom

A CIP catalogue record for this book is available from the British Library.

Print ISBN 978 1 78863 851 7
Ebook ISBN 978 1 78863 119 8

Look for more great books at www.canelo.co

Printed and bound in Great Britain by Clays Ltd, Elcograf S.p.A.

For my husband and children,
thank you for making our house a home.

Chapter 1

'Here we go...'

Holly Dryden took a deep breath, then placed her free hand on the heavy wooden door and pushed hard. It groaned loudly as it swung open, making her cringe, and the tiny bundle in her arms wriggled in protest at the noise.

'It's okay, Luke,' she whispered, before kissing the downy head then pressing him tighter to her chest. She closed the door, keeping her eyes down, delaying the moment when she would have to look at the scene she'd had nightmares about.

But eventually she had to look...

The flames of votive candles flickered in their red glass holders on a rack to her right, under the shadow of a large iron cross. Tall, heavy candles burned in stone holders fixed to the windowsills that ran the length of the building, and the air was thick with their liquid wax scent. The old stone church was full, the congregation mid hymn. Every pew was occupied by mourners in a uniform of black coats, trousers and skirts.

She made her way along the aisle, avoiding eye contact and keeping her son close to her body, until she reached the front.

Then she froze.

Because there it was.

The coffin that held the body of her grandpa.

Her legs weakened and she stumbled forward, her cry swallowed up as the organ chimed the final notes of 'How Great Thou Art'. All heads turned at once, and Holly felt the weight of every eye in the church upon her as she scanned the pews, hoping desperately for a space to squeeze into, however small. She felt lost, afraid and exposed, and the seconds that she stood there felt like hours.

'Holly!'

A figure emerged from her left, tall and broad in his dark wool suit, and Holly's throat closed up.

Dad…

He hurried towards her, wrapped a strong arm around her shoulders and led her towards the front pew.

'I didn't think you were going to make it,' he whispered, his familiar features etched with concern.

'I'm sorry. I got held up.'

A cough that travelled through the microphone at the altar and echoed around the church signalled that the service was about to begin. Bruce Dryden nodded his understanding at his daughter, then squeezed her hand. They'd have time to talk after the service, and she could explain then why she'd been late, why she'd almost missed the final farewell she'd ever get to say to her grandpa. Although of course she'd never really said farewell at all; she'd missed his last moments and the chance to say a proper goodbye.

–

'Thank you so much for coming.'

The phrase was repeated over and over as Holly's dad shook hand after hand, accepting condolences and nodding sombrely. Holly stood at his side, her arms around her baby son, her grandmother flanking her, smiling and nodding at people she knew and those she didn't recognize, aware that her grandpa, Henry Morton, had been a well-respected man, and that some of the congregation would have travelled far to attend his funeral in the old stone church set on a Cornish hillside. Some of the faces that passed made her determination not to cry waver, especially when Rich Turner's mother, Lucinda, paused in line and peered at little Luke. Holly knew that her ex-boyfriend's mother would be wondering if there was a chance the baby was his, and that wasn't a conversation she wanted to have at the moment. Thankfully Lucinda had offered a brief smile then moved on, but not before Holly had seen the burning question in her eyes.

Holly glanced at Granny Glenda, and the older woman squeezed her arm. Holly was full of admiration for Granny's bravery, for how she'd kept her pointed chin raised high throughout the service, and for how she was, even now, the epitome of elegance and composure as she shook hands with those who had known her husband of sixty-six years.

Finally the church had emptied out and the only people remaining were Holly, her dad, her granny and the elderly vicar.

'Thank goodness that's over,' Granny said, rubbing a shaky hand over her eyes.

'Are you all right, Mrs Morton?' the vicar asked.

'Yes, I'm just tired.'

'Can I get you anything?'

'No thank you. I'd like to get this day over with.' Granny pulled a lace-edged handkerchief from her sleeve and blew her nose, then tucked it away again. 'We need to get my granddaughter and great-grandson home. I suspect the baby will need a feed before long.'

Holly nodded, although she'd fed Luke just before the service, which was one of the reasons why she'd been late. Arriving outside the church right before his next feed was due had been poor timing, part of a morning of poor timing, with the train from Exeter being delayed, then the taxi driver taking the country lanes from the station to the church at a frustrating crawl. She had hoped to go to Greenacres first to drop off her suitcase, but it would have meant missing the service altogether, so instead she'd tucked it behind a bush around the side of the church, along with Luke's three-in-one pram with its detachable car seat. With it being such a quiet spot and a serious occasion, she hoped no one would think about taking her belongings, even if they did spot them. But then who would want a battered suitcase on wheels filled with her clothes – a lot of them maternity garments, since her body hadn't exactly pinged back into shape – and a pram that wasn't anywhere near top-of-the-range, as she'd been very careful with her money since leaving home?

'Ready, Holly?' Her dad slid an arm around her waist and pressed a kiss to the top of her head, just as he'd done since she was a little girl. It was such a caring gesture and she leant into him, glad to accept his comfort.

'I guess so.'

'Let's say goodbye to Grandpa, and then we can get you home.'

Holly followed her family out into the spring sunshine, thinking that going home to Greenacres sounded like a very good idea indeed.

–

Rich Turner drove through the green-hedged country lanes that he knew as well as the back of his hand. He'd been aware that this morning wouldn't be easy; had known that it would, in fact, be one of the hardest days of his life to date, but even so, seeing her after all those months, the same yet different, was just…

He swallowed hard.

My beautiful Holly.

Although she wasn't his any more, was she? He'd always thought Holly was far too good for him: intelligent, pretty, popular, funny and out of his league. But she'd liked him; loved him, and he hadn't been able to believe his luck. How many people were fortunate enough to fall in love with their best friend?

Then he'd ruined it all and pushed her away. And now she had a baby; probably a boyfriend or even a husband too. Unless… unless the baby was his. Was it possible?

A tractor coming towards him snapped him from his thoughts and he pulled in to allow it to pass. You couldn't afford to lose your concentration for a second in these Cornish country lanes; it could be fatal. He lowered the windows and let the country air enter the car. It was sweet, fragranced with the aromas of grass and flowers and the heady undertones of the rich, fertile earth. It was a familiar and comforting smell that grounded him, and he'd missed it when he'd been away.

Once the tractor had passed, he continued through the lanes until the hedges opened out and before him lay one of the most beautiful views in the world. He had seen some sights over the past eight months, but nothing compared to the place where he'd grown up, the place where he'd fallen in love. If only he'd known how important it was before he'd left and made the second biggest mistake of his life.

The fields spread out in front of him, green and luscious following a mild winter and the spring rains, a pretty patchwork of emerald, avocado, olive and pea… so many shades of green. Then there were the bright-yellow fields full of rapeseed, like golden squares breaking up the green, promising a season of plenty for the Cornish farms. The grey road weaved around the fields like a snake, descending gradually until the big old house at Greenacres came into view. It was Holly's childhood home and a place Rich had spent a lot of time in over the years; one that held many memories.

Surrounding the house were the barns and winery where the wine was manufactured and stored, along with the small shop that Holly had run, then the rows and rows of vines, the lifeblood of the vineyard. It was a breath-taking sight and one that Rich knew he hadn't always fully appreciated. Perhaps it was his heightened senses, tingling with nerves and anticipation, that made it all the more beautiful today.

After another five minutes, he indicated left, then drove through the open gate, underneath the sign that read: *Greenacres House and Vineyard – Fine Cornish Wines*, and made his way along the gravel pathway until he reached the house. He parked around the side of the building and cut the engine.

It appeared that no one else from the funeral party had arrived yet. Rich had sneaked out of the church early, but he knew that Glenda Morton had hired caterers for the wake, so the house would be open. He'd head on inside and see if he could make himself useful. It was the least he could do, especially at a time like this. Especially after what he'd done last year...

–

Holly pushed Luke's pram along the uneven path, following closely behind her granny and her dad. The vicar had gone ahead with the caretaker of the graveyard to ensure that everything had been prepared.

Holly focused on Luke, settled now in his car seat, which clipped on to the lightweight frame. She'd wrapped him up warmly, despite the sunshine, because a breeze had picked up and it was spiked with the cooler air that swept in across the Atlantic. A lifetime spent in north Cornwall meant that Holly knew how chilly the winds could be. She certainly wasn't going to allow her three-and-a-half-month-old baby to suffer because of the cold.

'Are you ready, Glenda?' the vicar asked as they reached the end of the path.

'As ready as I'll ever be.' Glenda Morton gave a wry laugh, and Bruce took her hand, tucking it into the crook of his arm, then led her across the wooden boards that had been laid over the grass to enable them to access the graveside.

Holly followed them, parking the pram to one side and pushing down the brake. She peered at Luke, gathering strength from his innocent beauty and her deep love for him, then went to join her family.

As the vicar spoke, she found herself tuning out, his solemn words drifting away on the breeze like puffs of cloud. Instead, she was acutely aware of the hard boards beneath her feet, the bright green of the fake grass covering the mounds of soil either side of the grave, the rich brown hue of the earth and the fact that her grandpa lay in the mahogany box that had been lowered into the hole. She felt as though she should be screaming or crying hysterically like people sometimes did in movies, but the situation was surreal and she felt detached from it – practically numb.

Because, of course, this couldn't be happening.

Only eight months ago, Grandpa Henry had already been in a slow decline – he had been succumbing to dementia for a while – but he'd still been so big, so broad and so loud. Gosh, he'd been loud, his laughter and his booming voice capable of filling the house and travelling across to the barns, the vineyards and beyond. He had been filled with a zest for life, so convinced that his way was the right way, and had steadfastly refused to change how he ran the vineyard; had denied Bruce the chance to bring in new methods or machinery, or to embrace new ways of promoting their wines, insisting that change would destroy the equilibrium that had existed so well for so long. He had been a stubborn old man, and Holly found it hard to believe that he would have let death claim him.

She wiped at her cheek, then looked at her hand. It was wet. Tears were streaming from her eyes and she hadn't even realized. She wasn't as numb to her loss as she had believed. She'd been lost in her memories, in her love for a man who had been at once admirable and intimidating, a man she had loved deeply yet feared disappointing as her mother once had. Yet the reason had been the same – an unplanned pregnancy for an unmarried mother. It was one of the reasons why she had not returned in time to say goodbye, one of the reasons why she had missed his final months at the vineyard. If he had known about her pregnancy, and then about Luke, she didn't think he would have taken it well. Her mum and dad had married quickly when they'd found out they were expecting her, but getting married hadn't been an option for Holly, even if she had wanted to. However, she didn't know if she could ever forgive herself for failing to say goodbye to her grandpa, even though, deep down, her reasons for staying away had been down to more than an unplanned pregnancy.

The vicar finally fell silent and Holly watched Glenda drop a single red rose into the grave, then press her hand to her heart. It made the lump in her throat expand and she inhaled shakily, trying to prevent any more tears escaping. She must already look enough of a mess, and she worried that her own emotion would be her grand-mother's undoing. But as Granny turned to her and saw her distress, she opened her arms. Holly leant into her embrace and hugged her tight, breathing in the lily of the valley perfume that had always reminded her of spring mornings, the flowers' verdant foliage dressed with morning dew. It was so familiar, evoking a whole host of memories and emotions, that the final silken thread of her strength broke and she sobbed in Glenda's arms.

When she managed to compose herself, she looked up and met her granny's pale green eyes surrounded by bright white eyelashes.

'It's all right to be upset, Holly. Goodness knows I've cried my fair share of tears this past few months.' Glenda wiped Holly's tears away with her thumbs, then kissed her cheeks. 'But it was Grandpa's time to go, my sweetheart. He was very tired and it was painful to watch his struggle. We have to remember, though, that he was a good man and he loved us all, and now we will go on for him. You…' she looked over at the pram, 'and that beautiful baby boy are his legacy.'

Holly nodded, then accepted a tissue from her dad. As she wiped her eyes and her cheeks, and blew her nose, her granny shook the vicar's hand and spoke quietly to him. When she rejoined them, they made their way over the boards and back to the path.

'Shall we go and see Mum?' Holly asked. It had been over eight months since she'd been to her mother's grave, and the yearning to do so now was overwhelming. Visiting the place where her mum had been buried gave her a sense of connection that she had missed terribly.

'Of course.' Her dad released the brake on the pram and they walked the short distance to the grave. Her grandparents had reserved their plot many years ago, but Holly's mum's passing had been sudden and unexpected, following her shock diagnosis with breast cancer when Holly was fifteen. Bruce had requested a particular plot for his wife near a large old oak tree that overlooked the fields, and beyond them, the sea. He had told Holly that her mum would have liked the view.

When they reached the grave, Holly gazed down at the headstone, then leant forward and pressed a hand to the cold marble.

'Hi, Mum, I'm back. And I've brought your grandson to say hello.'

Chapter 2

Holly entered the kitchen at Greenacres with her granny holding onto her arm. Her father was in front of them, carrying Luke in his car seat, and she was relieved that her son was sleeping soundly after the car journey to the vineyard. She needed some time to take stock and found it hard to concentrate on anything else when Luke was awake and in need of attention.

Two women from the catering team bustled around them, offering polite smiles as they removed trays from the oven and set small pasties and pies onto large trays that they carried through to the dining room.

'I'll pop the kettle on, shall I?' Bruce asked, and Holly noticed his eyes wandering over her granny's face. She had turned very pale.

'Granny? Are you all right?' The question seemed ridiculous in light of Glenda's loss.

'I'm fine, dear. Except... it hit me that Grandpa is never coming home again.' She sighed, long and low, seeming to hunch over with the weight of her knowledge. 'And yet the strangest thing is that another Morton heir has just entered our home. Little Luke has come to fill the void your grandpa left behind.' She blinked hard, and Holly looked away, her own vision blurring at her granny's sentiment.

'Yes, you're right.' Bruce smiled down into the car seat. 'Luke has come to help us through our loss and to take us into the future. Nothing like a baby to keep you moving forward.'

'I could do with that cuppa now, Bruce, please.' Granny released Holly's arm, then removed her black wool coat.

'Your room's ready for you,' Holly's dad said. 'I got your old cot down from the attic and cleaned it up, and Granny insisted on ordering a few things to make it comfortable for Luke. Since she learnt how to shop online, we're always having deliveries!' He shook his head. 'Anyway, everything should be there, but let me know if you need anything else. I can always pop into town.'

'Thanks, Dad. I'm sure it will be fine.'

'I'll get the kettle on, then bring your suitcase up from the car.'

Holly took the car seat from him and walked through the kitchen and the dining room. She smiled at some of the mourners who'd come for the wake but gestured at Luke in his car seat to let them know that she needed to take him upstairs. She suspected that more people would arrive within the hour, having stopped off at home or even the pub first, and that some would already be in the cosy lounge.

Entering the house had been an assault on her senses as familiar sights, smells and sounds rushed to greet her, but she'd tried to maintain her composure for her grandmother's sake, although when Granny had made the comment about Luke taking Grandpa's place in the household, she had struggled not to break down completely.

The big old house hadn't changed a bit in the months she'd been away, but then she hadn't expected it to be any different. The same aroma of woodsmoke and baking hung in the air, the house still creaked and groaned as the wind moved around it outside and sneaked through the gaps around the white sash windows, and the decor hadn't altered since Holly had first entered the house in her mother's arms, fresh from hospital – she'd seen the photographs to prove it. Only... it *was* different now, because Grandpa was gone. His deep voice used to echo through the hallways, his loud laugh bounced up the stairs, and his anger caused the floorboards to vibrate when he unleashed it. Which wasn't often, thankfully, but he had been a strict man with old-fashioned values, as well as unrelenting in his pursuit of what he believed was the right way to raise a family and conduct his business.

Holly had grown up well aware of these facts. She had loved him – how could she not, when he had such a good heart? – but she had also feared him, and the idea of letting him down. The fact that she had been conceived before her parents married had been a family secret, as if it was something to be ashamed of, but Holly had been aware of it from an early age. She'd heard her mum and grandpa arguing one day, Grandpa ranting about his daughter disappointing him. Her mum's reply had been sharp and quick: she had given him a beautiful granddaughter; how could he claim to be disappointed with that? Holly had loved to hear her mum debate with people. She had been so intelligent and articulate, and even Grandpa had been forced – on more than one occasion – to swallow his words. Holly didn't think she was as brave as her mum had been, which was one of the reasons why she'd run away. She hated conflict, and in that way, she was more like her dad than her mum. Bruce tended to bite his tongue and walk away rather than get involved in an altercation, but Holly found that just as admirable; sometimes it took more strength of character to walk away than to stand and fight. Her parents had been so different and yet so perfectly matched, and she loved them both dearly.

If only her mum hadn't passed away when she was so young. Too young to lose her. Too young to know how to cope with saying goodbye.

She climbed the stairs, then turned left and walked along the wooden floorboards of the corridor, passing the closed door of her dad's bedroom and the door to the right that led to one of the two family bathrooms. At the other end of the landing, directly opposite Holly's room, was her grandparents' bedroom, and next to it, their bathroom.

She turned the handle and pushed at her bedroom door, expecting it to groan on its hinges as it swung inwards, but it didn't make a sound. Another thing to thank her dad for, no doubt – he'd had the foresight to oil the hinges in order to avoid them disturbing her son.

She set Luke's car seat down on the floor at the end of the double bed. Her room was as she'd left it, a mixture of teenager and twenty-something, with band stickers all over her built-in wardrobe doors – from Madonna to Whitney to Bryan Adams – and posters on the walls featuring Leo and Kate in that iconic pose from *Titanic*, and Sarah Michelle Gellar in her classic *Buffy the Vampire Slayer* stance. The shelves on the wall still held her books, and she gazed at their spines, reading the familiar titles: *Pride and Prejudice*, *Salem's Lot*, volumes on business law that she'd bought back in her teens when she was considering a career in that direction. She shook her head at her younger self, at the naïve girl she'd been before her mum had died, before life had changed for ever.

Growing up, Holly had been filled with a zest for adventure that her mum had nurtured, and had believed she'd travel far and become a successful lawyer. But when her mum died, it was as though the spark in Holly was doused, and the idea of straying from Greenacres suddenly seemed terrifying. It was, she knew now, a perfectly natural reaction to her loss, but at the time, she had thought fear would rule her life. Time had helped her to overcome her grief, of course, but she had never been the same. Her plans to go away to university to study business law – which she aimed to use to help her family and other small businesses – were abandoned. She sat her GCSEs and A levels, achieved good grades and had unconditional offers from three universities – in London, Bath and Cardiff – but when it came down to choosing one, she decided not to go.

Her dad and grandmother had tried to encourage her to leave and experience a different life, to expand her horizons, but her grandpa had been happy to keep her close. He'd told her once, not long after she'd declined all three universities, that he was glad she'd stayed at Greenacres. He'd lost his daughter and didn't want to lose his granddaughter. Holly had been happy to have his approval, as it made her decision feel justified. Instead of leaving, she had focused on running the shop at Greenacres and helping out in the vineyard, on being a good daughter and granddaughter and on enjoying a simple life near the village of Penhallow Sands. It had taken something big to make her leave her childhood home, and when she had made the decision to go, she hadn't known if she would ever return.

The large bay window in Holly's bedroom overlooked the rear garden and the fields that lay beyond. It was a beautiful view and one that she had spent hours gazing at. Her heart fluttered as she looked at it now. Eight months away and such a lot had happened in the meantime; the view was the same, but the family had changed. It would never be the same again.

This room had seen so much as Holly grew into a woman: tears, anger and laughter, excitement and love. She flopped onto the bed and ran her hands over the patchwork bedspread that her mum and granny had made for her before she was born. Soft and worn, it had been a constant in her life even when other things had changed. She'd wrapped it around her to keep warm on frosty nights, sobbed into it when she'd been grounded as a young teenager for going night swimming with a group of friends, and later on, when she'd lost her mum. Then, last year, when she'd known that she'd lost Rich too. The bedspread had stayed here when she'd left, almost as if it were waiting for her to return. It might only be a blanket, but her mum had helped make it, and had done so with love for the child that was growing in her belly. Holly knew now how it was to love a child, and how awful it would be to have to leave the world before that child was fully grown.

The fluttering in her chest grew into a pain so red hot that she gasped and sat upright. She couldn't do this at the moment, didn't have time to grieve for her mum right now. She was home and she had a responsibility to be there for her granny and her dad. Today of all days. But coming home with her own child made her wish more than ever that her mother was here to greet them. Mum would have loved Luke, and knowing that she would never see him was devastating.

She stood up and walked around to the cot that her dad had placed on the other side of the bed. It was pine, with a drop-down side, crafted by her talented grandfather. She'd heard the story numerous times about how Grandpa had worked late into the night in the weeks before she was born. He'd been determined to get the finish right, to ensure that no rough edges remained to hurt his precious grandchild when she arrived. The beautiful elaborate carvings on the outside of the cot were of vines and grapes, representative of the business that he would one day pass on to the Morton heir. Grandpa had been dedicated to his family, expecting no less of everyone else than he did of himself. Whether he had expected to have more grandchildren after Holly was something he never mentioned; Holly knew that her parents had wanted more children but it had never happened. So she had remained an only child, adored and showered with love and attention.

The cot was already made up with a new mattress, a clean fitted sheet and soft wool blankets. Holly lifted Luke gently from his car seat and laid him on the bed. She removed his jacket and deftly changed his nappy, holding her breath when his eyelids flickered open and a frown passed over his smooth forehead, worried that she'd wake him. When he was dressed again, she placed him in the cot and covered him with a blanket. She watched as he tried to settle himself, but the smells and the mattress were unfamiliar, so she fetched his soft bunny from the car seat and tucked it in next to him, knowing it would be of comfort.

There was a quiet knock at the open door and her dad came in.

'Your suitcase,' he whispered, placing it on the floor next to the car seat. 'I've put the pram base in the cupboard under the stairs.'

'Thanks. I'll be down once he's settled properly.'

He nodded, then tiptoed over to the cot and gazed down at Luke. A wave of love swept over Holly. Bruce Dryden was such a big man and yet so gentle; he had been a kind and caring father and she knew she was lucky to have him. He had been her grandfather's polar opposite in many ways: the calm to his storm on numerous occasions. Holly had never clashed with her father over anything; instead, it had been Grandpa who'd evoked the teenage angst and rebellion in her. It had been Bruce she'd told about her pregnancy, and who'd come to see her and Luke, bringing what he could spare to help them out, offering love and support and trying to encourage Holly to return to the vineyard, though not before she was ready, of course. He had been supportive and never judgemental, understanding and never expectant.

Now she stepped closer to him and hugged him tight, wanting him to know how precious he was and how grateful she was for his love. When she released him, he kissed her forehead, then quietly left the room.

Holly pulled the baby monitor from her suitcase. The first one she'd bought had been a video monitor, but then she'd watched a documentary about people who knew how to tune into the unsecured video links and were able to spy on babies and their families. It had scared her into binning it and replacing it with an audio one. Even if someone could hear her and Luke, at least they couldn't watch them.

Once the monitor had been plugged in and the receiver tuned, she closed the curtains and left the room, pulling the door behind her. If Luke woke and needed her, she could be with him in seconds, but she had a feeling that the train journey and the busy morning had tired him out, and that he'd sleep for a while.

–

Rich had been circulating at Henry Morton's wake for an hour, pouring drinks and directing people to the kitchen and the downstairs toilet, as well as the back door if they wanted somewhere to smoke or vape. He'd been tempted to have a beer but wanted to keep a clear head for when he saw Holly, though her failure to put in an appearance so far had made him start to wonder if she'd actually turn up.

'Wine?' He held up the bottle of red he was carrying and filled the proffered glasses.

Moving on, he found himself with his parents, Lucinda and Rex, who were talking to Catherine Bromley, the deputy head teacher of the local primary school. Catherine declined wine, but Rich's mother held out her glass. His father was drinking coffee, his lips set in a thin line. Rich knew that their own memories would be haunting them right now; how could they not after what they'd been through? And yet they stood there, dressed in their smart black clothes, making polite conversation and refusing to allow their pain to drag them away from showing their respects to a man who'd been a pillar of the warm Cornish community.

Rich listened to them for a while, glad of the distraction, but when Catherine started talking about league tables and literacy strategies, he tuned out and moved on. She had been in his year at school and she'd been a pleasant girl, but always so serious. As a teenager, she'd preferred to stay home, do her homework and keep her mother company rather than going out or dating anyone. Her mother had been in her forties when she'd had her, and some of the kids had teased her about that, but if it bothered her, she never let on. Rich had found it strange that Catherine didn't seem to want a social life, but when he'd asked her about it once, she'd replied curtly that she wanted a good career and that she wouldn't let having fun get in the way of that. He had always admired how single-minded and determined she was, but also wondered if she ever let her hair down.

He realized that the bottle of wine he was holding was empty, so he returned it to the kitchen and put it with the others for recycling. His shoulders were tight and the tension was spreading through the rest of his body. More than anything he wanted to get out for a walk in the fresh air, but now wasn't the right time. He'd go later, if he had a chance. This level of tension couldn't be good for anyone.

A familiar voice carried through from the dining room, bringing a rush of sensations and emotions that made him breathless: a first kiss in the rain, the taste of bubblegum on her pale pink lips; the swish of her waist-length golden hair as she turned; the feel of her against his naked chest, her skin warm from the sun as they lay on the sand; the pain in his heart that day when she'd turned and walked away...

Holly was here.

At last.

—

Holly smiled politely, shook hands and accepted kisses on her cheeks, all the while holding tightly to the baby monitor. She knew from past experience that wakes weren't easy to get through and had vowed to leave instructions not to hold one when she passed. She wanted to spare her loved ones the awkwardness, the expense and the exhausting rounds of socializing and sharing stories that these events demanded. Losing someone was hard enough without having to put on a show of strength afterwards.

She knew some people found it helpful, that ultimately it was a celebration of the person's life, but after losing her mother so young, Holly struggled to deal with anything that reminded her of that awful time. Just when she thought she'd put her loss behind her and was dealing with life well, something would happen and she'd end up grieving all over again. Losing her mum before she'd even turned sixteen had left a huge hole that no one had been able to fill. Her dad, granny and grandpa had tried to help her, and they'd been wonderful, especially as they were dealing with their own grief too, but Holly and her mum had missed out on so much, and nothing could ever change that.

Since Luke had arrived, death seemed even more terrifying, because he needed her and she wanted to be there for him for as long as possible. Becoming a mum had brought her such joy, but it had also opened up a chasm of vulnerability that hadn't been there before. Holly was no longer responsible only for herself but also for another tiny human being; she was the most important person in his life right now and she was convinced that no one could ever love him as much as she did. Except, perhaps, for his father…

'Holly.'

Her name, uttered from between those perfect lips. Sending a shiver up and down her spine. Creating sensations at her core that sent her reeling. The last time she'd seen him had been so dreadful.

'Rich.'

Their eyes met, and it was all she could do not to throw herself against his chest and sob, then pound it with her fists until she'd released the pain she'd carried for what felt like a lifetime.

'I'm… sorry for your loss, Holly.'

She licked her lips, gripping the monitor tightly in front of her as if it could protect her from pain. 'Thank you. I can hardly believe he's gone.'

'Me neither. It doesn't seem right somehow. He was always here, and part of me thought he always would be.' Rich shook his head. 'Would you like a drink?'

She nodded and followed him through to the kitchen, her heart pounding and her throat tight with emotion.

'Wine?' he asked, holding up a bottle.

'No thanks. Something else. Not alcohol.' She pushed her hair behind her ears, aware that he was gazing at it. The last time she'd seen him, it had still been long; she'd had it cut after having Luke. She was used to it now, but it probably looked strange to Rich.

'Lemonade?'

'Please.'

She placed the baby monitor on the table and watched as he opened two cans, then poured the lemonade into glasses before handing her one.

'Thanks.' She stared down at her glass, willing the whooshing of blood through her ears to stop, wanting words to come that would not cause hurt or pain, sound bitter or strangled. This wasn't about her or Rich now; it was about their son and what was best for him.

'How are you?' Rich asked. 'You've had your hair cut. It suits you.'

'Thanks.'

A murmur from the monitor made her pick it up again and watch for the lights that flashed at any noise Luke made.

'Is that a baby monitor?'

'Yes. Luke's in my room.'

'Luke? That's the baby's name?'

She ran her gaze over his face, but it remained expressionless. Only his eyes betrayed his emotions, his deep, dark eyes.

Did he know? Had he guessed?

'How... how old is he?'

'Three and a half months.'

Now Rich frowned, and she knew he was trying to work out if Luke could be his, but she'd left the previous summer not knowing she was twelve weeks pregnant, and Luke had been born early, at thirty-three weeks. Would he ask her, or had he decided that her grandfather's wake wasn't the time or place for such an intimate conversation? Or did he have no idea? Did it hurt him that she had a child he might believe wasn't his? Worse still, what if he didn't want to find out?

He raised his glass and sipped his drink, his face etched with uncertainty. 'Is he... I don't know how to ask this, really, but... is he mine?'

She had to tell him and it had to be now. It had been too long already.

'He is yours,' she blurted, then held her breath, watching as myriad emotions passed over his face. She'd wanted to break it more gently, but they might only have minutes alone and she couldn't bear to keep it from him any longer.

'He's mine?' he squeaked eventually.

'Yes. Do you need to sit down?'

He shook his head.

'I'm a dad?'

'Yes.'

'Why didn't you tell me before... before you... before I... before...' He was shaking his head, his eyes shining and his breath coming in shaky gasps.

'I'm so sorry, but I didn't know I was pregnant when I left. I cut off all social media and changed my mobile number, so I had no way of contacting you. I was so angry, I couldn't bear to keep any links between us.'

He dragged his hands through his hair. 'I did the same.'

'You did?'

'So even if you had tried to contact me, you'd have struggled. Damn it, Holly, what have we done?'

They gazed at each other for a while as their confessions hung in the air between them. Exhausted, Holly pulled out a chair at the kitchen table and sank onto it, then Rich did the same.

'You know… I never imagined we could end up like this.' His voice was tinged with sadness.

'Like what?'

'Like strangers.' He looked down at his feet, exhaled, and raised his eyes again. 'We're parents. I have a son I didn't know about. I thought we'd be…'

'Yes?'

'I thought—'

'There you are!'

Holly jumped as a hand landed on her shoulder and she turned to find her old friend Francesca Gandolfini smiling at her.

'Fran!' Instinctively she got up and hugged her friend, but the hug she received in return was stiff and formal.

'Good to see you, Holly, although I'm really sorry it's in these circumstances.'

'Thank you.' Holly tried to pull herself together, to focus on what Fran was saying, but it was hard when all she wanted to do was continue her conversation with Rich. They couldn't leave it like this. She realized Fran was staring at her, so she shook herself. 'I guess eighty-eight is a good age, but even so… is it ever time?'

'I don't think so.' Fran shook her head. 'I know my grandmother says she feels the same at seventy-eight as she did at eighteen. She Skyped me yesterday and was going on about how her body is letting her down because she can't run up the stairs any more but her mind's as sharp as ever.' She smiled.

'Your grandmother Skyped you?'

'Oh yes!' Fran nodded, causing her silver and amethyst earrings to sway. 'Since Dad went back out to Italy, he's got Nonna Gandolfini using every technological device possible. She's madly in love with her voice-activated virtual assistant.' Her dark blue eyes twinkled.

'I'll have to see if I can get Granny to try out some new technology. Dad said she loves online shopping, but I don't think she's tried video calls yet.' Holly tried to picture her granny using Skype or FaceTime, but it wasn't easy.

'You should.' Fran sipped her wine. 'How long are you back?'

Holly glanced at Rich, then back at Fran, two of the people she'd cared about most in the whole world but who were now like strangers. She'd been away for less than a year, yet it could have been a lifetime for the gulf it had created between them.

'I'm not sure.' She didn't want to commit to anything yet, had tried not to make any decisions.

'And you have a baby?' Fran frowned, hurt clouding her eyes.

Heat crawled up Holly's throat and into her cheeks.

'Yes.'

'Well that's something you kept to yourself.'

Holly winced at Fran's bluntness, but she knew her friend was right. They'd been so close, but she hadn't contacted Fran at all while she'd been away.

'Uh… I'd better be going.' Rich stood up and shifted from one foot to the other while running a finger under his shirt collar. Panic filled Holly. He couldn't leave now, not when they had so much to discuss.

'Can't you stay for a while?' she asked, hating the desperation in her tone. But she wanted to get this over and done with, couldn't bear the thought of it hanging over her for another hour, let alone another day or longer.

'I can't. I'm sorry. I need… some time to think.' He stared at her hard and she understood. He needed to process what she'd told him before he did anything. It was a shock for him, of course it was, and coming on the back of their difficult break-up and subsequent estrangement…

'I'll see you soon?' she asked, filling her eyes with meaning.

'Yes. Let me give you my number and you can text me yours.'

He scribbled on the back of an envelope that was propped up next to the kettle, then handed it to Holly.

'It's good to see you, Rich.' Fran smiled. 'Your mum said you've been busy with a new job.'

'Yes. That's right. With an accountancy firm in Newquay. We'll have to catch up.' He turned to Holly. 'I'll see you soon. The sooner the better, I think.' He gave her a small nod, then walked away.

Holly bit down on her bottom lip. Too many things were happening here and she didn't know which fire to try to extinguish first. Rich was absolutely bewildered at the bomb she'd dropped on him, and although Holly was still mad as hell at him for what he'd done last summer, she also felt guilty that he'd been oblivious to Luke's existence. On top of that, Fran was clearly still smarting from being abandoned. Holly had made such a mess of everything, and she felt like running up to her room, slamming the door and hiding under the duvet. But that was something for her teenage self; she was an adult now and she had to face up to what she'd done.

'Fran… I know I owe you an explanation. I'm so sorry for running off and not contacting you.'

Fran sipped her drink, eyeing Holly over the top of her glass.

'I'm just glad you're all right,' she said eventually. 'You're one of my oldest friends and I care about you.' She ran her free hand over her short red-brown hair, then sighed. 'I can't believe you have a baby and I didn't know anything about it. Is it a boy or a girl?'

'A boy.'

At that moment, the lights on the monitor flickered and Luke let out a squawk.

'And it seems he's hungry. Want to meet him?'

Fran nodded enthusiastically.

'Come on then.'

As Holly weaved through the bodies in the dining room, then climbed the stairs to her old room, she let the guilt settle on her shoulders. Running away had seemed like the only option last summer, but now that she was back, she had some bridges to build.

She just hoped her friends and family would be able to forgive her.

Most of all, she hoped Rich could cope with the information she'd just divulged, because if he couldn't, she had no idea where to go from here.

Chapter 3

'He's beautiful!' Fran smiled as Holly lifted her son out of the cot.

'*I* think so, but then I'm biased.'

'How old is he?'

'Fourteen weeks.'

'So is he…' Fran bit her bottom lip and Holly knew what her friend wanted to ask.

'He is. I've just told Rich… He didn't know before. It's complicated, but we haven't had a chance to speak about it properly yet, so please—'

'Of course I won't say anything. It's not my place to. But then… you must have been pregnant when you left?'

'I was but I didn't know it. Because of my polycystic ovaries, I rarely had periods anyway, so I had no idea anything was wrong. I felt a bit under the weather but blamed a cold, then the stress of me and Rich breaking up. Look, I need to make Luke a bottle, so let's get him downstairs and we can talk more.'

Fran squeezed Holly's arm. 'We won't have an opportunity to talk downstairs. As soon as people see Luke, they'll be all over you like a rash. Let me give him a cuddle now and we can get together at the weekend or something and have a proper chat.'

Holly handed Luke over, and Fran cooed at him until he grabbed hold of one of her earrings.

'Here, let me help you.' Holly gently prised Luke's fingers from the antique silver drops, then took him back. 'He clearly likes your choice of jewellery.'

'He has good taste then.' Fran chuckled. 'Don't fancy having my ears torn in half, though.' She removed her earrings and tucked them into a pocket, then held out her arms again. 'You get his bottle ready and I'll bring him down.'

'I did try to feed him myself.' Holly felt the old urge to explain herself emerging. 'It was all I heard when I was pregnant – how important it was to breastfeed and give the baby the milk my body had made especially for him. He was born prematurely, and I did express milk at the hospital, which they gave to him in tiny bottles. I fed him for six weeks after taking him home, then I developed mastitis and it was agony. I was in tears all the time. After three rounds of antibiotics, I gave up and put him back on the bottle.'

'Holly.' Fran looked her straight in the eye. 'Is this baby fed, warm and safe?'

'Well… yes. Of course.'

'Then stop beating yourself up about breastfeeding.'

'I can't help it. He's still so young, and every time I see a woman feeding her child, or read something about it, I feel so guilty that I can't do it properly.'

'You're doing the best you can. My mother told me that she fed me until I was seven months old, but I know some women who popped their babies straight on the bottle, and there's nothing wrong with that at all. You gave Luke a damned good start, so please don't be so hard on yourself.'

'Oh Fran, I've missed you.'

And she had. She'd missed her practical, no-nonsense approach to life, missed her reassurance and her hugs. Fran had always been able to make her feel better about things.

'I've missed you too.' Hurt crossed Fran's face again, and Holly's heart lurched.

'I need to explain some things to you, and I hope that when I do, you'll understand. There isn't a good enough reason for running off and not contacting you, but I was a mess. Ironically, I needed your friendship and support more than ever, but I couldn't ask for it. I had to cut myself off from everything at Greenacres and Penhallow Bay, and the only contact I had was with my dad.'

'I know. I asked him about you and he told me you were well but that you needed some time out. He was very good and didn't give anything away about where you were or about Luke.'

Fran moved Luke onto her hip, then took Holly's hand.

'You're here now and you're safe and well. I can see that you've had your hands full. Besides which, you've just lost your grandpa and I don't want you feeling bad about me today of all days. I'm fine; I survived. But please promise me one thing.'

'Of course.'

'Don't run off again… at least not without letting me know how to get hold of you.'

Holly took a deep breath. 'I promise you, I won't.'

It was a promise she intended to keep.

–

Holly gave the bottle one more shake, then tested the heat of the milk on her wrist. It was perfect. She walked to the door, and froze as Lucinda Turner filled the doorway.

'Hello, Holly.'

'Lucinda.' She pulled herself up to her full height. She didn't want any conflict, but this was her home, and if Lucinda wanted a repeat performance of last year, then Holly had a few things to say in return.

'I'm very sorry for your loss, Holly.'

'Uh… thanks.' Holly recalled seeing Lucinda at the church, noticing the question in her eyes when she'd looked at Luke. Then she remembered the last time Lucinda had spoken to her before that, and she shivered.

'He was a good man, your grandpa.'

Holly nodded.

'I see congratulations are in order too.' Lucinda's brown eyes fixed on the bottle in Holly's hand.

Holly could sense the questions bubbling. No doubt Lucinda thought she had got together with someone else as soon as she'd split up from Rich. It hurt her to feel that this woman who she'd spent so much time with, who she'd once cared about and respected, could believe that of her.

'It's not how it looks, Lucinda.'

'It's not for me to judge you.' Rich's mother shook her head sadly.

'Judge me?' The words were out before she could stop herself. She swallowed hard, pushing down the rest of what she wanted to say. The last time she had seen Lucinda, the older woman had judged her very harshly indeed.

'Here he is!' Fran squeezed past Lucinda with Luke in her arms, and Holly sagged with relief at the interruption. 'He says he wants his bottle pronto.'

Fran pulled out a chair at the kitchen table, then shifted Luke around in her arms, as naturally as though she held babies every day. Holly handed her the bottle and Luke started to feed, gazing up at Fran as he did so, as if he'd known her all his short life. He was so trusting, such a happy, settled baby, and Holly knew she was lucky in that respect. It could have been very different if he'd been born even earlier, or if he'd not been as strong as he was.

She pulled out a chair and sank onto it, wishing she could go and lie down, but with Lucinda in the room, her fight-or-flight instinct was on high alert. Lucinda crossed the kitchen and crouched down in front of Fran.

'He's perfect.' She stroked Luke's cheek gently, which made Holly bristle. If Holly hadn't been good enough for Lucinda's son, would she think the same of her child? But then, as she watched, Lucinda's eyes filled with tears. 'He looks so much like…'

'I know.' Holly nodded. She'd seen the photographs, had known Rich and his brother Dean as children. Of course she was aware that Luke was the image of them. 'He's Rich's son.'

She had wondered about telling Lucinda when she saw her, had wondered if the woman would even want to know, but witnessing her reaction to Luke had made the decision easy. In spite of how badly Lucinda had treated her the last time she'd come to Greenacres, it was clear now that meeting her grandson had moved her.

Fran looked up and met Holly's eyes.

'Tell you what,' she said. 'I think he needs changing. I'll just pop him upstairs.'

Holly smiled her thanks, then she and Lucinda were left alone.

'I can hardly believe what's happened to us all,' Lucinda said as she sat down. 'What a mess we've made of things.'

'Lucinda… I've only just told Rich about Luke. It's a difficult situation and I hope you'll understand that I couldn't tell you before. After the way you spoke to me last year…'

'I know, and I am truly sorry. I was so angry and upset when Rich left that I couldn't think straight.'

Holly's stomach was somersaulting with anxiety, but she knew she had to get the conversation over with or she'd never be able to relax in Penhallow Sands. She'd learnt the hard way that delaying difficult conversations didn't always help. She'd been afraid of what her grandpa would think about Luke, and afraid of how Lucinda and Rex would treat her and her son, so she hadn't come home; and because of that, she hadn't been able to hug her grandpa again or kiss him goodbye.

'Lucinda, I was broken-hearted when Rich let me down the way he did, and then to have you coming here and saying such hurtful things was like having vinegar poured over a wound.' Holly's stomach churned at the memory of Lucinda standing at the back door, her eyes red and puffy, her hands planted firmly on her ample hips. When Holly had answered the door, she'd expected Lucinda to hug her and cry with her because Rich had left, but instead she'd been subjected to a tirade in which Lucinda had blamed her for the fact that her only surviving son had upped and left without an explanation.

Lucinda shook her head sadly and released a deep sigh.

'Holly, I know the truth now. I know it wasn't your fault at all.'

'Rich told you?'

'He did. He told me that he let you down by not turning up at the solicitor's office to sign the contracts for the cottage, then when you tracked him down, he hurt you even more.'

'I wanted to explain to you that I hadn't made him leave, that I loved him and that he'd broken my heart, but you—'

'I blamed you because it was easier; because I couldn't bear thinking that my only son had left me and his dad. I didn't mean what I said.'

Holly nodded, but the pain ran deep. She'd known Lucinda throughout her childhood, as she and Rich had been good friends long before there was anything romantic between them. Lucinda had tended to Holly's cut knees, hugged her when she'd cried over losing her mum and taken her shopping so they could enjoy girlie days out together. Then, that awful day, she had told Holly that she was to blame for Rich leaving the village, that she had never been good enough for him and that she never wanted to see her again.

'When I found out I was pregnant, I fell apart. I had no idea what to do. In the past, I'd have come to you and asked your advice. Especially in light of the fact that Luke is your grandson. But because of what you'd said, I had no idea if you'd even care. I thought about coming back to Greenacres so many times, but the knowledge of how much you hated me was one of the things that kept me away.'

Lucinda's mouth was open and tears were running freely down her cheeks.

'There's no excuse for what I did, Holly.'

'I do understand that you lost your son, and that made certain things harder for you...'

'No. That was why I reacted as I did, but to treat you so appallingly – a young woman who was like a daughter to me – was inexcusable, and I understand if you can't forgive me. It took me a while to realize what a mistake I'd made, and it wasn't until Rich came home and explained everything that I understood how bad that mistake was. But love, please believe me when I say that I never hated you.'

Holly sniffed. She had abhorred being angry at Lucinda and it had contributed to her own misery.

'Please try to forgive me, Holly. I'd really love to get to know my grandson and to make it up to you.'

Holly nodded. 'I'd like that too.'

She did want Luke to know his family, but she also knew that it would take time. There was a lot of hurt to work through first, and months of pain wouldn't disappear overnight.

'I'm glad you're okay, Holly. We were all worried when you suddenly left, and I knew it was partly my fault. What with Rich going too, it was like losing two members of our family.' Lucinda wiped at her eyes as she stood up. 'But the most important thing is that you're all right. And your baby son too. How... how old is he?'

'Three and a half months. He came seven weeks early,' Holly added.

'That must have been a worrying time for you.'

'It was. I need to speak to Rich about it all.' She met Lucinda's gaze. 'We didn't have much time to talk earlier, but obviously there are conversations that need to be had.'

'Of course there are.' Lucinda pushed her shiny bobbed brown hair behind her ears. 'You're not rushing off again, though, are you?'

Holly shook her head.

'Come and see us at the bakery? Please.'

'I will.'

'And bring Luke?'

'Of course.'

'And remember that I am sorry, Holly. I'd do anything to take my words back.'

Holly nodded. If only it was as simple as that, but once things were said, they were out there. All she could do now was try to move on, for Luke's sake.

–

Ten minutes later, Fran returned to the kitchen with Luke and an empty bottle.

'Looks like people want your mummy to stay around for a while, Luke.' Fran spoke to the baby but Holly knew it was for her benefit. 'She's been missed.'

'Did you hear what Lucinda said?'

'I bumped into her in the hallway as I was bringing Luke back down. She cooed over him for a while but wouldn't hold him. She said she didn't want to without asking you if it was okay. She clearly feels bad about something.'

Fran sat down and Holly shuffled her chair closer to her friend and leant her head on her shoulder, just as she used to when they were growing up. Things were different now, with Grandpa gone. Only a few months ago, she'd have faced his disapproval if she'd come home, and worried about Lucinda's reaction too. Plus, there were other ghosts at Greenacres that she didn't have the strength to confront.

But as with everything in life, things had to be dealt with eventually, and Holly knew that time had come. There would be no more running away.

–

'Would you like anything else to eat?' Granny asked as she stood up.

'No, that was lovely, thank you. The caterers you hired were fabulous.' Holly stood too. 'Sit down, Granny, and I'll make you a cup of tea.'

Glenda nodded, but as she sat back down, Holly noticed how she gripped the edge of the table.

'Granny, what is it?'

'What is what?'

'You're in pain.'

'Holly, I'm past eighty and it's been a long day. Some aches and pains are to be expected.'

'I know, but you should try to rest more.'

'I can rest when I'm dead, dear.'

Holly winced.

'Oops! Sometimes I can be so inappropriate. Talk about poor timing. Your grandpa would've frowned at me for that one.'

'I say the wrong thing all the time.' Holly grimaced as she recalled occasions when she'd put her foot in her mouth.

'Your mother was the same; I think you both get it from me.'

Holly filled the kettle, then went about making tea as her granny talked.

'It was strange today, wasn't it?'

'Very.'

'Seeing my husband buried not far from my daughter was surreal. No mother should lose a child. Losing a spouse, well, it's to be expected for one or the other, and Grandpa and I were lucky to have each other for so long, but losing a child goes against the natural order of things.'

'I understand that now more than ever.' Holly carried two mugs of tea to the table and set one in front of her granny.

'Yes, you're a mum now and it's wonderful. Luke is such a gift.'

'I'm sorry I didn't come home in time to say goodbye.'

'You wouldn't have known your grandpa at the end, dear. He was very different.'

'How so?'

'Well, he wasn't himself before you left really, was he? Not the man you knew growing up.'

'No... he was a bit forgetful, but I put it down to age and tiredness. The hours he was still working must have been taking their toll.'

'He was always the same, determined to keep going day and night to make the vineyard a success. It was just a shame he wouldn't listen to your father and try something new. Sun, rain or snow, he was out there somewhere dealing with something. I believe that's what kept him fit for so long.'

Holly sipped her tea and gazed around the kitchen with its dark green Aga, heavy oak cupboards and green and red tiled surfaces. The large window above the apron-fronted sink overlooked the same view as her bedroom window. Outside, the sky was dusky pink, painted with purple and peach streaks. It was beautiful, and made her aware of how much she'd missed that view, the sense of openness that being at the old house created. Unlike the flat she'd rented in Exeter, with its view restricted to the buildings opposite, Greenacres was detached and set in its own land; the only nearby buildings were the barns and winery. She knew that if she stepped outside now, she'd be able to inhale the sweet spring air, to feel its soft caress on her skin and to watch as the sky changed from pastels to navy then black. She also knew that if she kept walking, she'd cross the vineyards and the fields, eventually reaching the open expanse of the clifftops with their panoramic view of the sea and the paths that led down to the golden beaches of Penhallow Sands.

'He was a good grandpa.' She nodded.

'He was, but he was very strict, with your mother when she was a child and then even more so with you. But he loved you both and wanted the best for you, because of his own upbringing and because he wanted more for his family. After a childhood spent in children's homes and foster care, he worked his fingers to the bone to make this vineyard a success. He didn't always go about things the right way, or the most sensitive way, but I'm pretty certain that he was very hard on himself a lot of the time and that he felt he'd failed your mother when she got sick.'

'He didn't fail Mum. How could that possibly have been his fault?'

Glenda shrugged. 'I swear he thought he could scare the cancer out of her. He hated that it beat him. At least that was how he saw it. I told him there was nothing more he could have done, but he wouldn't listen.' She blinked, then wiped her cheek.

'Oh Granny, don't get upset.'

'I've cried many tears over your mum and Grandpa, Holly. A few more won't make a big difference.'

They fell quiet for a while, both lost in their memories.

'I don't know if I ever told you, but your grandpa was such a handsome man in his youth.'

'I've seen the photos, and you weren't so bad yourself.' Holly was glad of the change in the direction of their conversation.

Granny chuckled, then raised her mug.

'To the only man I ever bedded, and that's because we were wedded.'

Holly raised her mug too, feeling her cheeks glowing. She was a bit embarrassed that Granny was talking about sex. She also wondered if it was an unintentional comment on her own situation, because she had slept with Rich and got pregnant by him even though they weren't married. But times had changed, and judging by the distant look in Glenda's eyes, she hadn't meant to comment on Holly's lifestyle choices or her morals.

'The marriage thing was different when I was young,' she continued. 'We felt we had to be married before we had sex… or some of us did, at least! I know it's not something you want to think about your grandparents doing, but don't ever be shy about sex. It's a part of life and a damned good part. Of course, Grandpa didn't like to think it happened, especially to his daughter, which was why he was so shocked when she told us she was pregnant with you. He said that if Bruce didn't marry her right away, he'd crush him with the grapes and bottle him.'

'Goodness!' Holly could imagine her grandpa saying exactly that.

'Your mother fought her corner for a while, insisting that she didn't need to be married, but she and your dad were in love, so they were happy to say "I do" before you arrived.

'He was a passionate man, your grandpa,' Granny carried on, clearly back in the past. 'He knew a thing or two about making love—'

'That baby is good as gold.' Bruce entered the kitchen and set the baby monitor on the table, and Holly breathed a sigh of relief. Her granny clearly needed to talk about Grandpa, but the direction the conversation had taken was making her uncomfortable.

'He went down okay then?' she asked him.

'Oh yes, he wasn't averse to a bit of that.' Granny smiled, a faraway look in her eyes.

'Oh God, no...' Holly shook her head, but Granny wasn't listening.

'He did.' Bruce frowned in the direction of his mother-in-law. 'I won't ask what you two have been talking about. I'd love a cuppa if there's one going.' He took the empty baby bottle to the sink and swilled it out, then set it on the draining board while Holly made him a mug of tea the colour of mud. Her dad liked his tea strongly brewed with a tiny splash of milk.

'Right, I'm off to bed.' Granny got up and picked up her own mug.

'I'll sort that. Leave it there.'

'Thank you, Holly. It's so wonderful to have you home again. Love you both.' She gave a little wave, then left the room.

'Was she talking about sex again?' Bruce asked as he pulled out a chair.

'Again?'

'Yup. She's been doing it quite a lot lately and it can be very awkward, especially when she misunderstands what someone has said. It's like some kind of innuendo bingo.'

'Is it the grief, do you think?'

'It could well be.' Her dad nodded.

'At least she's thinking about something nice.'

'True. Not really what other people want to think about, though... especially not the vicar, although he did deal with her comments quite well when he came to the house after Grandpa had died. She was going on about one time when she and Henry got naked and rolled around in the grapes in the winery.'

'Best avoid that vintage then.' Holly giggled.

'Doesn't bear thinking about, does it?' Her dad raised his eyebrows.

Holly drained her tea, then picked up the monitor and automatically checked that the volume was turned on.

'Don't worry, I checked it already.'

'Force of habit, I guess. Living alone means that I check everything about a hundred times.'

'I hate to think of you being on your own, Holly. I'd have come to see you more often if they could have spared me.'

'I know that, Dad, and I appreciated you visiting when you could. I'd have come back sooner too if I hadn't been so worried about Grandpa's reaction to Luke. Now I feel dreadful that they never met.'

'Some things just aren't meant to be. Grandpa declined so much in the last six months that he might not even have understood who Luke was.'

'Was it that bad?'

Her dad nodded. 'Poor man.'

'And you and Granny?'

'We're okay... especially now that you're home.'

He met her eyes and the love in his gaze filled her heart. She'd left Greenacres in a moment of panic and pain and hadn't really thought it through, but then she'd found out she was pregnant, and coming back had seemed too big a mountain to climb.

She'd told her father that she and Rich had rowed, but not the things they'd said, nor why she'd been so hurt. She'd been unable to voice her feelings, fearing that freeing them would make her pain even worse, so instead she'd given him a summary and left it at that. She was also afraid that telling him might make him see Rich differently, or prejudice him towards the young man he'd loved as a son. That was something she'd never want to do. Rich was Luke's father, and in spite of how he'd treated her, she knew that she had to try to ensure that both families could accept that fact.

'I'm so grateful to you for trusting me when I told you I couldn't talk about me and Rich, and not pushing me to tell you more.'

Dad nodded. 'As long as you're good, then so am I. Tell me if you want to, but forget about it if that suits you better. I'm just here for you whenever you need me.'

'Thank you.'

'Right… I'm going to head up to bed now, if you don't mind. It's been a tough day and I have an early start tomorrow.'

'At the vineyard?'

'I wish it *was* outdoor labouring. It's with the accountant.'

'Old Mr Seymour?'

'Yes. He's still doing the books for us. Though he still insists he can't abide computers and needs everything in writing. It makes keeping the books straight so much harder. I guess we should think about changing to an accountant who's a bit more with it, really.' Her dad rubbed his eyes.

'It would make sense. I remember Grandpa saying that Mr Seymour had given up all his other clients and only did Greenacres' books as a favour to him.'

'It's something I'll try to look into soon.'

'Everything okay, though?'

His eyes dropped to his slippers and he shook his head. 'It'll be fine. I need to go over some figures with him, that's all, and see how the land lies.'

'Okay, well if you need me there too, let me know.'

'Will do.' He kissed her cheek, then left the kitchen.

Holly stared at the surface of the old pine table and ran her finger over the grooves and lines etched into its surface. There were straight lines, wonky lines and even some numbers, probably left over from her maths homework or her grandpa working out the vineyard accounts. Towards the edge was what appeared to be a pattern, but when she looked more closely, she could see that it was actually a smiling face surrounded by a mass of wavy hair. It was her mum, a childish sketch Holly had drawn years ago, when everyone had been here, sitting around the table together; a whole family, not one fragmented by death and distance, pain and loss.

Time moved on. People changed, left the area and passed away.

But this was still a family home, and Holly was back. She hoped she could piece together what was left of her family before it was too late, before anyone else was taken away.

She stood up and yawned, took the mugs to the sink, checked the back door was locked, then picked up the baby monitor and headed upstairs. It wasn't even nine, but she was exhausted, and knew she'd need her strength for the next day. A good sleep would help; she had to hope Luke thought so too.

Chapter 4

When Holly awoke the next morning, dawn was creeping through the gap in the curtains, bathing her bedroom in cold grey light. The dark, bulky shapes of the furniture she'd grown up with lurked at the edges of the room, and for a moment, she felt disorientated, slightly uneasy. This was quickly replaced with joy when a gurgle caused her to turn and see Luke lying in the cot, waving his hands in the air. They had both slept through, in spite of the unfamiliar surroundings, which Holly had worried might unsettle the baby.

She got up and went to the cot. Luke smiled as she reached for him.

'Good morning, little man.'

She carried him to the window and pushed the curtains aside, then peered out into the morning. There was a gentle haze across the fields and she knew that if she walked out there now, the dew would soak her legs and feet – fresh and cold, pure and new. The yard was quiet; it would be an hour or so yet until the working day began at the vineyard. Growing up, she'd often walked through the fields with her mum, dad and grandpa, completing a variety of essential tasks: stripping leaves from the vines, which aided ripening by exposing the grapes to the sun; removing secondary fruit as harvest approached so the pickers didn't collect unripe grapes that would affect the quality of the wine; and checking for any sign of pests or disease. On hot summer days, she helped Granny take cool drinks and sandwiches to the seasonal pickers, and warm drinks on cooler autumnal days. Harvesting occurred any time between late August and October, depending upon the type of grape.

Sometimes, as a teenager, she'd lain down between the vines and gazed up at the sky, watching as the clouds sailed along, listening to the birds singing in nearby trees as planes passed overhead, wondering where they were heading. She had been taught to respect the earth and the fruits it produced, to love the smell of fresh, fertile soil, and in the middle of spring, in the seemingly momentary week or two of bloom, she'd enjoyed pressing her nose against the silken grape clusters and inhaling their sweet, subtle aroma.

'All of this could be yours one day, Luke.' She kissed his soft head and he patted her arm, as if reminding her that it was breakfast time.

Downstairs, she wandered through to the kitchen and found her dad at the table, a mug of coffee and a plate of toast in front of him.

'Good morning!' His face lit up and he held out his arms.

Holly handed Luke to him and began to make up a bottle. When it was ready, she gave it to her dad so he could feed his grandson, then sat down and sipped at the coffee she'd just poured.

'Mmm. This is good.'

'Freshly ground.'

'I can tell.' She sighed with contentment. 'Luke slept through the night.'

'I thought I hadn't heard him. Granny got up twice to use the bathroom. I was listening out for her… It's a habit I've developed. But she went straight back to bed both times.'

'Is she still asleep?'

'I think so. Didn't want to wake her in case she'd had a rough night.'

Holly nodded. 'It's a tough time.' The contentment she'd felt just moments ago slipped away, and unease at the hard times ahead filled her. She still had to speak to Rich; still needed to grieve for her grandpa, whose death hadn't properly sunk in yet.

'It'll help her having you around, Hols.' Her dad cleared his throat but kept his eyes on Luke. 'Any idea how long you might be staying?'

Holly watched the steam rising from her mug. She wished she knew. Everyone would want to know: her dad, Fran, Rich probably.

'I just need to see how things go.'

He met her eyes then. 'No pressure, angel. It's your life and you'll always be welcome here, but I understand that you might not want to stay.'

She exhaled slowly. Was her dad right? Did she really have a life in Exeter to go back to? She'd fled there last summer in a whirlwind of emotion; stayed there because circumstances had taken an unexpected turn and she couldn't face returning to Penhallow Sands. But did she have a reason to go back there now? To her one-bedroom flat and lonely nights in front of the TV while Luke slept? To ready meals eaten alone as she wondered how she could possibly afford childcare when she returned to work, in whatever capacity that might be? Before she had Luke, she'd done an admin job with a temping firm and had intended to work right up until the end of her pregnancy. Luke had come early, so her working days had come to an abrupt end.

But she had things to do before she made any decisions about her future. Most important was finding a way forward with Rich so he could be a father to Luke, if that was what he wanted. She had no idea how he was feeling about what she'd told him yesterday. Besides which, there were things to worry about here at the vineyard too. She had a feeling there was something her dad wasn't telling her.

'Dad, you would let me know if everything wasn't all right, wouldn't you? Last night, when you told me about the meeting with Mr Seymour, you looked worried.'

Her dad shook his head. 'Everything's fine, Holly, absolutely fine. Don't you worry about a thing.'

She watched him carefully, but his expression was one of adoration as he lifted his grandson to a sitting position then gently rubbed his back.

'This little lad has a good appetite.'

'He does.'

'When I get back later this morning, I can watch him for you if there's anything you need to do.'

'Thanks. I do need to meet up with Rich at some point, but I'll try to spend some time with Granny first. I don't know when Rich will be free, as he's got work.'

Her dad nodded, a smile on his lips, but she could see the concern in his eyes.

Rich poured himself a coffee from the pot, then opened the back door of his parents' cottage and went out into the garden. He had to leave for work soon, but he hoped some fresh air would clear his head, as he'd barely slept all night.

The morning was mild, the air sweet with the fragrance from the bedding flowers his father planted religiously every year. Then there were the pretty roses that climbed around the back door and over the pergola that he had built from one end of the house to the other. For as long as Rich could remember, his father had always been occupied with one DIY project or another, especially after his brother had passed away. It had been his way of clinging to life and trying to give it meaning again. He worked at the bakery alongside his wife throughout the day, then came home and started again. Rich could barely remember a time when his father hadn't been flat-out busy, a time when he'd been able to sit and relax and enjoy his home and garden.

His mum was the same, but her hobbies involved book clubs, knitting and charity appeals. She was always rushing off to a meeting with her fellow readers, raising funds for an animal shelter or the local church roof, or perched on the sofa late at night, mug of tea to one side, TV tuned to a soap rerun and knitting needles clacking away in her hands as a garment or blanket expanded rapidly on her lap.

Rich had grown up believing that staying busy was the best way to keep the demons at bay. Even before their lives had changed so dramatically, his parents had been active, but afterwards... after the initial raw agony of grief had passed, the numbness set in, and his parents seemed to vow to charge through the rest of their lives barely stopping to draw breath.

Rich had done the same. Secretly blaming himself for Dean's death, he'd carried a burden throughout his teens and twenties. As a teenager, he'd lived hard and fast. He went out on pub crawls with his mates from college and university, drinking heavily. Alcohol helped to block out the guilt and the memories. The problem was that they always came back the next day, and with a hangover, everything felt even worse.

He learnt to drive, first a car, then a motorbike – much to his mother's horror – and every time he rode it, he did so as if it could be his last ride. Going away last year had opened his eyes to how he'd been living, and to the areas in his life that he'd neglected, the big mistakes he'd made. In many ways, he'd been lucky; a good brain and some last-minute cramming meant that he had achieved an upper second-class honours degree at Southampton University. Ironically, in spite of studying accounting and finance, he'd got himself into some financial difficulties, but his parents had bailed him out unquestioningly. They had never reprimanded him, never shown any doubt in him and he had taken full advantage of that.

And now... he felt so guilty about it. Guilt on top of guilt – it was no wonder he'd ended up snapping under the pressure. He had gone, for want of a better description, off the rails, and it had taken him eight months away from his normal life to see it clearly. It wasn't even as though he was in his teens or early twenties when it had all come to a head. He'd raced through his twenties, freelancing in accountancy, earning sporadically, never putting down roots. He'd got together with Holly by chance at a friend's wedding, and he really cared about her, but he had struggled to give her all of himself. Not only did he feel unworthy of her, but he couldn't shake off the thought that Dean had never had a future ahead of him to enjoy. It held him back and led him to a point where he'd been unable to go on. And so he'd let Holly down.

He had left Penhallow Sands with his head in a mess; jetted off to Ibiza intending to drown his sorrows. One evening, he'd met up by chance with Sam, a friend from university, and they'd gone for a drink to catch up. It was then that his old friend had told him about the quieter side of Ibiza. Initially Rich had been sceptical, believing it wasn't what he was looking for, but with Sam's encouragement, he'd headed over to Cala d'Hort and it had taken his breath away. He'd stayed on at the peaceful retreat for several months, using Sam's family home as a base. Here in this older part of the island, he had found something completely different. He'd been clinging on to his youth, the belief that he needed freedom, as if it would stop time from passing, but of course, no one could do that. Time waits for no man, and Rich felt sad that he'd wasted years of his life trying to stop the clock.

The months away had given him what he'd needed for so long: time to think, to take stock, to grieve and to begin to heal. It had made him feel that he was on his way to becoming a new man, and when he'd returned to Penhallow Sands just over a month ago, he'd been ready to seize the reins of his life and move on. He couldn't fully heal until he had confronted his past back in Cornwall, until he had apologized to those he had hurt, and until he had accepted that life was as it was.

Sam had suggested that he should apply for a position at the prestigious accountancy firm in Newquay where Sam was a junior partner. Much to his own surprise, he had agreed. For so long he hadn't wanted to commit to a stable job, preferring the flexibility of freelancing, but what if he could make a go of this? Get a foot on the career ladder; develop his skill set and client list? At least numbers could be controlled, and they never surprised him; in fact they grounded him and helped him to feel that at least some things in life could be explained. He had applied for the job, and with his qualifications and Sam's recommendation, he'd been successful. He was still new at the firm but his colleagues were warm and supportive and he felt that he belonged there.

Of course, some things had changed in his absence, the main one being Holly's disappearance. Rich had deactivated all his social media accounts before he'd left, because he'd believed it would set him free. When he'd returned to Penhallow Sands, he'd rejoined Facebook and Twitter, but Holly hadn't been on either. Her mobile number was dead, and when he'd gone to the vineyard to speak to her father about her whereabouts, Bruce had remained tight-lipped, telling him only that Holly had left eight months ago and didn't want to be contacted by anyone from Penhallow Sands until she was ready.

Rich had felt the pain of losing her then, and it had torn through him as he realized exactly what he'd done. While he was away he'd thought of her often, but he'd accepted that he was in a bad place and that he had to heal himself from within. He'd returned home with the intention of apologizing to her, in the hope that she would forgive him. He wasn't expecting a romantic reconciliation, but he had thought he might make peace with her. Unable to do that, he was trapped in a form of limbo. He had thrown himself into his new job, dressing the part, working long hours and hoping that one day Holly would return to Cornwall and he'd get the chance to apologize for how he'd treated her in the past.

It was the least he could do when – if – he saw her again.

The wake had been the wrong place for that, and, of course, she'd had the baby. His baby. He was a father, had been a father for over three months and he'd had no idea at all. He knew that feeling angry at Holly for that wouldn't do any of them any good, and it was pointless anyway, as she'd had her reasons for staying away. Rich had learnt a lot about forgiveness and patience while he was abroad, and he was trying to apply what he'd learnt to this current situation. It was a challenge, as he desperately wanted to meet up with Holly and spend time with Luke, but this couldn't be rushed. He had to respect Holly's wishes regarding the matter.

He also knew that his parents were keen to get to know their grandchild. His mother hadn't put any pressure on him last night, but he'd seen the hope in her eyes. She'd told him that she'd gone to Greenacres and been quite cruel to Holly the day after Rich had left, but that she'd apologized to her yesterday at the wake for how she'd treated her. Rich had been shocked to hear what she'd done, and he'd felt even worse for running off as he had, but he'd had a long talk to both his parents and they all clearly wanted to do what was best for Luke.

He pulled his mobile from his pocket and sent a text to Holly, asking her if she'd be able to meet up the next day.

He'd have suggested today, but he had meetings that he couldn't avoid and he suspected that Holly would be busy with her family too. At least she was home now. At least he knew she was okay. Even though he'd seen the hurt in her eyes, hurt that he had caused, and hated himself for it.

–

Luke had gone down for a late morning nap, giving Holly the chance to shower and dress. When she emerged from the bathroom, a towel wrapped around her hair, she found a text on her phone from Rich. She'd sent him her number before going to sleep the previous night, and told him to let her know when he was free to meet. He had work today but asked if she'd be available to meet the following afternoon. He apologized for the fact that he couldn't see her in the morning, but he had three client meetings lined up that day that he couldn't miss. In spite of everything, it made her smile to think of Rich having a permanent job. He'd got himself a good degree, then used it to freelance, working with several clients and businesses but not making a commitment. It had worried her, that failure to commit in his work life, as she had felt it reflected on his life outside of work too, but she had thought that sooner or later he would find a position to suit him – even set up his own accountancy firm – so she'd kept quiet. Rich hadn't pushed her about her decision not to go away to university, and she hadn't pushed him about his career. They'd had money coming in and it had been enough to fund their lifestyle.

After she'd dressed, she went down to the kitchen to make some more coffee. Just as she was pouring some into a mug, her granny appeared in the doorway.

'I'd love one of those, please.'

'Of course.' Holly poured a second mug, then took both to the table. 'Can I make you some breakfast?'

'Breakfast?' Glenda laughed. 'More like lunch now, isn't it? I had a restless night, then drifted off about dawn and only woke ten minutes ago.'

'How about toast, or a sandwich?'

'I'll take a piece of toast, please.'

'Granny, I wish there was something I could say to help.'

'You being here is a help, Holly. Really, there's nothing to be said now. Terrible as it is, Grandpa is gone and I have to keep going or give up. And as you know, Grandpa insisted that we Mortons are not quitters. He'd be furious with me if he thought I was throwing in the towel.'

'He would.' Holly shivered as the image of her grandpa's frown popped into her head.

'So today I'm going to start sorting things out.'

Holly dropped two pieces of bread into the toaster. 'Things?'

'Grandpa's things.'

'Is it not a bit soon?' She gazed at her granny's face; at the deep grooves around her mouth, the high cheekbones – which Holly had inherited – and the crows' feet either side of her eyes. Even though Granny was in her eighties, she was still beautiful. It was life etched on her face; the journey she'd been through, who and what she'd loved and lost – the story of time.

'I need to make a start. Who knows how long I have left before I pass on or dementia gets me too.'

'Don't say that.' Holly's throat constricted.

'Holly, I'm already quite forgetful, and although that's to be expected at my age, I'm also well aware that since Grandpa's condition deteriorated, my own memory has become worse. Not my long-term memory, but my short-term one. I can recall my youth now with startling clarity. Funny, that! Yet I can barely remember what colour tights I wore yesterday.' She pressed a finger to her temple. 'Oh, I can, yes… black. For the funeral.'

'That's right.' Holly steeled herself, preparing for an emotional day. Or rather an emotional few weeks, if she stayed that long. 'Where did you want to start?'

'With what?' Granny appeared confused. She ran a hand over the long white hair that hung over one shoulder in a plait. 'Ah… with this!'

'You mean you want to do your hair?'

'Yes, it's time to cut it, I think.'

'What? Why?'

Granny had always had long hair. When Holly was a little girl, she had loved to brush it and style it, and Granny had been happy to sit there and let her do as she liked.

'You cut yours, Holly dear.'

Holly touched her short bob.

'Yes, but that was after Luke came along. It was too much hassle to take care of, and quite a bit of it fell out, so I thought it would be better to have it chopped.'

'My hair was never the same after I had your mother. It's linked to hormonal changes, they say. During my pregnancy, it was long, thick and shiny, but after I gave birth, it became brittle and dull. I didn't cut it because Grandpa liked it long, but now… I think I'd like a change.'

'I could take you into the village later, if you're sure you want it cut.' Holly's voice sounded uncertain even to her ears, but if it was what Glenda wanted, she could hardly deny her.

'Can't you do it?'

'Me?'

'Well, yes. You used to style my hair all the time.'

'I didn't cut it.'

'You did. A few times.'

'That was only trimming the ends.'

'So you'll be trimming long ends. What's the difference?'

The toaster pinged, so Holly jumped up and grabbed the toast, then set it on a plate next to the antique farmyard print butter dish that was already on the table.

'All right, I'll have a go, but I'm not making any promises about how it'll turn out. You might need to go to the hairdresser to have it tidied up.'

Granny clapped her hands. 'Wonderful! And thank you for my toast.'

'My pleasure.' Holly drank her coffee as her granny ate, then went to the sink and washed up. They did have a dishwasher, but it was old and clunky, and washing up gave her something to do, something to delay having to go through Grandpa's things or cutting Granny's hair.

And yet in spite of knowing that things had to be dealt with, she was happy to be home, surrounded by the people she cared about.

Chapter 5

'What do you think?' Holly asked as she held up the mirror.

Granny patted her chin-length white hair, freshly washed, cut and blow-dried, and her face broke into a smile.

'Oh, I love it. You know, I even think your grandpa might have liked it, traditionalist though he was.'

'It really suits you.'

'We're like hair twins now, aren't we?' Granny chuckled as she preened in front of the mirror.

'We are indeed.'

They hugged, and Holly breathed in the coconut fragrance of the shampoo and conditioner she'd used on her granny's hair. Her heart was so full of love for this little old woman that she wondered how she'd stayed away for so long. All she could do was try to make up for it now that she was back.

They'd decided to do Granny's hair first, so they could spend the afternoon sorting through Grandpa's things without having to stop. Holly hoped it would give Glenda the boost she needed before she started the heartbreaking task of bagging up her husband's belongings. It had also given Holly time to gather her own strength ready to tackle the job.

Ten minutes later, they were in Granny and Grandpa's room, perched on the side of the bed with its faded pink and purple patchwork quilt. Holly had fed Luke, and now he was lying on his play mat on the floor, gurgling up at the zoo animals that dangled over him.

'Where do we start?' she asked, looking around the room. It was all exactly as it had been when she was a child. There were two heavy mahogany wardrobes to the right of the door, a tall chest of drawers took up the wall to the left, and an antique chandelier hung from the middle of the ceiling. It had been a wedding gift from her granny's parents. The bed was positioned between the two windows that overlooked the back garden.

'With his clothes.' Granny went to one of the wardrobes and opened the door. She stood there for a moment as if undecided, then reached inside and brought out several shirts and suit jackets, which she carried to the bed.

As she set them down, their scent washed over Holly – Grandpa's cologne, woody and earthy, a fragrance she had always associated with the vineyard because it had seemed to trail behind him wherever he went, a smell that was uniquely his. She ran a hand over the top shirt and found it stiff and starched, exactly how Grandpa liked them. As a child, when he'd picked her up and carried her on his shoulders, she'd wrapped her arms around his neck, feeling his shirt collar pressing against her inner arms. It had been a part of who he was, stiff and formal on the outside, but with a heart of gold. Holly had known that anyone who could reach that heart was very lucky indeed, because Grandpa would always care for those who did. Knowing how much he loved her had made her fear of disappointing him stronger, because there was so much to lose.

Emotion surged inside her, so she went out onto the landing and picked up one of the cardboard boxes they'd brought up from the kitchen. Granny had asked Bruce to get them from the barn before he left. Holly stood for a moment, taking slow breaths as she tried to conquer her pain. Being home meant that it was gradually sinking in that Grandpa was actually gone. It felt as though something inside her was coming loose, and if she wasn't careful, she would completely unravel.

When she felt a bit calmer, she took the box into the bedroom and set it on the floor next to the bed.

'Are you sure about this, Granny?'

'It has to be done.'

Holly nodded. She removed the shirts from their hangers and folded them neatly before setting them in the box, then did the same with the jackets. It was terribly sad and also quite surreal packing away his things, a final confirmation that he was gone, that he'd never return. But Granny was right: it had to be done.

They worked quietly, Granny getting things out and Holly folding and packing, until they'd emptied the wardrobe of hanging garments. The room was filled with Grandpa's scent and Holly could imagine that he was right there with them. She wondered how her grandmother was finding it, and if she too felt as though her husband was there.

'How are you doing?' she asked.

Granny turned to face her.

'It's difficult. I knew it would be, but… it also doesn't feel real. It's like I'm watching a movie and this isn't me.' She held up her hands and stared at them.

'Do you need a break?'

'No, dear. Best get it done or I might find that the determination to be organized deserts me.'

She turned back to the wardrobe and leant forward, pulling out two shoeboxes.

'His best shoes. All his boots are downstairs, but these were for weddings and funerals.'

'Did he have shoes on… in the coffin?'

'Yes. But even though he was wearing one of his best suits, I decided to put his favourite work boots on him. They were so worn and soft and wouldn't have been any good to anyone else, and he loved them so much that I thought he'd prefer them to a hard, shiny pair.'

Holly nodded.

'I did polish them first, though.' Her granny smiled, but her eyes suggested she was far away in her mind. Perhaps that was best; perhaps it would help her to get through the rest of this process. 'He'd have wanted them polished.'

'Of course. He was a smart man.'

Once the first box had been filled and sealed with packing tape, Granny went to the chest of drawers and started removing jumpers and pyjamas. She sorted them into those that could be given to charity and those that were too worn and faded. 'Dusters and patchworking for these old ones,' she explained to Holly.

As the afternoon wore on, Luke drifted off to sleep on his mat, so Holly picked him up and took him into her room, settling him in the cot. She watched him for a few minutes as his face moved in sleep, his tiny mouth pursing and his forehead furrowing, as if he were reliving the events of the past few days and trying to make sense of them. He was such a gift, such a precious part of her life now, and she knew that she would do anything for him. Her love for him had grown from the moment she'd known she was expecting him, and even though she had considered all the options available to her, she'd known that she couldn't get rid of him. He'd already been firmly rooted inside her, a part of her, growing there silently in spite of her ignorance of his existence, and as soon as she'd been aware of him, she'd changed her life to accommodate him.

Giving birth to him, enduring hours of contractions and days of worrying after his early arrival, had confirmed to her that he was now the centre of her world, and that no one could ever be that important to her. Except, perhaps, another child – should she ever have one. But that wasn't exactly on the agenda right now, or for the foreseeable future. Luke was her son, her reason, her life, and she'd do everything she could to give him the upbringing he deserved.

Back in Granny's room, she found the older woman sitting on the bed with a small drawer next to her. She was picking things up then putting them back. She looked up when Holly approached the bed.

'What's in there?'

'His watch, cufflinks, odds and ends… buttons he might need, unused toothpicks, some old coins.'

'What will you do with them?'

Granny picked up the watch with its brown leather strap and gold-plated back. The face was white with plain black numbers; a smaller circle showed the date, and another one the phases of the moon.

'Here.' Granny held it out.

'I know, I remember it well. Grandpa used it to teach me to tell the time.'

'It's yours.'

'Oh… I couldn't take it.'

'Yes you can. What else am I going to do with it? Your father never wears a watch, and I'd hate to give it away to someone who wouldn't value it. I mean… it's hardly a Rolex, is it? The value is purely sentimental.'

Holly touched the winder on the side, then traced her finger over the glass that protected the watch face. To her, it did have value. To her, it represented her grandfather: his efficiency, his work ethic and his desire to see her well educated and well brought up.

'Thank you.'

She fastened the watch around her left wrist, but it slid up her arm, even on the smallest setting.

'Get your dad to make another hole in the strap.'

'I will do.' Holly smiled. For all that Granny was a strong woman, she was still old-fashioned in some ways. She knew she'd probably be able to make another hole herself. As she gazed at the watch, though, she made a decision: she would put it away and keep it safe for Luke to wear when he was old enough. It was a thought that gave her comfort.

Cufflinks were put into a box for Bruce and other bits and bobs binned or packed for charity, then they carried the boxes out on to the landing and set them in a row.

'It's not much for a lifetime.' Granny stared at them.

'That's not his life, though, is it?' Holly said.

'No, you're right. He made your mum, and then she made you, and you made Luke. These things are just... things. His love and his hard work at the vineyard are his legacy, and that will go on through you. We'll always carry him in our hearts and minds.' Granny's voice wavered, and Holly slid an arm around her shoulders.

'We definitely will.'

A row of boxes might hold Grandpa's clothes, shoes and coats, but it didn't hold who he had been or what his life had been about. They stood staring at the boxes for a while, then Granny turned into her embrace, and Holly held her tight, tears rolling down her cheeks. She cried for her granny, for her grandpa and for herself. Letting go was so hard, and all they could do was try to find comfort from one another and from their memories of a man who had once been the backbone of their family. Now that he was gone, Holly wondered what the future held for them all, as well as for Greenacres.

It was more uncertain than she cared to admit, even to herself.

–

Over dinner that evening, Bruce talked about people he'd seen during his trip into the village, and about how he hoped for a good summer for the vineyard. But as much as he smiled and gesticulated, his eyes told a different story. Holly could barely wait to get him on his own; she had a feeling he was hiding something from them.

After they'd cleared the dinner things away and she'd bathed and fed Luke and settled him in his cot, she went into the lounge to find her granny and her dad in front of the TV. Glenda was sitting on the battered old brown leather sofa with her slipper-clad feet up on a small stool. The log burner was lit because the spring evening had turned chilly, and Granny was crocheting what appeared to be a blanket. Bruce was in the chair by the window, scrolling on his tablet, the blue light of the screen reflected in his reading glasses.

Holly placed the baby monitor on the coffee table made from half a wine barrel, then sat on the sofa next to her granny. She gazed at the TV screen, where images of the day's news flickered: tragedies and politics, public concerns and scandals. Although she was usually keen to keep up with what was happening in the world, she found it difficult viewing now that she had a child. The world she left behind would be his world, so she wanted it to be a good one.

Her eyes kept moving to the large leather chair in the corner. Grandpa's chair. Its emptiness was like an elephant in the room, reminding them that he wasn't there, that his chair was vacant and always would be. That chair held so many memories for Holly. Grandpa had bought it right after her mother, Sarah, was born, and refused to get a new one, even when the seams had become worn and the cushions had to be reupholstered. He had said that it could never be replaced. It was where he'd sat and held his baby daughter, then his granddaughter, where he'd made plans for the vineyard, where he'd watched as his family decorated the Christmas tree each year. It had been, in a way, his throne, with him the king of all that he surveyed.

A smile danced on Holly's lips, because for all that Grandpa had been strict and set in his ways, he had been the glue that held their family together: unwavering, unrelenting and unchangeable. His mindset had been something they could all rely upon to remain the same, and even if they didn't always agree with him, they had respected him. If it hadn't been for Grandpa's strict ways, her mum might have left Penhallow Sands and travelled, or done something else with her life instead of staying on to work at Greenacres. If it hadn't been for the vineyard, Holly's dad would never have settled in the area, and probably wouldn't have met her mum. Everything that happened in life was reliant upon something else; it was like a long chain of events that stretched back over the years and would stretch forward into the future too. It was a chain that linked them all together; even Rich, now that she'd had his son.

She swallowed hard. This loss was so difficult; Grandpa had been there all her life and he would be missed. She reached out and squeezed her granny's hand, and the elderly woman looked up and met her eyes. Granny was feeling it too; how could she not be?

'Shall I make some tea?' Dad asked, breaking the spell.

'I'll do it.' Holly stood up. 'Actually, how about hot chocolate?'

'Fabulous idea.' Bruce stood up too. 'I'll show you where the marshmallows are.'

As they walked through to the kitchen, Holly didn't mention that she knew where the marshmallows were – that they were in the same place they'd been for the last thirty-odd years – because she suspected her dad had an ulterior motive.

While she warmed some milk in a saucepan, Bruce paced in front of the door.

'What is it, Dad?'

He cleared his throat.

'Dad? I know something's wrong.'

'I didn't want to burden you with this, Holly. In fact, I still don't. I'll sort it out. It's fine.'

'Please tell me, Dad. You need someone to talk to.'

He cleared his throat again, then pulled out a chair at the table and sat down. Holly turned the heat under the milk down but kept stirring it, not wanting it to scorch.

'Okay… You know I went to see the accountant today?'

She nodded.

'Well, the thing is, it doesn't look great. We're still making enough to get by, and the forecast for the next three years is steady, if things continue as they have done this year, but after that… if we don't do something, we'll probably be in decline. We need to do more to develop the business and to compete in the current market.'

Holly turned the heat off under the saucepan.

'How has this happened?' She'd had a feeling that this was coming from the moment she'd returned. 'Is it because I wasn't here to run the shop?'

He shook his head, a sad smile playing across his lips. 'No, Holly. As much as the shop was a help, it didn't make that much of a difference overall. This is bigger than that. See… there are lots of vineyards out there now that are undercutting us. It's really competitive as more vineyards start up, and our wider European sales aren't guaranteed any more either. We just can't afford to sell to supermarkets at the low prices some vineyards do, and people don't always want to pay more for good wine… especially if they haven't heard of it. Just running a vineyard isn't enough these days. We need to do something else to stay afloat.'

'Like what?'

'I tried to encourage your grandpa to think about some extra ventures, but as you know, he was very set in his ways and he didn't want to consider any changes. But we need to move with the times if we want to keep going. I hate that this is happening so soon after Henry passed away, but I feel responsible for trying to fix things, because if I don't, who will?' He spoke softly, but Holly heard the sadness and the weight of responsibility in his tone. Her poor dad was dealing with all this alone.

She got the cocoa powder out of the cupboard and mixed it with the milk and some sugar, then poured the hot chocolate into three mugs before sprinkling marsh-mallows over the top.

'I'll take Granny's in to her, but I'll be back. Stay there, Dad.'

She told Glenda that she was helping her dad with some numbers, then returned to the kitchen to find the back door open. Peering through the window, she could see her dad standing in the garden. She hooked the baby monitor to her belt, grabbed two blankets from the cupboard under the Welsh dresser in the corner, then carried them and the mugs outside.

They wrapped the blankets around their shoulders and walked over to the bench near the herb garden that had once been her mother's pride and joy. In the fading light, Holly could see that it was overgrown and neglected. She had taken over its care after her mother had passed, but it seemed that no one had tended it during her absence. She hadn't paid it much attention when she arrived home yesterday and had been busy today helping her granny, but now its evident deterioration saddened her. She used to grow lots of lavender in the garden, which she dried and

71

stuffed inside the little pouches that her granny crocheted, and they sold well in the shop. But now the lavender that remained was spindly and sorry-looking. She hadn't had time to venture inside the shop since she'd returned, but she was keen to take a look to see how it had fared during her time away.

'Sorry about the herb bed.' Her dad too was staring at the mass of weeds and herbs, wound together so they were indistinguishable from one another. 'I just didn't have time to sort it.'

'Of course you didn't.' Holly rubbed his arm. 'It's fine, I'll do it while I'm here.'

But when she left, would it end up like this again?

'Your granny misses having fresh herbs for cooking.' He shook his head. 'Sorry, Hols, I didn't mean that to sound like I was trying to make you feel guilty. You have to do your own thing, what's best for you and Luke.'

'I know you didn't, and it's fine, really. But tell me about the vineyard.'

'I've been looking into it and I know there are other things we could do to increase revenue. Greenacres will be yours and Luke's one day. Unless, of course, the worst happens…' He shook his head.

'What is the worst, Dad?'

'It won't come to that.'

'To what?' Panic filled her chest.

'Well… if things don't improve over the next three years, we could end up losing money, and that might mean we'd be forced to sell to cover our backs.'

'To sell?'

He nodded but didn't meet her eyes. This was as hard for him to admit as it was for her to hear. The idea of losing even an acre of the land, let alone the house, the garden, the barns… Holly had taken it for granted that Greenacres would always be in the family, but now it seemed there was a possibility that it could slip right through their fingers.

'Of course, if you were happy with that, then I would go along with your decision. I don't want to assume that you want to keep Greenacres in the family. I understand that you might be keen to return to Exeter, that you might prefer to sell sooner rather than later and to have your inheritance to do with as you want. None of it belongs to me and I'm sure Granny would be open to discussion, although doing that to her now seems a bit cruel in terms of timing. It's why I haven't told her about the financial concerns. It just doesn't seem fair to burden her with them. But you should know that there have been several expressions of interest since you left… as people learnt of your grandpa's decline. I dismissed them immediately, but if you did decide at some point that you wanted to sell, it would be an option.'

Holly blew on her hot chocolate, giving herself time to let the news sink in. After her mum died, she'd thought she wanted Greenacres, imagined herself living there and working there and her children doing the same. But last year everything had changed in more ways than one. It had always been Rich she'd pictured at her side, ever since they were teenagers, though for a long time it had just been as friends. They'd both had other relationships, though none of them lasted; then, when Holly was twenty-eight and Rich thirty-one, they'd attended a mutual friend's wedding. A dance and plenty of champagne had led to another dance, then a kiss, and it was as though Holly had been struck by a thunderbolt. All those things she'd never felt before in her relationships but had read about and longed for were right there in front of her. She had fallen madly in love with her best friend.

As time had passed, she had yearned for something more serious; had wanted to know that Rich felt the same way she did, but she'd sensed there was something holding him back from fully committing. She'd hoped that as they were friends as well as lovers, he'd soon realize how good things were between them, and she tried to put her concerns from her mind.

But things were bound to change, and everything had come to a head when Plum Tree Cottage had been put up for sale. Holly had set her heart on buying it. It had been, perhaps subconsciously, a way of finding out if Rich wanted the same things as her now that they were three years into their relationship.

The cottage was halfway between Greenacres and Penhallow Sands. It was set on two acres of land, within walking distance of both the vineyard and the coastal path. Holly had loved it from childhood. The owner had been an elderly lady who kept very much to herself. It had been rumoured that she fell in love with a soldier who was killed in the Second World War, and that when he died, she moved out of the village and settled in Plum Tree Cottage alone, hiding herself away from society. It was a sad story but one that Holly could understand. She had run from her own life, but been just as isolated in the middle of a big city as the old lady had been in her isolated cottage.

The place had a quiet charm and Holly had often imagined herself living there, popping back to the vineyard whenever she wanted to. She'd known that one day she'd move back into the house at Greenacres to take over there, but that had been something in the future, a long time away, when her own children would be fully grown and she'd return home to care for her ageing father.

But buying Plum Tree Cottage wasn't meant to be; life had got in the way, and her plans had fallen through.

Holly sipped her drink, savouring the sweetness of the marshmallows with the rich milky chocolate, and the warmth of the blanket around her shoulders.

'We used to come out here like this all the time. Do you remember?' Bruce gazed up at the darkening sky, where the stars were starting to show, faint pinpricks of silver against the vast navy blue.

'I do. I can remember sitting out here with Mum when I was younger.'

'Your mum loved to sit outside in the evening to look at the stars.'

'Do you think she's out there somewhere?' Holly wrapped her hands around her mug.

'Maybe. I know your grandparents have always been religious, but for me, it's more about the impact someone leaves behind.'

'Mum had a church funeral, though, and you married in the church, didn't you?'

He turned to her and smiled. 'Do you think Grandpa would have had it any other way?'

She shook her head.

'I was happy to go with the flow. As long as I got to marry your mum – and later to see her buried in the spot where she wanted to rest – I didn't mind. Why upset her parents when they wanted to do what they thought was best for her?'

'You're so easy-going, Dad.'

He laughed. 'Must be the Aussie in me.'

'I don't think I've ever seen you get angry.'

'It happens, Hols, I'm only human. But my anger always fades quickly too. I don't see the point in negative emotions. I'd much prefer to try to fix a situation than to waste time and energy moping about it.'

Warmth bloomed in Holly's chest. Her dad was such a good man. He'd always been the voice of sense and reason, but Grandpa had been so loud that sometimes Dad's common sense was drowned out. He never fought to be heard, though; just picked up the pieces and moved on.

'Are you happy here, Dad?'

He drained his mug, then set it on the bench next to him.

'I have been very happy here.'

'Did you ever want to return to Australia?'

'Sometimes. But your mum wouldn't have left the vineyard, and then, after she'd gone, I couldn't have taken you away from your grandparents. So I stayed. Besides which, I love Greenacres and Penhallow Sands. It's my home and has been for years.'

'Tell me about your ideas, Dad.'

'My ideas?'

'For the vineyard. The ones Grandpa didn't want to consider.'

'They're just ideas at the moment. I haven't spoken to anyone else about them.'

'That's fine. I want to hear them.' She reached out and took his hand. 'It's time you were heard.'

And as the sky turned indigo and the stars glowed, they talked and laughed, sharing ideas, memories, hope and dreams, and Holly's life in Exeter seemed even further away than before. She didn't know what the future held, but she did know that she wanted to see her family happy, and that she hated the thought that they could lose Greenacres; that one day she might have to leave and would never be able to return. So she made a pact with herself: she would do whatever she could to make sure that didn't happen. She didn't know exactly how yet, but she knew they'd find a way.

Chapter 6

Rich was trying to concentrate on what a client was telling him, but his mind kept drifting to the text he'd received from Holly. She did want to meet with him today. He'd known it would happen sooner or later, but he'd thought it would take her a while to settle back in and to grieve for her grandpa. He'd also thought she might not want to see him, that she might try to delay it, as he couldn't imagine that he was her favourite person – father of her child or not.

There were cafés and pubs in Penhallow Sands, but the chances of being left alone to talk for any length of time were slim, as people who hadn't seen Holly for some time would want to pass on their condolences and catch up with her. He could suggest heading into Newquay, but again, they might not get any privacy, and that was something he thought their conversation would require. There was only one place he could think of for what he imagined was going to prove to be an emotional meeting.

As soon as his client had gone, he replied to Holly's text, asking her to meet him at 5.30 that afternoon at the old spot. Holly would know where he meant. He'd be able to get there by then as long as he clocked off straight after his final meeting of the day.

Since the funeral on Monday, the atmosphere at his parents' cottage had been strained. His mother was trying her best not to pester him about Holly and the baby, but it was obvious that she was struggling with it. She wanted to know if Holly would stay in Penhallow Sands, if she would be able to spend time with her grandchild. Rich too wanted to know the answers to those questions, and yet he was terrified of finding out either way. He knew now that Luke was his, but he and Holly had always used contraception and it had never failed them before, so he was confused about how it had happened. If Luke had been conceived despite contraception and Holly's condition – which she'd been told in her teens could affect her fertility – then he was meant to be. Against the odds, he had arrived – a beautiful, healthy baby boy.

Then there was the other matter to consider. Rich had always believed he never wanted children. After what had happened to Dean, he'd sworn never to open himself up to hurt like that again, never to put himself through what his parents had endured. Why would anyone take that risk? And it had all been his fault – Dean's death, their parents' suffering; all because of Rich's stupidity and weakness.

His heart was racing and his palms were clammy; he knew what was happening. He had to get control of this before it consumed him. His life had moved on to a better place; he would not let the old anxieties resume their hold on him.

He closed his eyes and focused on his breathing – in for four, out for four. He felt the air rushing into his lungs, then he pushed it back out, emptying his chest until he needed to fill it again. He opened his mind to the scenery from Ibiza, imagined the sounds of the waves lapping at the shore and the sensation as he walked into the water and felt its warm, soothing embrace.

Tension gone, he drifted…

'Rich?'

He opened his eyes to find Sam standing in the doorway.

'You okay?'

He nodded, blinking away his meditation.

'Just overthinking things, so I needed to mentally check out for five minutes.'

Sam smiled. 'Did it work?'

'Like a charm.'

'Good. You want to grab an early lunch then have a walk along the beach? Get some fresh air?'

'Wonderful idea.'

Lunch and a walk would be just what he needed before an afternoon of work. Sam really was a good friend.

–

Holly pulled into the large car park of the Seaview Diner and cut the engine. It had been a while since she'd driven her grandpa's Range Rover, but when her granny had announced over breakfast that morning that she needed to go into town, Bruce's eyes had widened. Although Glenda still had her driving licence, she rarely drove, and Bruce was concerned for more than one reason about her being on the roads. Holly had picked up on his concern and suggested that she take her granny and Luke into town – she needed more nappies and baby formula anyway – then they could go for lunch if Granny felt up to it.

They had gone into the centre of Newquay to do their shopping and Granny had pushed Luke's pram, smiling proudly as they walked along the high street. Whenever they bumped into someone they knew – which happened a lot – they stopped, and Granny told them all about her precious new great-grandson. Holly could see how much it helped her to focus on Luke, and how whenever someone mentioned Grandpa, she quickly moved the conversation back to the baby. She was glad that Luke had given Granny something to focus on other than her grief, and today she seemed brighter than she had done since Holly had returned home.

Holly climbed out of the vehicle and got Luke's pram from the boot, then placed his car seat on top and locked it into place. It would be nice to have lunch at the diner. She hadn't been there in over a year and it had always been one of her favourite locations to eat out in Newquay. They'd often celebrated family occasions such as birthdays and anniversaries there, enjoying the beautiful view over Fistral Beach and sometimes burning off their meal by taking a walk along the sand afterwards.

They crossed the car park and entered the diner, and were led to a table in front of the floor-to-ceiling windows that overlooked the beach. When they sat down, Granny clapped her hands.

'How delightful! I do love this place.'

'Me too.'

'Haven't been here in ages. The last time was… Gosh, it must have been Grandpa's birthday last year.'

Holly's heart plummeted at the memory. She'd pushed it from her mind in her desire to return here; her yearning to recapture some happy memories. Grandpa's birthday last year had marked a turning point in her life. She had tried not to let it affect her enjoyment of the evening, but it had been hard, especially as the man she loved had been absent. Earlier in the day, Rich had failed to turn up at the solicitor's office to sign the papers for Plum Tree Cottage, forcing her to go looking for him, but even after seeing how much he'd upset her, he'd still failed to show for her grandpa's birthday meal. She'd known then for certain that he didn't love her in the same way she loved him. And her heart had broken.

She looked into the pram next to the table, keen to forget her pain. Luke was waking up, so she lifted him out and held him close. To think that from so much sadness, a beautiful baby had emerged – an innocent child who had no idea what had happened before his arrival – was incredible. There was no denying that for Holly, at least, Luke had been conceived in love, but his birth had been overshadowed by her sadness that Rich was not there. At the time, still deep in her pain and anger that he had treated her so badly, she'd thought it might well be a good thing that he didn't know about Luke. Seeing him since then, she wondered if she'd been right.

'Shall we start with a cocktail?' Granny asked, a twinkle in her eyes as she ran her finger with its swollen knuckles down the menu. She'd never had any pain from her arthritic lumps and swore it was down to how active she was, especially with crocheting, as it kept her fingers nimble in spite of the swelling.

'You have one, but I'm can't – I'm driving.'

'Oh dear, I forgot that. I do love the names of some of these.' Granny's eyes twinkled mischievously. 'Shall I have a Slow Comfortable Screw, a Slippery Nipple or Sex on the Beach?' She started chuckling, her thin shoulders shaking.

'Have whatever you want, Granny.'

'I do wish you could join me.'

'Drink mine for me.'

'Order two?' Granny's pale-brown eyebrows rose up her lined forehead.

'Why not?'

When the waitress came to their table, Holly ordered a lime and soda with plenty of ice, and Granny took great delight in asking the young woman for a Screaming Orgasm and a Horny Southerner. Holly felt like covering Luke's ears with her hands.

'We should do this every week now you're home,' Granny said as she sipped the first of her brightly coloured drinks.

'That would be lovely.'

Holly gazed out of the window at the golden sand of the beach, and beyond that at the white crests of the waves as they crashed against the shore. When she would leave remained to be decided, but the thought wasn't particularly appealing, especially since her conversation with her dad last night, when he'd shared his concerns about the vineyard. It could really make a difference if she stayed and helped him. Trying to turn things around would involve a lot of hard work, and it would be too much for him on his own. Besides which, it was her responsibility too. In the past, Grandpa had kept them in the dark about the vineyard's finances, preferring to shoulder the ups and downs himself, but Holly knew now that her dad had been aware that things weren't right. If only Grandpa had shared the information with them, they might have been able to start putting things right before now.

But her dad had seemed convinced of one thing: it wasn't too late to turn things around.

'Granny, I need to explain why I left,' Holly said. 'I'd hate that you might think I was being selfish running off like that.'

Granny drained her cocktail.

'I don't think you're selfish, sweetheart. I know you had a lot going on. We were a bit shocked, but that week before you left, it was obvious that you weren't yourself at all.'

'Was it? I'm sorry.'

'It wasn't your fault, Holly.' Granny sniffed. 'Your grandpa disapproved of Rich, you know.'

'I knew he had some reservations about him, and that was why it was even more difficult to talk to you both about what had happened. I thought that if I went away for a bit and took some time out, then I could come back feeling stronger and carry on with my life. But when I found out I was pregnant, I couldn't face coming home and dealing with Grandpa's disappointment.'

'He always thought you were too good for the baker's boy.'

'The baker's boy?' Holly's tone betrayed her shock at the epithet.

'I know. Such a cliché looking down on people like that. But it wasn't because he was the baker's boy so much as because he always seemed so... restless.'

'Restless?'

'Your grandpa didn't think the lad would ever commit to you. He liked him, thought he would turn out okay, that he had a certain strength of character, but he didn't think he was going to settle down with you. It was clear how much you loved him, but we were concerned that he didn't feel the same. Grandpa said he should have proposed to you long before you started discussing moving in together.'

Holly smiled. She could imagine her grandpa saying exactly that.

'I think I was always in love with Rich.'

'Even before your mum passed away?'

'Yes. In an immature way back then, of course. I just didn't realize it for a long time.'

'I remember him coming to the house for tea, but oh gosh… you were so young.'

'Too young for love, I know, but there was always something between us. Rich was special, because he was my best friend too.'

'Some of those others you dated over the years…' Granny cackled. 'They weren't brave enough to return and face Grandpa for a second time.'

'No.' Holly's grandpa had scared the life out of some of her boyfriends, intimidating them with questioning the marines would have been proud of resisting, and none of them had been keen to return to the vineyard. But Rich had seemed to be unfazed by Grandpa, to respect the old man's strength of character and tendency to speak his mind without adopting the tact that most people would.

'That little man will be just as strong a character. He has your grandpa's resilience, and, I suspect, some of Rich's too.'

Holly needed to speak to Rich. Waiting until later might be necessary, but the sooner it was done, the better. Rich had a right to know everything.

When they'd ordered their food, and Granny had finished her second cocktail and requested an Afternoon Delight from the waitress, they both gazed out of the window, lost in thought. Holly heard a familiar voice and turned towards the entrance, where a couple had just entered: a well-dressed, handsome couple with broad smiles and the look of two people who were very fond of each other, if the way the woman touched the man's arm as they followed the waitress to their table was anything to go by. As they took their seats, Holly positioned the menu at the edge of the table to hide her face, and leant forward, hoping they wouldn't look over.

'Holly? What on earth are you doing?' Granny asked loudly, following it up with a hiccup.

'Shh.' Holly placed her finger over her lips and gestured at the table in the corner.

'Who is it?' Granny squinted. 'I can't see that far these days, and I brought the wrong specs.'

Holly winced as her grandmother's words carried across the diner, but nothing happened, so she tried to relax. Perhaps he wouldn't even see them. Perhaps they could have their lunch then leave unseen.

But when their food arrived, she pushed hers around the plate. Her stomach had closed over and the salmon and dill fishcakes and rustic potatoes had lost their appeal. It was all she could do not to turn and stare at Rich and the beautiful woman he was having lunch with.

It was all she could do not to burst into confused and broken-hearted tears.

Would she ever get over him?

–

Rich looked up from the menu, still smiling at a comment Sam had made about juggling everything in her life. He couldn't help but admire her and how she managed her career, her extensive and rather demanding family and the work she did for several mental health charities. She was very caring and supportive, and if she hadn't come along when she had, he might be in a very different situation.

His eyes drifted over the people in the restaurant and fell on a young woman with a short blonde bob sitting at a table with an elderly lady. The younger woman was helping the other one into her coat, and struggling by the look of things.

Was it…?

Yes, it was.

Holly and her granny, and the pram. She must have the baby with her.

He got up and excused himself, then hurried over to their table.

'Holly.'

She froze, holding her grandma's arms in the sleeves of the coat behind her, like some kind of straitjacket. Then she looked up at him, and colour rose in her cheeks.

'I thought it was you.' He smiled, but Holly's mouth remained set in a tight line.

'Richard!' Glenda Morton grinned, revealing a sprig of broccoli that was stuck in her front teeth. 'Hellooo.' Her eyes were glassy and her lipstick had been applied generously around her thin lips; so generously that she could have given a clown a run for its money.

'Are you all right, Glenda?' he asked, concerned that Holly's grandma had been rendered unstable by her grief.

'Oh yes, darling boy! I've had such a grand afternoon. I've had a Slow Comfortable Screw and a Screaming Orgasm.'

'What?' Rich ran a finger under his collar.

Glenda's eyes widened. 'The Sex on the Beach was out of this world!'

'Granny's had a few cocktails.' Holly raised her eyebrows.

'Oh, right. Of course. I thought… Gosh…' Rich released a breath through closed teeth as he tried to stifle his laughter. 'So you've had a nice lunch?' he asked, his eyes now on Holly, his fingers itching to tuck away the stray strands of blonde hair that had fallen over her cheek.

Where had that impulse come from? Clearly old habits died hard.

'It was lovely, thank you, but Holly didn't eat much of hers.'

'I did, Granny.' Holly finished getting Glenda's arms into her sleeves, then turned her round and buttoned the front of her coat.

'No you didn't.' Glenda hiccuped. 'I saw you pushing it around your plate and trying to hide it under your napkin.'

'Well I was still quite full from breakfast.'

Glenda shook her head. 'One minute you were fine, and the next it was as if you'd seen a ghost.'

Rich cleared his throat, concerned. Holly had always enjoyed her food; it was one of the things he'd loved about her. She didn't pick at salads or follow fads; she ate well and it showed in her eyes and her skin. Or it had. She was so pale now, and he was certain that she'd need to eat properly to keep her strength up. Caring for a young baby couldn't be easy.

'Why don't you come over to my table and meet Sam? She's my—'

'No!' Holly's reply was sharp and icy, cutting right through him. 'We can't. We have to go.' She glanced in the direction of Rich's table and he thought he saw her shiver, but it was so quick that he couldn't be certain.

'Okay. Maybe another time.' He stepped towards the pram. 'How's Luke?'

'He's fine.'

Rich gazed down at the baby and the baby peered up at him, his tiny mouth forming a perfect O. 'He's...' What was the right thing to say? Beautiful? Cute? Small? Practically bald? He didn't have much experience of babies at all. And this one was his!

'I'll see you later as planned?' Holly looked at him, and then away quickly, as if she couldn't bear to maintain eye contact.

He nodded. 'Be good to catch up.'

'Yes. It will.'

Then she turned away, wrapping her free arm around Glenda's shoulders as they made their way out of the diner.

Rich watched them leave and cross the car park. He hoped Holly would manage to get Glenda into the car okay. He considered following them outside, but thought better of it. The tilt of Holly's chin and the way she'd all but avoided eye contact suggested that she didn't want his help or concern.

He returned to Sam with a heavy heart. Getting through this afternoon might be even tougher than he'd first anticipated.

Chapter 7

Holly walked briskly along the beachfront at Penhallow Sands, enjoying the sensation of the spring sunshine on her face and the wind in her hair.

Above her seagulls soared, screeching to one another then swooping into the waves, chasing after some tasty morsel or other. The sky was a flawless blue, and looking up hurt her eyes, as if she'd been indoors in the shadows then come outside for the first time in a long time. She blinked as she adjusted to the bright coastal light. She had her sunglasses in her bag but she didn't want to put them on just yet; she wanted to enjoy seeing everything properly, unhindered by lenses.

The tide was coming in and its slow movement was hypnotic, reassuring. This would happen every day for as long as the earth existed; for a long time after Holly had gone. She shivered. Such a maudlin thought wasn't conducive to happiness, but she knew it was linked to her recent loss and to the fact that she'd returned to her childhood home, the place where she'd had to accept death early on with the passing of her mum. It was a part of life, the one thing that was guaranteed; but now, more than ever, Holly wanted to be around for a long time. Having Luke had made her determined to be there for him for as long as he needed her.

Could she come home permanently and raise Luke here? It certainly was a beautiful place. Yes, in high summer it got busy, but even so... There was the pretty, award-winning beach flanked by the steep grey cliffs where birds nested and reared their young. The cliffs were like muscular arms, cradling the beach and providing protection from the expanse of the sea that lay beyond. On clear summer days, the sea and skyline were hard to distinguish from each other, their blue mingling so perfectly. But as twilight fell, and the sky was dyed with hues of lavender and peach, the water seemed to turn navy blue, a base colour that had seeped from the blended palette above. The view was breathtaking and Holly had missed it, had missed the sense of freedom that came with living here.

She had gone to Exeter because she knew and liked the location. The university there had been one of the places she'd looked at as a possibility for further study. Exeter was far enough away, yet also not too far – it provided the security of giving her the space she needed while also being only a few hours away from her family. She had liked the vibrancy of city life, but Penhallow Sands was home.

And there was nothing quite like home.

She had needed this: to get outdoors and get her heart beating naturally, instead of that awful anxious pounding it had been doing since she'd seen Rich and that woman at the diner in Newquay. She'd been happy enough sitting there with Granny, finding her comments amusing and hoping that Granny was enjoying herself too. Then Rich had walked in with that beautiful woman, and Holly's stomach had turned over. Her lunch had been wasted, her throat too tight to swallow more than sips of water. She'd been tempted then to order a cocktail, could have murdered a Bloody Mary, but she was responsible for Luke and her granny, so she'd had to manage her feelings instead.

She had no right to care if Rich was in a new relationship. What they'd had was long gone, and as she'd found out last year, he'd never cared about her in the way she had done for him. She had always been the one to make all the effort, to phone and text, to book restaurants and romantic breaks in cosy cabins, to send Valentine's cards and pick out Christmas and birthday gifts that would have a special meaning. If she was being honest with herself, a lot of the time it had been as though Rich was absent from their relationship. She wondered now if he had merely been keeping his options open in case someone better came along. Someone like that woman in the diner... what had he called her? *Sam...*

She stopped suddenly, nearly running over a dog that had dashed in front of the pram.

'Stupid dog!' she spat, her frustration channelled towards the scruffy mongrel but stemming from her feelings towards Rich.

'So sorry, Holly!' A woman flew past her and grabbed the dog by the scruff, then clipped a lead to its collar. 'You naughty boy. You could have been run over.'

'Fran?'

Her friend straightened up and nodded. 'Yeah... thought I'd take this boy for a walk on the beach, see how his recall was, and before I knew it... whoosh! Off he went.'

'Is he yours?'

'I'm fostering him at the moment, but if no one comes forward to adopt him, I might well have to keep him.'

'Is he a mongrel?'

'A lurcher, and from his shaggy coat and small build, I'd say he's most likely a cross between a greyhound and a terrier. He's daft as a brush.'

The dog tilted his head to one side and gazed at Fran, then cocked his leg and peed over the wheel of the pram.

Holly grimaced. 'He clearly has no manners.'

'He's barely more than a pup; he was found wandering around an abandoned warehouse on an industrial estate. Goodness only knows what he's been through. He'll learn... he just needs love and patience.'

Holly looked at the dog, who was now sitting at Fran's feet as if butter wouldn't melt in his mouth, then back at Fran, who was smiling warmly.

'Anyway, Hols, how are you doing?'

To her horror, Holly's eyes filled with tears.

'Sweetheart, what is it?' Fran reached out and rubbed her arm. 'All a bit much for you? Come here.'

She pulled Holly into a hug, and they stood that way for a while, until Holly managed to stop sniffling.

'It's okay, Hols. You're bound to feel rubbish. Losing your grandpa and coming back here with a young baby was always going to be tough.'

Holly nodded, then pulled a tissue from the changing bag hooked over the handles of the pram and wiped her eyes. 'It's a bit more than that, though.'

'Rich too?'

'Yes.'

'Come on, I know what you need.'

Fran slid her arm through Holly's and they crossed the road, making their way along the path that led behind the row of shops on Beach Street, and along Dolphin Drive until they reached Shell's Shack.

'How did you know?' Holly laughed as Fran held the door open and she pushed the pram inside.

'Nothing like one of Shell's shakes to make you feel better.'

She hoped Fran was right.

–

The smell in Shell's Shack was heavenly. A combination of sweet and savoury pastries, freshly baked bread and cakes. Shell used locally sourced produce as far as possible, but her inspiration came from around the world, and in the summer holidays she ran cookery classes for children from the village and those holidaying in the area.

Holly wheeled the pram over to a table in the corner and put the brake on, then removed her coat and sat down. Fran joined her after she'd said hello to Shell and her daughter, Bella.

'This place never changes.' Holly looked around her at the eclectic decor. The low ceiling beams were draped with fishing nets and colourful shells looped together with lengths of blue string. Dried lavender and rosemary bouquets filled sea glass vases on the small round tables and the open fireplace to the right of the counter. There were a variety of lobster pots and an anchor on the hearth; above it was a driftwood mirror complete with sea horse carvings. The plump cushions on the chairs had herb prints with their Latin names, like *Lavandula* and *Ocimum basilicum*. Against the one wall was a two-seater sofa covered with a deep burgundy and red patchwork quilt, and in front of it sat a table made entirely of driftwood.

'It is cosy and quaint.' Fran nodded. 'Sit.' She pointed at the dark wooden floorboards, and the dog stared at them then at her.

'He doesn't look like he wants to.'

'Training doesn't happen overnight, sadly.' Fran didn't look sad, though; she looked quite amused, as if the pup's antics were all part of the fun.

'Sit!' She tried again, and this time the dog obeyed. 'You're such a good boy!' she cooed at him, rubbing his fluffy ears.

'It looks as though he's smiling.' Holly peered over the table.

'Of course he is.' Fran frowned. 'What's that grunting?'

'Oh…'

Holly checked on Luke. He was stirring after his nap, and as she gazed at him, she felt that familiar tug in her chest. She would do anything for this child, anything at all to make sure that he was happy and safe, that he had the best life she could give him.

She unbuckled the harness of the seat and lifted him out. He grunted again and she wrinkled her nose.

'Filling his nappy,' she whispered to Fran as she grabbed the changing bag. 'Won't be long.'

'What'll you have?' Fran called after her, waving the menu.

'Surprise me.'

In the toilets, which were fully equipped with a baby changing unit complete with side guards and nappy bin, Holly changed Luke, then washed her hands and picked him up again. As she unlocked the door, she caught sight of herself in the mirror and paused.

Seeing herself holding a small baby never ceased to surprise her, as if she was living someone else's life. It wasn't that she'd never wanted children, because she had, but Luke hadn't been planned. She'd thought she'd have a beautiful home, a secure job, a loving husband and all the traditional things her grandpa would have expected of her before she had a baby. But it hadn't happened that way. Luke had come along as a surprise, but she couldn't love him more if she tried. He was her world now and everything was about him, for him, because of him.

And that was why he had to know his daddy too. She couldn't allow the situation to continue as it was. Luke had a right to know Rich and Rich had a right to know Luke, even though the thought of how it would all work filled her with unease – especially now that there was another woman on the scene. What if she didn't like babies, or what if she was mean to Luke? What if she had babies of her own and Luke ended up feeling left out or abandoned?

Her chest squeezed as she imagined her son being hurt emotionally or physically, and that urge to run resurfaced in her. At least in Exeter it was just the two of them, with fortnightly visits from her dad. At least she controlled their routine, their environment and their social circle. Not that it had been much of a circle. But here, back in Penhallow Sands, things were out of her control and there would be other people involved in Luke's upbringing. How would she cope with that?

She just didn't know. But for Luke's sake, she had to try.

Back at the table, Fran was reading something on her mobile and the pup was lying down at her feet. Fran was so pretty, with her reddish-brown hair, thick-rimmed black glasses and bright red lipstick. Her purple tunic with slashes of blue on the bell sleeves reminded Holly of the clothing she'd seen on a documentary about the Tudors. She loved Fran's dress sense and her short hair. She'd almost had her own completely chopped, but decided to see how she got on with a bob first.

'All clean?' Fran asked as Holly buckled Luke back into the car seat.

'Yup. But…' Holly held her nose, 'stinky.'

'That bad?'

'You wouldn't believe how bad considering he only drinks milk. I mean, it's not like he had a curry last night or anything.'

'Dogs are much easier.'

'Really?'

Fran pushed her glasses up her nose. 'Really. At least they do it outside, then it's a case of pooper scoop and into the waste digester.'

'What's that?'

'It's a bit like a bottomless bucket that I've buried in the garden. I have four, actually, dotted around, because the garden's so big that otherwise I'd have to carry the poop for miles. I have to add an enzyme to the buckets once a week, which turns everything liquid, and it drains into the soil.'

'Eww!'

'Hey, don't knock it! We have to think of the planet for future generations. With four dogs, five cats and two bearded dragons, how else would I dispose of everything?

97

I'd be putting out hundreds of bags of rubbish, and that would be such a bad thing.'

'Of course it would.'

They smiled at each other for a moment, then Holly asked, 'How are you doing? With your art and your sculpting?'

Fran was a talented artist and ceramist. She had converted the small extension on her parents' house into a studio, where she painted and sculpted. It meant that she could work from home, allowing her to be there to take care of her menagerie.

'I'm doing okay.' She nodded. 'I've had some orders for pots and vases from a few shops in town and from one in Newquay, and my paintings have been selling well too.'

Fran's Cornish landscapes were incredible, especially the ones of the vineyard. When Holly had run the vineyard shop, she'd stocked them and some of Fran's sculptures too. They'd sold well, and she had been proud to tell customers that the artist was a close friend.

'Sorry you lost the business at Greenacres.'

Fran shrugged. 'It was only a small part of my income, Hols. I'm managing.'

'I'm glad to hear it, but even so, when I left, I didn't consider the impact it would have on your sales.'

'Your dad returned my stock, so it's fine.'

Holly knew that Fran had already forgiven her, but she couldn't push away the gnawing guilt. She'd let Fran down and it saddened her.

Shell arrived at the table, her daisy-print apron with its frilled trim hugging her generous curves. She set two tall glasses on the table. 'Madagascan vanilla shakes with plenty of Cornish ice cream. I'll be back with your cake in a moment.'

She went to walk away, then paused.

'Is that your baby, Holly?'

'Yes, this is Luke.'

Shell leant over the car seat and gazed at him. She gently touched his cheek, then inhaled noisily.

'I just adore that baby smell, don't you?' Her big blue eyes widened. 'You ever want a babysitter, let me know.'

'Join the queue,' Fran said.

'I can't believe my own baby is seventeen.' Shell nodded at the counter, where Bella, who looked like a stretched version of her mother, was ringing something through the till.

'Seventeen!' Holly gasped. 'How did that happen?'

Shell had been a few years ahead of them at school and got pregnant just before she went to college to study catering. She'd had Bella at seventeen, something that had sent the traditionalists in Penhallow Sands into disapproving whispers, but she had held her head up and got on with it. With the support of her family, she'd finished her college course then got a business loan and set up Shell's Shack. She was strong and determined, and Holly and Fran had always been full of admiration for her.

Now she stood up straight and patted her mop of blonde curls, which were currently held back by a headband. 'She'll be heading off to university next year. She's at college at the moment studying law, psychology and sociology. Must get her brains from her father. Bastard!' She grimaced. Bella's father had been a holiday romance, a slightly older boy who'd come to the bay for a week, got Shell pregnant, then walked away. Apart from maintenance, he'd refused to have anything to do with Bella – something that had shocked everyone who knew the beautiful child.

'He's lost out,' Holly said.

Shell nodded. 'He has, but so has she. I've tried to make up for it, but I know she'd have loved a daddy too.'

'She's happy and ambitious and she'll be just fine.' Fran patted Shell's hand. 'She has you and your family and she's a bright girl. She'll go far.'

'It's wonderful that she's doing law,' Holly said. 'I studied business law at A level. It's hard work, but fascinating.'

'I know, I'm so proud of her.' Shell gazed at her daughter and Holly recognized the expression of maternal love on her face – she saw it in the mirror every day since she'd had Luke. 'Who's Luke's daddy, Holly, or shouldn't I ask? Is it Rich? Of course it is, right? You two were always together.'

Holly opened her mouth, then closed it again.

'Oops!' Shell bit her lip. 'None of my business. I'll just take my big mouth away.'

She sashayed over to the counter and picked up two plates of cake, which she brought to the table and set in front of them.

'It's lovely to see you, Holly. Really lovely. You must come to one of my girls' nights in while you're home. I promise to keep my nose out of things that don't concern me.'

'Sure.' Holly nodded. 'And it's fine, honestly.'

When Shell had gone to serve another customer, Fran leant over the table.

'Her girls' nights in can be a lot of fun. It's basically a chance to eat delicious food and drink wine while laughing… a lot.'

'Sounds great. And this cake looks amazing.'

The slice of cake was enormous and she wondered if she'd be able to manage it, but after not eating her lunch, she was quite hungry now. And it was so tempting. Rainbow layers of sponge were sandwiched together with thick whipped cream, and the surface was slick with marble icing. She stuck her fork into it, and when she put it in her mouth, she moaned.

'I know, right?' Fran giggled. 'Delicious.'

They ate in silence, people-watching as customers came and went and Shell and Bella bustled around serving and clearing plates away. A few familiar faces came over to say hello and to admire Luke, and each time Holly could see the question in their eyes. They all wanted to know if Luke was Rich's child. Why would they think anything else?

When Fran went to the toilet, Holly pulled her mobile from the changing bag and read Rich's text again, where he'd suggested meeting at their old spot. She started to compose a text with a question about Sam, asking if she'd mind Rich meeting his former girlfriend, but she thought better of it and deleted it. Better just to keep it simple.

She had a lot to deal with, and this afternoon would involve a tough conversation, but for now she had Luke, Fran, cake and vanilla milkshake. Who could ask for more than that?

Chapter 8

Later that afternoon, Holly steered the Range Rover up the winding road that led to the car park she'd been to so many times before. Luke was chatting happily to himself in his car seat, and the sounds he was making made her smile in spite of her nerves.

The tyres crunched on the gravel as she pulled in next to an old Fiesta that she recognized as belonging to Rich's mum. Lucinda had had that car for years and it seemed that Rich had borrowed it to come here today. Holly doubted he'd have brought his mum too; that would have been a bit much and they'd never manage to speak frankly with her around. She meant well but could sometimes be a bit overbearing.

There were no other cars in the car park, so Holly hoped the walk would be quiet and give her time to gather her thoughts. She got out and unfolded the pram, then clipped the car seat onto it and slid the changing bag over the handle. The air was fresh and cool, so she tucked a soft blanket over Luke and gave him a kiss before raising the hood to keep the chill off him. Where they were going, it could get breezy.

She walked briskly for ten minutes along the tree-lined path, enjoying the chance to stretch her legs and get her heart beating. As the trees thinned out, the path opened up to reveal a grassy verge at the top of the cliffs. Standing at the railing, gazing out to sea, was Rich.

Holly paused, seizing the opportunity to look at him properly. He was wearing blue jeans and a black shirt with the sleeves rolled up. He had never seemed to feel the cold. Throughout his teenage years, Holly had heard Lucinda shout at him to take a jacket or a jumper when he went out, and Rich had always laughed then left the cottage without either.

His tall, broad-shouldered frame stood out against the glorious backdrop of the sea and the coastline with its golden sand and grassy dunes. He could have been a model on a photo shoot. His dark hair shone in the late-afternoon light, and she could even make out the line of his jaw in profile.

Then he turned.

She gasped as she was hurtled back through the years to the first time they'd come here as a couple, a few years ago. When they'd set out from the village, the weather had been fine. Rich had driven his own car then, a black Audi that his parents had got him for his birthday, and as they'd climbed the road to the pretty spot, Holly's belly had fizzed with excitement and nerves. They'd only recently got together, and their relationship was still very new.

They'd reached the car park at the same time as heavy grey clouds, and when they'd got out of the car, it had been cold, the air filled with the threat of a storm. Rich had taken her hand as they walked to the railing and peered out at the haze over the sea, where rain had already started to fall. He had pulled her closer when she'd shivered; then, as droplets started to wet their hair and shoulders, he'd turned her in his arms and raised her chin. His dark-brown eyes had held hers and her heart had threatened to burst as he slowly lowered his head and kissed her. It wasn't their first kiss, but it felt like the first time.

He'd tasted of the salt air and sunshine, and his skin smelt of cedar and spice. His lips were soft, his kisses firm, and feelings had unfurled inside Holly that she hadn't experienced before. She'd pressed herself against him, and when he'd slid his hands down and pulled her even closer, she'd emitted a moan that was raw and primal.

Then the rain had really come down, drenching Holly's red cotton summer dress, filling her white-laced pumps and even soaking her underwear. They had broken apart, laughing, then run to the car and jumped back in. Rich had pulled a blanket from the back seat and draped it over Holly, then started the engine with the blowers on full to warm them up.

But in spite of her wet clothes and hair, Holly had been warmed by an inner glow that Rich had lit within her. His kiss, his embraces and the desire she felt for him had only confirmed what she'd already known: Rich was the only man for her.

'Holly!' He waved, snapping her back to the present.

'Hi...' Her voice emerged croaky with emotion, and she coughed to clear her throat.

As he walked towards her, she took a deep breath.

'Shall we sit down?' He gestured at the bench off to their right.

'Sure.'

She pushed the pram over to it and set the brake, then checked on Luke. He was patting his mouth with his hand and cooing, clearly enjoying the noise it made.

'So, we need to talk.' It was a statement, not a question.

She nodded and turned slightly on the bench to face him. Her neck and shoulders felt stiff, and she knew it was the stress of being here with Rich again, of having to deal with the tension that now existed between them.

'It's still so beautiful here,' she said.

'I know. I've come here a few times since I got home, and it seems even more beautiful than before.'

Just like you…

Stop it, Holly! Focus.

'What happened last year, Rich…'

'I know, and before we go any further, I have to say that I'm so very sorry.'

She allowed her eyes to roam his face, taking in the slight dent to the left of his nose where he had a chickenpox scar, the shadow on his jaw that suggested he hadn't shaved this morning, and the fine lines at the corners of his eyes. Lines that had formed over the years but that only added to his allure. And his hair… Up close, she could see silver glints where there were a few odd greys. Had they been there last year? She didn't think so. She wondered if he'd go completely grey as he aged, or bald like his father. Either way, she knew he would still be the same Rich; that she would still yearn to hold him whenever she saw him. But he had moved on, he had someone else, and that was his business. What he did was up to him now, as long as he treated Luke right.

He'd said he was sorry…

'You're sorry?'

He nodded. 'I am. For so long I didn't value you or what we had. Letting you down like I did was awful. Unforgivable.'

'Oh…' She'd been expecting fireworks as she'd seen in the past; for Rich to argue that he'd been justified in leaving her hanging as he had, but instead he seemed to be accepting responsibility for what he'd done.

She wanted to pour everything out, to ask him why he'd behaved as he had, why he'd let her down, why he hadn't loved her as she wanted him to, but another, stronger impulse was driving her now. Her own feelings didn't matter as much as her child's, and it was Luke she'd come here to talk about. The past was the past and couldn't be changed. Rich had someone else now, so it was up to Holly to fight for her son, to find out whether Rich was prepared to commit to him. It was better to know now while Luke was so young, while she could protect him.

So she squashed the yearning to know more, to beg for answers that would soothe her and ease the pain she'd carried for so long, and pulled her maternal instincts to the forefront instead.

'Holly… I'd like to explain—'

She held up a hand. 'It's all right, Rich. There's no need. That was then. Life is very different now.' She glanced at the pram. 'This isn't about us, it's about Luke.'

'I can't believe he's mine.'

She nodded. 'I wasn't lying to you.'

'I know, but even though I've had two days to let it sink in, I'm struggling to accept that I'm a dad.'

His eyes were filled with confusion. It made him look younger, more vulnerable. Holly had seen that look in his eyes so many times before as he'd struggled to deal with losing his brother.

'I understand why you didn't let me know, but I also feel... I feel angry, Holly, as though I've been robbed of his first few months.'

'I know, and I'm sorry for that. But when I left, I didn't know I was pregnant. It took me by surprise too.'

'When did you find out?'

'I was fifteen weeks along.'

'Wow.'

'I know, but what with my periods always being so irregular, I wasn't surprised when I didn't have one for months. I also attributed it to the stress of what had happened after you let me down.' Pain and anger flickered in her chest.

Rich rubbed his eyes and blew out his cheeks. Something passed over his face and it tugged at her heart. She'd seen that look before; it surfaced when he was struggling to deal with something, when he was hurting but didn't want to show the world. Her hand shot to his face before she could stop it, and she gently stroked his cheek. His skin was cool, rough with stubble. His pupils dilated and he covered her hand with his own. As angry and hurt as she had been, and still was to a certain degree, she had loved him deeply.

'Holly...'

'Oh Rich, how did it come to this?'

She pulled her hand away and pressed it into her lap, lacing her fingers together to stop herself from touching him again. It wouldn't help the situation.

'I didn't know what to do when I found out that I was expecting. The timing couldn't have been worse. And we'd been using protection, so I was completely confused about how it had happened. The chances were so slim.'

She took a deep breath. Out on the sea, a ship sounded its horn, and a few seconds later, another replied.

'As soon as I discovered that Luke was growing inside me, I knew I would do everything I could to protect him.'

'That's why you stayed away?'

'Yes. You'd left, and I knew I couldn't return home pregnant. Grandpa—'

'Would've gone mad.'

'That's an understatement.'

'I'm so sorry.' His voice was thick with emotion.

She shrugged. 'You didn't know.'

'But I left you.'

'You did, and I can't deny that you hurt me.' She released a shaky breath. 'But it's not about me now. I can deal with my own feelings. I just wanted you to know that Luke is your son and to ask how you feel about it.'

'It's a shock, but obviously when I saw you at the funeral I suspected he could be mine. When was he born?'

'The eleventh of January. He was premature, born at thirty-three weeks.'

'You coped with all that alone?'

'What choice did I have? Dad came to see me when he could, but I managed.' A bitter taste flooded her mouth. She was angry with Rich, but she knew it was for the wrong reasons. How could he have been there to help when he knew nothing about the baby? He wasn't a mind-reader, was he? Besides which, her own pride had prevented her from trying to contact him. And yet… Rich had made it clear that he didn't want her last year, so he was the last person she would have turned to for help. She'd been furious with him at the time for how he'd behaved, for not wanting her, but she'd also not wanted his charity, had feared that he might suggest getting back together out of pity or a sense of obligation.

'You're amazing, Holly.'

'I had no option other than to keep going.' This was harder than she'd imagined it would be.

A squeal from the pram made her jump, and she pushed down the hood to reveal Luke's red, scrunched-up face. She undid the straps and lifted him out, automatically kissing his soft cheek, then turned back to Rich, holding their son on her lap, taking strength from her fathomless love for the baby they'd created.

Rich gazed down at Luke and reached out to him, and the baby grabbed his forefinger and shook it up and down, then pulled it towards his mouth.

'He wants to eat everything at the moment,' Holly explained.

Rich smiled, his eyes fixed on Luke.

'Could I hold him?'

'Of course.'

Holly handed the baby over. He looked tiny in Rich's arms, yet he seemed to belong there. Rich murmured to him, sniffed his head and kissed his cheek, and Holly realized what was happening: he was falling in love with his child.

As if the meeting hadn't been emotional enough, her heart filled until it was fit to burst. She'd imagined this moment for so long, pictured it in the grey hours of dawn when she'd been pacing the floorboards with a grizzly Luke, when she'd cried at how lonely she was and how she wished that life had turned out differently.

But now it was happening… and it was beautiful.

'He's perfect,' Rich said, settling Luke in the crook of his arm and taking the rattle that Holly offered him. He held it in front of Luke's face and the baby tapped it, then smiled when it made a noise.

'How do we do this, Holly? I would like to be involved in Luke's life and to help you in whatever way I can.'

'We both need time to adjust, I guess.'

'But when are you leaving? If you are, I mean...'

'I don't know if I will.' The words escaped and Holly ran them over in her mind. She had made the decision without being aware of it. 'I'm needed here, and to be honest, I need to *be* here.'

'What about work? Did you have a job?'

'Briefly. I did some temping, but when Luke came early, I had to quit.'

'How did you manage?'

'I had savings, remember.'

There was ice in her tone, and Rich's shoulders stiffened.

'You used the deposit for Plum Tree Cottage on rent?' He sounded devastated for her.

'Some of it, and what I'd earned while I was able to work. Apart from rent and food, and some baby things, I wasn't exactly out partying my money away.'

'No, of course not.' He kissed Luke's head. 'I'm glad you're going to stay. It'll give us time to work things out in terms of this little man. And please let me know what you need.'

'I have most things already.'

'But surely you need nappies and clothes and so on? I mean, I don't know much about babies, but I do know that they grow.'

'I'll let you know. I haven't had much time to think about all that since I came home.'

'It must be difficult at Greenacres.'

'More than you know.' Holly's mind strayed to the problems the vineyard was facing, and she realized that despite everything – the hurt, the tears, the recriminations and the grief – she had to stay and help fix things.

'Holly… my mother… she'll want to see Luke too, if you can find it in your heart to let her. And my father, of course.'

'We need to take this one step at a time. I haven't let him out of my sight since he was born. Those first weeks were so tough, and I worried I'd lose him.' Her throat tightened and she tried to relax her shoulders, to elongate her neck and breathe slowly.

'He was ill?'

'He was strong, so he didn't suffer any infections like some premature babies do, but even so, he had to stay in hospital for three weeks until they were sure his lungs were sufficiently developed. It's hard for me to think about being without him.'

'I understand that, Hols. I really do. We'll do this at your pace. As I said, I don't know much about babies, but I'll learn quickly, I promise.'

She nodded, then held out her arms for her son. She pressed him to her and breathed him in, holding him tight and keeping him safe. That was her job and she'd do it well, come what may…

–

Rich watched as Holly strapped the car seat into the back of the Range Rover. While she folded up the pram and packed it into the boot, he leant into the car and said goodbye to little Luke. It was one of the strangest mornings of his life, finally accepting and facing the fact that he was a father now, and that the woman he'd spent so many years of his life with was the mother of his child. But it wasn't a bad feeling, not at all. Rich had once thought he'd never want children, never want to settle down, but sometimes life had a way of surprising you, of letting you know what you needed.

He closed the door gently, then went round to Holly.

'Any idea when I can next see him – and you?'

'You have my number, so text or ring and we can sort something out.'

He nodded. 'I guess the weekend is too soon?'

Holly paused. Was it too soon? Their meeting had gone well and she did want him to be involved in Luke's life.

'No. Come for lunch if you like, on Sunday.'

'I'd love that!' He smiled, then stepped towards her as if he was about to hug her, but she moved backwards and her cheeks flushed.

'Sorry, I… Old habits, I guess.'

'It's okay. Just… you know… it's probably not a good idea to get too close, is it?'

Holly was right. He'd let her down badly last year and she had every right to be angry with him. He'd had time to think things through and he knew that he had cared about her, but he also knew that he'd held his feelings back, that he'd allowed fear to dominate his life.

'No… I guess not.'

'It would only make everything even more confusing, and I just… I can't, Rich. Not now.'

Holly got into the car and closed the door behind her. The electric window opened and she smiled at him. 'See you Sunday.'

Rich stood and watched until the Range Rover had disappeared down the country lane, then he turned and walked back to the railings and gazed down at the sea below. It swirled around, lapping against the rocks, pulled this way and that, uncertain of its intended direction. Until he'd gone away, Rich had felt like that for as long as he could remember. His head was so much clearer now, and he was glad, because the news that he had a child he hadn't been aware he had created was mind-blowing. In fact, it was downright terrifying. What an enormous responsibility! But Luke was here now and Rich had to get used to the idea, and fast, or he could ruin this chance to be a dad to his son.

Seeing Holly again, being close to her, had also opened his eyes to how badly he had behaved and to what he had lost when he threw their relationship away. She was a good woman, a loving mum, and his son was lucky to have her to care for him. It was obvious that she adored Luke and would do anything to protect him. Everything she'd been through showed just how strong she was, and how brave; she could have crumbled, but she hadn't. She'd kept going for their child, through difficult times, and she'd done an amazing job of motherhood so far.

Rich felt ashamed that he hadn't been there for them, that he'd let her and their son down. What kind of a man did that make him? But then last year he'd been at his lowest ebb and would likely have been more hindrance than help. There were no excuses for the past, but he would make things better for them all from here on in.

He had a job now, he had prospects, and would provide for his son if Holly would let him.

It would be too much to hope that she might also want him in her life again, and he wasn't sure that it would be right for any of them. Her love had been deep and true, and a positive force in his life, and he'd brushed it off as though it was dust on his sleeve. He could see the hurt in her eyes and could tell that she was still wounded, cautious, hesitant. If he pushed her, she might flee, and he didn't want that. He wanted to earn her trust, to prove that he was a decent human being who could be a decent father, even though that idea also unnerved him because he had no idea how or where he was going to start with it.

But he had to start somewhere, and helping with Luke, getting to know his son, was probably a good place to begin. He was terrified of doing something wrong – after all, he had no idea about babies and their wants and needs – but he aimed to learn quickly. Gone were the days when he focused on fast cars and drinking games, on wild holidays and trying to forget about Dean. He knew he was still on a journey and that he had to monitor his own behaviour and reactions to situations; that he couldn't take anything for granted, because if he took his eye off the ball, he could sink again. This new responsibility would be a challenge, but it was one he wanted to live up to. Holly had been his best friend, and if he wanted to have her friendship again, he'd need to prove that he was worthy of it.

There was one other thing he could do; something he should have done a long time ago. He wanted to pick up a few things, so he'd head into town at the weekend to search for some inspiration. He had a feeling that a certain person would want to help.

After all, this was a very big deal for his mum too.

Chapter 9

The next morning, Holly left Luke with her granny so she could take a look around Greenacres. The three days since she'd returned had been chaotic, and she hadn't had a chance to explore her old home.

She let herself out of the back door and headed across the yard in the direction of the winery building. As she passed the window, her dad waved at her. He was engaged in conversation with one of the long-term employees, so she decided not to disturb them, but to go and take a look at the shop instead.

There was a sign on the door telling customers the opening hours, which had been reduced considerably since Holly had last worked there. There was also a mobile number in case the shop was unattended for some reason, so customers could alert someone at the vineyard to their presence.

Holly pushed the key into the lock and it turned easily. It was like stepping back in time.

The smell of lavender and paper hit her first, followed by the smell of furniture polish. There was the counter with its mural of the vineyard in summer that Fran had painted, the old-fashioned till sitting on top, and the shelves that took up the walls to the right and left. However, unlike in the past, the shelves were almost bare.

There were some bottles of wine, a few of the decanters that Holly had ordered in as an add-on sale and some boxes of complimentary glasses that they'd given away with larger orders.

The wall behind the counter was naked. Previously it had been adorned with Fran's beautiful paintings, and now that they were gone, Holly could see how much they had added to the shop. To her right, the shelves that had held Fran's olive bowls, vases, jugs and tiny models of Greenacres were empty except for a film of dust. On the top one, a can of furniture polish sat with a yellow duster, clearly abandoned mid clean.

It made her sad to see this small corner of the vineyard in disarray. As a child, she had helped her mum out in the shop. On quiet days, her mum had told her stories about the grapes, and about her own childhood, as they'd sat on stools behind the counter and drunk endless cups of tea. Sometimes her dad had joined them, and he'd spoken about his life in Australia and about coming to Cornwall and falling in love with Holly's mum. She had loved to listen to her parents, to watch how they gazed at each other and to feel that she was a part of something very special indeed.

After her mum had died, Holly had run the shop and built it into a successful part of the vineyard business. Customers came to buy wine, and Holly would ensure that they went away with extras like the lavender pouches and Fran's artwork. She had been good at anticipating what people wanted, then selling them something else too. It had been enough for her, the small world that she had lived in. Her dreams of travelling had been put away like the dolls she'd played with as a child, and she'd stayed where she felt safe and loved. And there had been Rich. He had been everything she'd wanted and needed and she had clung to what they had. She had thought she could love him enough for both of them.

She had been wrong.

She went behind the counter, pulled out a stool and sat down, resting her elbows on the counter. Then she buried her face in her hands and cried.

She cried for her mum, for her dad, for her granny and grandpa, for Fran and her lost sales, and she cried for what she herself had lost when Rich had pulled out of buying Plum Tree Cottage. She had thought she had her life sorted, then everything had spiralled out of her control and changed beyond recognition.

At last she sat up and wiped her eyes on her shirtsleeve.

Today was a new day. She was home.

She was going to help her dad to save Greenacres, only this time it would be better than ever before. And she knew exactly how she was going to start. She pulled her mobile from her pocket and dialled Fran's number.

—

'I'm not so sure about this, Dad.' It was two days later, and Holly was sitting in the passenger seat of her dad's Range Rover.

'It'll be fine and it will do you good. I bet you've not had an evening out in at least eight months.'

'No, but… I don't mind.'

'Holly, you'll only be at Fran's, and I'll come and pick you up later.'

'At ten?'

'Yes, or earlier if you want. Luke will be fine.'

Holly peered into the back of the car, where her son was strapped into his seat.

'What if he needs me?'

'I did raise a baby, you know, and you're sitting right next to me. I know how to feed and change Luke, how to sing to him and read to him if he's fractious. And Granny will be there too.'

'Okay...' Holly unclipped her seat belt and opened the car door. 'Promise you'll ring me immediately if there's a problem.'

'I promise. I love him too, you know.'

'I do know that.' She smiled at her dad. Of course he loved Luke too. He was a kind, big-hearted man who had always doted on her. Loving her son would be second nature to him.

She closed the door gently to avoid disturbing the sleeping baby. It was fine; it would all be fine. She had the chance to spend an evening with Fran, to relax and let her hair down. Hell, she could even have a glass of wine. Or two...

She opened the gate, then walked up the path and knocked on the door. From within came the barking of several dogs and the scratching of claws on the flagstone floor. She heard a stern command to sit and stay, then the door opened and Fran stood there wearing denim dungarees covered in wet patches, with a spotted scarf tied around her head and a small grey dog wriggling under her right arm.

'Holly!' Fran grabbed her and gave her a one-armed hug. 'Come on in.'

Holly wrinkled her nose at the strong doggy aroma that wafted off her friend, but composed her features and stepped into the hallway. Three dogs sat in a row, their tails wagging as they eyed Holly excitedly.

'Stay!' Fran pointed at the dogs.

'They won't rush me, will they?' Holly asked, only half joking.

'No, they're all well trained. It's this little scamp I have to watch at the moment.' Fran rubbed the scruffy grey head and the dog squirmed, trying to break free from her embrace. 'He's desperate to say hello.'

'Oh…' Holly held out her hand and let the lurcher sniff her palm. He gave it a swift lick, and she grimaced as the warm, wet tongue met her skin.

'Worse things you could do than accept a canine kiss.' Fran waggled her eyebrows, then indicated the row of dogs. 'You'll remember Crosby, my golden Lab, and Scamp, the whippet, then this is Dust Bunny… I have no idea what her parents were.'

'Yes, I met Crosby and Scamp before I left… Hello, Dust Bunny.'

The dog blinked up at her and shuffled closer.

'I'm watching you, Dust Bunny,' Fran warned, and it shuffled backwards with a gentle whine.

'What's the new one called?' Holly asked.

'I don't know. I've tried to name him, but I can't come up with anything that seems right. Perhaps you can help me.'

Holly gazed at the dog, trying to think of a suitable name. It had been hard enough choosing one for her son; in the end, she'd named him after one of the nurses at the hospital who had cared for him in the days after his birth.

'I'm going to set him down now. Are you ready?'

'I guess so.'

Fran put the dog on the floor and Holly braced herself. The pup's eyes widened, then he shook his head, wagged his tail and leapt at her, causing her to take a step backwards. Even though he was small, his enthusiasm gave him momentum and power.

She reached down and patted him, and he immediately flipped over onto his back. She looked at Fran, wondering if she'd done something to upset him.

'He's offering you his belly to stroke. It's a sign of trust and submission. He likes you.'

As Holly rubbed the dog's belly, she heard Fran say, 'Go on then.' She was suddenly flanked by the other three dogs, and she held her breath as she was licked, sniffed and showered with canine affection.

'That's it, dogs! Enough for now. Let Holly get up.'

Holly staggered to her feet and Fran grinned at her.

'They love you as much as I do.'

'Ha! Now I stink.'

'My dogs are clean.' Fran's grin had dropped from her face.

'I know that. What I meant was that they all licked me and…' Holly looked down at her black top and jeans, which were covered in hair. 'I didn't mean to sound rude, Fran, gosh…'

'You're still so easy to wind up.' Fran winked at her. 'I know you weren't being rude. Doggy drool does tend to be a bit whiffy. Anyway, come on through and I'll pour you a drink.'

Holly followed Fran through the airy hallway with its flagstone floor, open staircase and doorway to the lounge. The cottage kitchen was just as she remembered it, with dark beams on the white ceiling, ancient yellow

Aga against the back wall, apron-fronted sink and green wooden cabinets with chips and missing handles. She was hit by a wave of memories from childhood as she walked over to the round table and pulled out a chair. She'd sat here with Fran while they'd revised for exams, talked about school, boys and the future; while they'd played games at Christmas time with Fran's parents and while they'd put the world to rights.

The dogs settled, two of them on the old sofa near the Aga and one in a fluffy round bed in the corner. The grey lurcher came and sat at Holly's feet. She smiled at him but kept her hands in her lap, not wanting to encourage him to start licking her again.

The kitchen smelt of spices and woodsmoke, a familiar combination that made Holly relax, and as the tension seeped from her shoulders, she realized how tightly she'd been holding herself.

'Red or white?' Fran held up two bottles.

'Do you know, I was in such a rush that I forgot to bring wine. And my family owns a vineyard!' Holly shook her head.

'It's okay, chick, I have plenty here… the advantages of having an Italian papa. The cellar is well stocked.'

'I'll have white, please.' Holly removed her coat and hung it on the back of the chair.

'You okay?' Fran asked as she set two glasses on the table.

Holly blinked hard. 'Yes… it's just been a challenging few days.'

'Your grandpa?'

'In part. It's so strange at Greenacres without him around. I keep expecting him to call me for dinner or to find him sitting in his chair in the lounge.' Her throat ached as emotion welled. 'I miss him so much.' She covered her eyes and took a few slow breaths as she tried to control herself.

Fran hugged her, resting her chin on top of Holly's head. 'Let it out, Hols. It's okay.'

Holly gave a small laugh. 'Sorry. I came here to see you and to catch up, not to cry on your shoulder.'

'Hey, it's what I'm here for.'

'I don't deserve you.' Holly looked up at her friend.

'We've been friends for years, Holly, and I hope we'll always be friends. I've cried on your shoulder too, so please don't turn all formal on me.'

'Okay,' Holly squeaked. 'Thank you.'

Fran sat down. 'How are things with Rich?' she asked gently.

Holly filled her in on their meeting. She hadn't told her about it when she'd rung her yesterday, as she'd been keen to discuss her plans for the vineyard shop, then Fran had needed to rush off to deal with a puppy emergency.

'How do you feel about it now?' Fran pushed her glasses up her nose, with its tiny diamond stud.

'Confused.'

'I'll bet.'

'He said he wants to be involved in Luke's life, which is wonderful, but it will be strange being around him now that we're no longer together and he's seeing someone else.'

'Is he?' Fran looked surprised.

'Well… I don't know for certain, but when I saw him at the diner in Newquay, he was with a woman. A very beautiful woman.'

'Didn't you ask him about her when you met up?'

Holly shook her head. 'It didn't seem like any of my business really.'

Fran nodded.

'Fran?'

'Yes.'

'Why are your dungarees wet? I meant to ask when I got here, but I was distracted.'

'I ran the bath for scruffy dog there, because I wanted to get him cleaned up before you arrived, but as I lowered him in, he escaped. The water was only a few centimetres deep and I managed to save myself from a complete soaking, but I still got splashed when he jumped out.'

Holly looked down at the dog, who was resting his chin on his paws and gazing up at her.

'But he looks so cute. I can't imagine him being any trouble.'

'He's not. He just likes his own whiff.'

They giggled then and Holly picked up her glass.

'This is good.'

'Dad never scrimped on wine.'

'It's one thing you shouldn't scrimp on.'

'How are things at the vineyard?'

Holly sighed. 'In a bit of a mess.'

'Want to talk about it?'

She nodded.

'Tell you what... I'll get changed out of these wet dungarees, then you can tell me all about it. I've got pizzas for dinner.'

'Sounds wonderful.'

'Back in a bit.'

When Fran had left the kitchen, Holly leant forward and stroked the dog's head. He emitted a low sound that startled her, and she pulled her hand back. Had he just growled at her? He raised his head and nudged her hand. No, that couldn't have been a growl. He wanted her to do it again. This time, she kept stroking him, and he closed his eyes and his body relaxed.

'You're a little cutie, aren't you?'

She had always liked dogs, but never had one herself, and that made her slightly nervous around them. But this little lad was sweet and had the most adorable eyes. Fran had said he needed a home, but Holly had enough on her plate without thinking about adopting a dog.

Didn't she?

–

After they'd eaten, they moved into the lounge, and Holly told Fran a bit more about the financial forecast for the vineyard, to clarify why she'd rung her yesterday.

Fran nodded. 'I've had a good think about what you asked me, and I can definitely help.'

'You can?' Holly squealed.

'Of course. I still have some of the paintings of Greenacres here, and I'll get to work on the order of clay condiment bowls and goblets after the weekend.'

'I was thinking that perhaps we could have them in a variety of colours.'

'Definitely. Blue always looks nice, but so do multi-coloured ones.'

'I was thinking that if I set up a proper website, then I can sell everything on there too. Although I might need some help at some point, I think I can do the basics.'

'That sounds amazing. I could even design a logo for you.'

Goose bumps rose on Holly's arms. 'Oh Fran, I'm getting quite excited about it. Grandpa wouldn't hear of us using the internet or consider modern ways of promoting the vineyard, and it could do so much for Greenacres. I have lots of ideas, and so does Dad, and with your help, I'm sure we can build the business up again.'

'I'm happy to be involved, especially if it means you'll stay local.'

'You know what, Fran... I'm pretty certain that's what I'm going to do now.'

They clinked glasses and drank to a successful future, and Holly was happy to think about something other than the past. Yes, it had been tough in many ways, but there was today and tomorrow, next week, next month and next year to consider too.

Fran began to regale her with some of her dating app stories, or rather tales of dating disasters.

'You really pretended to work there?'

'Well, yeah... I walked into the restaurant and saw my blind date sitting there, looking more like David Cameron than David Beckham, and... well let's just say the ex-PM is not my cup of tea. So I followed the waitress to the table, and as she walked away, I asked him for his drinks order.'

'Didn't he recognize you from your online photo?'

'I might have used a few filters myself, you know, to ensure that if I did enter an establishment and find someone there that I didn't like the look of, I'd have an escape plan.'

'Oh Fran, you crack me up!' Holly held her belly. It was full of pizza and aching from laughter. Coming here this evening had been a good idea; she couldn't remember the last time she'd laughed so much. Fran had always been able to take her mind off her worries, and Holly hoped that over the years she'd supported her friend just as much. Her life had changed dramatically since last year, but being with Fran made it all a bit easier to deal with. Holly was still the same person, regardless of what she'd been through, and she'd missed spending time with her friend. Over recent months, she'd felt at times that she'd lost a part of herself, that she'd changed beyond all recognition. Now that she was back, she felt that the original Holly was still there, just below the surface, and it was good to know. She had needed to evolve in order to deal with what had happened, but it was only an evolution, not a complete transformation.

Fran was sitting at the other end of the squishy sofa wearing her pyjamas – she'd changed into them after removing her dungarees, because they weren't going out anywhere, and what was better than pyjamas – with Scamp curled up in her lap. Her other dogs were lying side by side in front of the log burner, and the pup was on the sofa next to Holly. She didn't know whether it was the three glasses of wine, or the fact that she was having such a good time, but she hadn't protested as the lurcher had gently placed his paws on the sofa cushion, then tentatively climbed up next to her.

Her mobile buzzed on the coffee table, so she picked it up. The message was from her dad, telling her he'd be there in ten minutes.

'Wow, is that the time?'

She told herself to get up, but her body stayed where it was.

'I don't feel like moving at all.'

'Me neither. I'll probably wake up here at about three a.m., flanked by dogs and with a stiff neck from being squashed.' Fran drained her glass, then set it on the table. 'Thanks for coming, Hols. It's been great to catch up. I'm so happy you're thinking seriously about staying in Penhallow Sands.'

Holly smiled as she finished her own wine. 'I know. Me too. I just hope it's for the best.'

'What's for the best is what's right for you and Luke.'

'I don't think I actually want to leave again, Fran.'

She rubbed the lurcher's head, then slid carefully off the sofa, trying not to disturb him, and stood up. When she looked back at him, he was yawing and wagging his tail.

'He'd come home with you right now.' Fran extricated herself from underneath Scamp and walked out into the hallway with Holly.

'I can't take on a dog at the moment, lovely as he is.' Leaving him there was proving more difficult than she'd expected; she'd grown fond of the pup over the course of the evening.

'I know that.'

'I need to know what my next move is… if that makes sense.'

'Of course it does.' Fran hugged her.

'Fran… I didn't get to explain myself properly. You distracted me with wine, food and laughter. I wanted to apologize again for running off as I did and not contacting you.'

'I understand. I've never really been in love, but I know how you felt about Rich.'

Holly slid her arms into her coat, then hooked her bag over her shoulder.

'I keep feeling as though I've forgotten something. It's strange travelling so light after months of being responsible for a baby.'

She'd sent three texts to her dad asking after Luke during the course of the evening, and he'd replied each time that he was fine and she shouldn't worry. It was so nice to have some help, to know that there were people around who would support her with Luke. It was another wonderful bonus to being home, and reminded her how lonely she had been in Exeter.

'Hope everything works out for you now.' Fran scuffed her socked foot on the flagstones. 'Don't be a stranger.'

Lights coming up the road shone through the glass pane to the side of the front door.

'I won't. I'll text you soon, and I'm looking forward to seeing what you come up with for the shop.'

'Don't worry, I'll make some beautiful things to help you boost business at Greenacres.'

Holly opened the door and walked down the path to the car. Once she'd buckled her seat belt, she turned to wave. Standing next to Fran in the pool of light was the little grey lurcher, his head on one side. If it was possible for a dog to look sad, he certainly did.

'Cute pup,' her dad said as he pulled away.

Holly nodded, unable to reply.

With everything else that was going on in her life, why was she getting emotional over a dog?

—

Holly stared at her reflection in the bathroom mirror. Bleary-eyed was an understatement, but it had been at least a year since she'd had a good drink, and the wine she'd put away last night had gone straight to her head.

She ran the cold tap and splashed water over her face, shivering as droplets landed on her chest and arms. She needed coffee and carbs, then she'd be in a better state to deal with whatever today had in store.

Luke had woken once in the night, but once she'd given him a cuddle and his dummy, he'd settled again, clearly enjoying the quiet of the countryside as much as she was. It was so different to her flat in Exeter, where sirens could be heard at all times of the day and night and her upstairs neighbours argued or played music into the early hours.

The air was different here too. When she opened the window, it rushed into the room, making everything feel cleansed and refreshed. If it stayed fine, she'd get their washing out on the line in the back garden later. Line-dried laundry was always nicer than clothes dried indoors.

She returned to the bedroom and lifted Luke from his cot, pressing her nose to his head and inhaling his scent. She'd know his smell anywhere; it was a part of her now. Did he have some of Rich's smell too? Was that even possible? She shook her head. It was probably silly to think so. Everyone had a unique scent, and Luke only carried some of hers because she held him all the time. But if Rich held his son regularly too, would the baby smell of him?

That would be a challenge to deal with.

Downstairs, her father was frying eggs and bacon.

'Morning, angel. Thought you'd appreciate a good breakfast this morning.'

'You were right, Dad. I didn't drink much, but I don't feel great.'

'You did seem quite merry when you got in the car, but I didn't think you were drunk.'

'I should hope not, seeing as how I had Luke to care for. But I do feel as though there's mist on the mountain this morning! Anyway, Fran and I got chatting about Greenacres and the shop, and I think I've managed to persuade her to make us some more stock. Pottery bowls and goblets and any other ideas she has. Plus she said she still has some paintings stored, so we can have those too.'

'Sounds wonderful.'

'I know you think it's only a small step, Dad, but I was also thinking of setting up a website.'

Her dad raised his eyebrows and nodded. 'I'm impressed, Holly. You'll have to tell me more.'

'I will.' She smiled. 'But for now, this boy needs his breakfast.'

She made Luke a bottle, then sat down. As she was feeding him, her granny wandered into the kitchen wearing a navy silk tea dress covered with bright red poppies, a lace and feather fascinator clipped to her bobbed hair. She shuffled over to the kettle in her slippers, and Holly caught her dad's eye.

'Morning, Granny.'

'Hello, darlings!'

'Are you going somewhere nice?'

'Why?'

'Well… you look very smart.'

Glenda peered down at her dress, then raised a hand to her head and straightened the fascinator.

'Yes, actually, I'm going out to lunch with the girls.'

Bruce frowned. 'The girls?'

'Yes, of course! My book club.'

'Who's in your book club, Granny?' Holly placed the empty bottle on the table and shifted Luke on her lap. Once he was sitting upright, she cupped his chin in one hand and rubbed his back gently with the other. His little head moved and his eyes roamed the kitchen. It was as though he was taking in his surroundings, learning where everything was.

'Oh... Yolanda Greene, Deidre Filpot, Hettie James. And others.'

'Where are you meeting?'

'At the library at two. I was hoping you'd drive me, Bruce dear.'

'Of course I will. So you're dressed this early just to be organized?'

She shook her head and emitted a little chuckle. 'I couldn't sleep, so I had a bit of a fashion show instead. I settled on this outfit but thought I'd check what you two thought first.'

'It's very nice.' Bruce smiled at her. 'You look lovely.'

'Why thank you! I know you both think I'm going potty, but I'm still here and fully present. Well, almost! However, I do know that I need to keep my mind active, so I phoned Yolanda last night and asked if I could attend a meeting. That husband of hers, Samuel, is such a flirt! I fancied him a bit when we were younger, you know? He looked just like Marvin Gaye.'

Luke let out a loud belch and Holly quickly dabbed at his chin with his bib.

Granny approached the table and stroked the baby's cheek. He gazed at her intently, then reached for the fascinator and grabbed it.

'Ouch!'

Holly tried to unclip the headpiece from her granny's soft white hair. When she managed to release it, Luke's hand flew backwards and the fascinator sailed across the kitchen, landing in the frying pan and splashing oil everywhere.

'Granny, I'm so sorry!'

'It's fine, darling. That's what babies are for... keeping us grounded. Luke clearly thought the lace and feathers were a bit much for book club.'

Bruce picked the egg-covered fascinator out of the pan and dropped it into the sink. 'I don't know if that can be saved, Glenda, and I'd better fry us some fresh eggs too, as I prefer mine without feathers.'

Granny took a seat next to Holly and held out her arms for the baby. Holly gently handed him over and then poured them all some coffee, hoping as she did so that the rest of the morning would run a bit more smoothly.

Chapter 10

'What's so important that you need me to come shopping, Richard?' Lucinda asked from the passenger seat as they drove through the country lanes on Saturday morning.

Rich glanced at her, taking in her rosy cheeks and ready smile, and realized that she probably knew already.

'Well… I thought you'd want to be involved, Mum, seeing as how I'm off to get some things for your grandson.'

Her face contorted and he wasn't sure if she was about to laugh or cry.

'That's wonderful, Rich. Thank you for thinking of me.'

'I know how you feel about him, and I want you to be part of his life too.'

'He's your double, Rich, just like your brother was. When Dean was born, he was…'

Rich waited for her to finish her sentence, but she didn't, and he knew why.

'I can't see it to be honest,' he said. 'Luke just looks like… well, like a baby to me. Mostly bald except for some fluff; small nose, big eyes, tiny hands and feet.'

'Men!' Lucinda shook her head and huffed. 'Your father said exactly the same thing.'

'Typical Dad!' Rich suppressed a laugh. His mother was a live wire at the best of times, but now that she had a grandchild, he wondered how she'd manage not to pop. 'Anyway, I'd really like to pick up a few things to take over to Greenacres.'

'This is very exciting!'

'It is.' He nodded, wanting to feel that sense of excitement, but he was still reeling from the shock of finding out he was a father. He hoped that if he embraced it with enthusiasm, it would sink in properly. Since the wake on Monday, he'd felt a bit strange, as though something was missing. Perhaps it was because he had a son but he wasn't seeing him every day; perhaps it was because Holly was back in Penhallow Sands but they weren't together, and without her he felt a bit... lost.

'So...' His mum opened her bag and pulled out her new smartphone. 'Where do we start with baby shopping?'

'What are you doing?'

'I'm having a look at a few websites, then I'll make a list to ensure we don't forget anything.'

'I only meant a few things, Mum, like some toys, clothes, possibly a highchair for when he's a bit bigger.'

'Shush, Richard. Let me decide.'

And shush he did, because he knew that his mother needed this. She had always been a positive force in his life, but her bubbly nature had been dulled by what had happened over twenty years ago. Losing her younger son so tragically had changed her for ever, and Rich missed the woman she'd once been. He'd seen flashes of the mum he'd grown up with emerging now and then, but the grief of losing her child had left her emotionally scarred.

Of course, it had impacted upon them all, changed them all irrevocably, so that at times it had seemed as though all hope was gone.

However, with new life came fresh hope. Luke was a sign for them all that love could go on, and love could grow anew. At one point, Rich hadn't believed it was possible, but every day was a new chance, and now life had given him a surprise in the form of Luke that he wanted to fully appreciate. He just hoped he wouldn't let his son down.

–

Rich sipped his coffee and gazed around the café. He'd practically had to beg his mother to stop for refreshments. Lucinda had been like a whirlwind around the shops, giving his credit card, and her own, a thorough battering. He was dreading seeing the bill next month.

But the smile on her face and the excitement flashing in her eyes made it all worthwhile. He just hoped that Holly wasn't going to be offended by the sheer amount of stuff they had bought for the baby. He was also wondering how his dad would react, seeing as how he hadn't yet spoken much about the fact that he had a grandchild. Rich suspected Rex was in shock too, and that given time, he'd come round to the idea. Perhaps, though, he was afraid to accept that he was a grandad in case Holly left Penhallow Sands and they lost Luke too. Of course, if she did go back to Exeter, it wasn't that far, but it wouldn't be the same as seeing her and the baby every day. And if she met someone else, it would all become a lot more complicated.

'That's better!' his mum exclaimed when she returned from the loo. 'Thought I was going to have an accident for a moment there.'

He laughed. 'Too much information, Mum. We could have stopped for a break sooner, you know.'

She settled on the round-backed red leather armchair opposite him and smiled. 'I know, but I was having so much fun. Ooh, just think, Richard, a new baby in the family. I'm so excited!'

He nodded. 'I know.'

'What will you and Holly do now?' Lucinda asked as she eyed him over her cup.

'In what way?'

'Well… it would be nice for Luke to have two parents around.' She sniffed. 'For him to have his parents together.'

'That's a bit traditional, Mum.'

'I *am* traditional, love. I've been with your father for over thirty-five years, as well you know. We had our ups and downs – some worse than others – but ultimately, we made it through. People today give up too easily.'

'Mum… I know you mean well, but this is something I don't know the answer to. I really hurt Holly last year. I messed up and let her down. Just because we have a baby now doesn't mean she's going to want me back.'

Besides which, after everything that had happened, he didn't know if that would be the right thing for Holly, Luke or himself.

'I know, love, but you could at least give it some consideration. For Luke's sake as much as yours. I know you still love her.'

He gripped his mug tightly. He did still care about Holly, he couldn't deny that, but he was afraid that he was in danger of confusing his feelings for her with something bigger. He hadn't felt that he could commit to her last year and had run off like a coward instead of staying around to face the music. If he rushed into something again, even after he'd learnt how to deal with his anxiety and his racing mind, then he could end up right back where he was before.

'She's a lovely person, from a good family. She's clearly a great mum. Just give it some thought.'

'Yes, Mum.' Sometimes it was easier to agree with Lucinda than to try to reason with her.

'I can't wait to see the baby again. Do you think she'll let me visit him soon?'

'I'm sure she will, but we must be careful not to overcrowd them or impose ourselves. This needs to be handled carefully. Holly's grieving for her grandpa and trying to settle in at Greenacres. I'm going over for lunch tomorrow, so I'll speak to her about it then.'

'Thank you.'

They finished their drinks in silence, exhausted by their shopping and lost in their thoughts. Rich was glad of the chance to be still, to catch his breath. When he did meet his mum's eyes again, he was surprised to see that they were full of tears.

'Hey, what is it?'

She waved a hand, her signal to him not to fuss, that she'd be okay in a bit.

'Sorry, love, it all welled up in me then. I think… I need to go and see Dean.'

'What, now?'

'Yes, love.'

Rich nodded. He wasn't surprised really, had almost been expecting it.

'Okay, we'll stop off on the way home.'

–

When Holly opened her eyes, it took her a few moments to register where she was. She'd returned from a walk around the vineyard feeling exhausted, so had eaten a light lunch with Granny and her dad, then taken Luke up for his nap. She'd lain on the bed and watched him for a bit as he babbled to himself before dropping off to sleep, then she'd done some research on her phone about setting up a website for the shop.

She must have fallen asleep too, because the light in the room had changed and was no longer early-afternoon bright. She slid her legs over the edge of the bed and stretched, then stood up. Luke was still sleeping, so she grabbed the monitor and padded from the room and down the stairs.

She made a coffee, then opened the back door. The air was cool on her face and she shivered in her T-shirt. She should've picked up a cardigan, but she didn't want to go back upstairs and disturb Luke, so instead she fetched one of the blankets from the cupboard, then went outside and sat on the bench.

From this point, the land seemed endless. It was bright with spring hope at the moment, but that would soon give way to summer, then the autumn harvest. Holly had always enjoyed watching the seasons change at Greenacres. It was comforting, solid and reassuring. They would continue to change whatever happened to her or her family. This land would be here long after she had gone, and perhaps one of her descendants would be running the vineyard then.

Or would they? If things were looking as gloomy as her dad seemed to think, then one day soon the vineyard might well close, the land sold to developers and turned into housing estates. The beautiful rich earth could be marred with concrete, the area heavily populated, and in a matter of decades, it would be unrecognisable. The thought was heartbreaking. She'd seen it happen before, to local farms and to other vineyards along the Cornish coast, and it had made her shiver. But she'd never thought it could happen here. Grandpa had been so certain that he'd never sell the vineyard, that it would continue to thrive and that it would be Holly's future and there for her children too.

But Grandpa was gone, and with him his determination, as well as his refusal to see the truth of the matter. Without some serious planning, the vineyard might not continue to be a viable business. Holly covered her mouth and blinked hard. If she left and returned to Exeter, she'd be turning her back on this life, taking it away from her son. She couldn't do that to him. He might not want to run the family business when he was older, but if it wasn't here, he wouldn't even have that option.

She wrapped her hands around her mug. There were ways to make money, to help the vineyard thrive without surrendering any of the land. She'd go inside and get her dad's laptop, then make a start on that website immediately. She'd made some notes about what to include and had got some good ideas from her research, so now was as good a time as any.

Rich parked in the church car park and got out. Apart from Holly's grandpa's funeral, he hadn't been here in years. He hadn't been able to face it but had known when he returned recently that he'd have to make the trip at some point. It was inevitable. Perhaps coming here with his mum was how it was meant to be.

He walked around the car and helped her out – it was her car, but she liked him to drive it when they went out so she could check her phone, and anyway she'd been a bit emotional after their shopping trip – then they made their way through the gates and around to the back of the church. The original graveyard dated back over two hundred years, but it had been extended to allow for more recent burials. His mum slid her arm through his and he looked at her. She'd blanched and was clutching her other hand to her chest. He wished he could reassure her, tell her that it was okay, but the words were trapped in his throat.

They took the winding path, then veered left. And there it was. Exactly the same as it had been twenty years earlier. The earth seemed to shift under him as they stood there, and he gripped his mum's arm tighter, sucking in shallow breaths to try to stabilize himself. Then, as if by magic, he heard the mantra the counsellor in Ibiza had used to help him deal with the anxiety attacks: *Feel the fear and do it anyway.*

He closed his eyes and repeated the words, letting them swirl around in his head then flood through his core and his limbs, loosening the tension until it evaporated and was swept away on the breeze.

Death was inevitable, he told himself. Not so early for most, thank goodness, but it was an unavoidable part of the human condition. He couldn't live his life in fear.

Not any more.

He felt to blame for what had happened to Dean and for how his parents had suffered. If it hadn't been for Rich, Dean would still be here, a grown man, possibly with a family of his own. Rich had wished thousands of times that he could turn the clock back; that he could change his mind about heading out into the sea, that he could persuade Dean not to follow him as he always had done. Letting go of that yearning to change what had happened was so hard. Some days he could rationalize it; other days he couldn't. Healing was a tough process.

He was learning gradually to treasure every day and to seize life, to enjoy the sensation of the breeze on his face, the bitterness of black coffee, the thrill as he dived into cold water and it caressed his skin. He had a child now, a precious gift, and although he might experience fear, anger and pain, he couldn't allow them to rule him.

Next to him, his mum sniffed, so he wrapped his arm around her shoulders and pulled her close.

'I'm here, Mum. I love you.'

She leant on him and her shoulders shook. Lucinda, the woman who had been strong throughout his life, who had refused to show the full extent of her pain or to crumble in front of her family, was now finding strength in him.

Chapter 11

Holly glanced at the clock for the tenth time that hour. She'd texted Rich that lunch would be served around one, and it was already gone noon. Her dad was in charge of Sunday lunch, but she was trying to help, seeing as how she'd invited a guest. She'd been up since six working on the website, tweaking pages and images, setting up widgets and contact details, and it was coming along nicely.

Granny was in the lounge with Luke, watching over him as he lay on his play mat. Again, Holly was aware of how comforting it was to have other people around, to have some help. Granted, she'd never bothered making a full roast for herself as it seemed extravagant and over the top. When she'd been younger, their Sunday lunches had been big affairs, with Grandpa at one end of the dining table and Granny at the other, Mum and Dad together then Holly on the other side, often with guests. Sometimes Rich had been there too.

They had talked and laughed, celebrated successes and commiserated over failures, and there had been a strong sense of family unity. Then Mum had passed away and it had changed. They'd still eaten lunch together, but an important part of their family dynamic was gone. It had affected them all. Holly had seen the same thing happen to Rich and his family after they lost Dean. Their shared understanding of loss was one of the things that should have made her and Rich closer, but at times it had seemed to take him away from her and she couldn't work out why. But then grief was different for everyone, so she had tried to be understanding and to support Rich in the way he supported her.

Today, Luke would be there at the table. He wouldn't be eating the roast lunch, of course, but he would be present. Holly wished her mum was here to see that; she'd have loved having her grandson in the room, would have adored the beautiful baby. It made her heart ache.

She shook her head. Nothing would change the past, nothing would bring her mum back, and this wasn't helping with her rising nerves. She shouldn't be nervous – Rich had been here numerous times before – but she was, because this time it was all very different.

'Holly, don't worry, everything's under control.' Her dad squeezed her shoulder.

'I know. I don't know why I'm feeling so anxious.'

'Because this matters to you, and that's fine. There's plenty of food and plenty of good wine, so we'll have a lovely lunch. It's good that Rich is coming over.'

'Yes. I know.' She bit her lip. She hadn't told her dad that she suspected Rich had a girlfriend, not wanting to complicate matters even further, but the knowledge would be there, the elephant at the periphery of the room. Although Sam had looked nothing like an elephant; she was completely stunning. And anyway, as Holly had already told herself, it was none of her business.

She went through to the dining room and checked the table. Crockery, cutlery, glasses... yes, everything was there. She was organized and could relax.

Couldn't she?

She was about to go and check on Luke when she heard a car pulling up outside. He was early! She rushed through to the kitchen, her stomach fluttering wildly, then out the door to see Rich parking next to the Range Rover at the side of the house. He got out, then Lucinda climbed out too. Holly paused. What was Rich's mum doing here? Not that she wasn't welcome, but she hadn't been invited. It didn't matter, as there was plenty of food, but...

'Hi!' Holly waved as she approached them. It dawned on her that she hadn't checked her appearance before coming outside. She'd washed her hair that morning in the shower and slicked on some lip balm, as well as some moisturizer that was meant to give her skin a healthy glow, but that had been the extent of her beautification. Not that it mattered, because who did she want to look beautiful for?

'Hello, Holly.' Lucinda approached her and gave her a tentative hug. 'I hope you don't mind, but I came to help Rich deliver the things we bought for the baby. I won't stay long and I promise I'm not here to bother you.'

'Sorry?'

'I said I'm not here to make a nuisance of myself.'

'No... not that. You said you bought things for Luke?'

'Yes, love.' Lucinda's eyebrows met above her nose. 'Oh gosh! Have I overstepped the mark? I only wanted to do something nice and I—'

'No! No, it's fine. I'm just surprised.' Holly smiled. 'Nicely surprised.'

'Thank goodness for that. I would've hated to upset you.' Lucinda's hand flew to her ample chest as she added, quietly, 'Again.'

'Hi.' Rich appeared at her side carrying a large box wrapped in blue paper with silver bows printed on it.

Holly tore her eyes away from his face as she felt her colour rising. It was almost as if she kept forgetting how handsome he was. His dark eyes seemed to bore right through her, and his freshly shaven face, white shirt and fawn chinos combined to create the image of Rich she had adored. How could he make such a simple outfit look so appealing? The scent that drifted over her was fresh and woody, cinnamon and bark, masculine and rousing. Damn him! Why couldn't he wear a sack and a balaclava and douse himself in antiseptic or cow poo or something?

Lucinda had gone to the boot and hefted out another large box wrapped in the same blue paper.

'A few things, that's all.'

'Goodness me! Uh… thank you. Shall I take that one?' Holly stared at the boxes.

'No, it's all right, Rich can carry them all in. Can I come and say hello to your… father and your granny?'

'Of course.' Holly glanced at Rich as Lucinda slid an arm through hers and walked with her towards the house. She had a feeling that by *father*, Lucinda actually meant son.

And that was fine with her.

In the kitchen, the aromas of roast lunch greeted them, and Lucinda sniffed appreciatively.

'That smells good, Bruce.'

'Lucinda!' Bruce turned from the sink where he was draining carrots and grinned. 'Great to see you. Have you come for lunch?'

'No, not at all, though the idea is tempting. I just came to help Rich with some things we bought for the baby.'

'You must stay, we have plenty to go round. Is Rex with you?'

She shook her head. 'Left him in front of the snooker.'

'Well, call him and tell him to come over. I insist!' Bruce left the colander on the draining board and gave Lucinda a kiss on the cheek. 'The more the merrier.'

'Are you sure?'

'Absolutely.'

'Then I shall.' She looked at Holly. 'If that's okay with you?'

'Of course.' Holly nodded. It might help them to build some all-important bridges.

Lucinda pulled her mobile from her bag and spoke quickly to her husband. 'He'll be here in about fifteen minutes. That okay?'

'Perfect.'

'Would you like to come and see Luke?' Holly asked.

'Yes please.' Lucinda nodded, her eyes bright with anticipation.

They went through to the lounge and found Granny kneeling on the floor next to the play mat. She was trying to unbutton Luke's tiny jeans but was struggling.

'These are so fiddly. Luke, dear, do stop wriggling so your great-granny can get you undone.'

'Granny!' Holly rushed to her side. 'It's fine, let me.' She suppressed a giggle. If she left Granny trying to change

147

Luke, they could end up with a dreadful mess, and right before lunch too.

'I could tell he was filling his nappy, so I thought I'd save you a job and change him, but I can't even do that.'

Holly helped the old lady to her feet. 'The poppers are fiddly but the jeans look so cute on him. You'd be fine changing him when he's wearing his dungarees or his little jogging bottoms.'

Granny nodded. 'I doubt that, but thank you for trying to make me feel better. Does your father need any help in the kitchen?'

'I think he's managing. Rich has arrived, along with Lucinda.' Holly gestured at Rich's mum, who was standing in the doorway, wringing her hands as if trying to stop herself interfering.

'Oh hello, Lucinda dear. I didn't see you there. I was so intent on my mission to clean up the poop.'

Lucinda gave a nervous giggle. 'Hi, Glenda. How are you?' Holly knew she was wondering how Granny was coping without Grandpa.

'I'm fine, dear. I have these two here to keep me busy now. I'll go and see if I can help in the kitchen.'

Granny tottered off and Lucinda knelt by Holly in front of the play mat. Granny had placed the changing bag next to Luke, so Holly quickly changed him, hoping Lucinda wouldn't be put off by the nuclear-grade stench. But as she popped the nappy into a bag and tied the top, she sneaked a glance at Lucinda to find her gazing at Luke with an adoring expression on her face.

'Are you okay to watch him while I take this out and wash my hands?' Holly asked.

'Of course. I'd be honoured.' Lucinda reached out and placed her hand on Holly's shoulder. 'Thank you, sweetheart. I know this must be difficult.'

'It's fine.' Holly smiled. 'We all need to get along now more than ever.' She didn't know if the hurt she'd felt at Lucinda's words would ever leave her, but she also knew that staying angry and bitter wouldn't help anyone.

She took the bag through to the kitchen, leaving Rich's mum alone with her grandchild for the very first time.

When she returned to the lounge, Lucinda was sitting on the couch with Luke lying across her knees. She was chatting away to him and he was cooing and babbling in his very cute way. Holly stood in the doorway watching them and her heart expanded. She'd once read that children could never have too many people to love them, and here at Greenacres, Luke would have that joy. Her fears that Lucinda wouldn't think her baby was good enough slowly dissipated like smoke on the breeze, and she felt herself relax. She was a natural with him, and from the look on her face, she already loved him.

Holly quietly backed out of the doorway. She'd let them have some time to get to know each other, to form a bond that she knew would benefit them both. Lucinda was a good person and she'd been through her fair share of suffering. Hopefully being with Luke would help her to heal. The happy, good-humoured baby had a way of helping those around him to feel better. She'd seen it this week as her granny had spent time with him and her dad had doted upon him. Now Luke had a whole extended family to care for him, and there was a wonderful sense of security in that. She was glad Lucinda had come to Greenacres with Rich today, and glad that Rex would soon join them; then they could eat as a family and start to put the past behind them.

Thinking of lunch, Holly hoped that her Yorkshire puddings would rise properly; it was the one job Dad had allowed her to do.

And no one liked flat Yorkshire puddings...

—

'Well, this is nice!' Bruce said as he gazed around the table.

'It is indeed lovely to have company.' Granny picked up her wine glass. 'I would like to make a toast...'

Everyone raised their own glasses, and Holly noticed that her granny's was wobbling. It must be difficult having guests round, with it being the first time since she'd lost her husband. There would be many firsts, but Holly knew that Granny would face each one with the same courage and determination. It made her feel that she should do the same.

'To present company, and of course... to absent friends.' Granny pressed her lips together and blinked hard before taking a long drink of her red wine.

'Absent friends,' they all responded, then clinked glasses.

'Thank you so much for inviting us,' Rex said.

'Our pleasure.' Bruce nodded. 'It's lovely to cook for company.'

They all filled their plates with meat and vegetables, then Holly held her breath as the Yorkshire puddings made the rounds.

'I have to apologize for the Yorkshires.' She got there before anyone could comment. 'I opened the oven too soon and they... uh... collapsed.'

'They look fabulous.' Rex stabbed one with his fork, then placed it next to his potatoes. 'Lovely and golden.'

'But like frisbees.' Holly grimaced.

'Holly, sweetheart, you are many things, but a great cook has never been one of them.' Her dad smiled at her. 'And what does it matter?'

'Not at all!' Glenda patted Holly's hand where it sat on the table. 'She has other talents, and at least she tries.'

Holly met Rich's eyes across the table and his smirk made her own laughter bubble. It was as though they were teenagers again, being patronized by their parents. So what if she couldn't cook? She could do the basics, and besides, Rich had always been better in the kitchen than her, so she'd let him and her dad crack on.

Rich's mouth widened into a grin, and Holly couldn't help it; she laughed out loud. It was as though the tension of sitting around the table had built up and now it could no longer be contained.

Lucinda looked from Holly to Rich, then back again, and released a giggle.

'Is everything all right?' Granny asked, her fork poised in mid-air. 'I didn't fart, did I?'

That made Holly and Rich laugh even more, and soon, everyone around the table had joined in.

When they finally fell quiet and Holly's sides were aching, Granny spoke again.

'I do that sometimes, you know, especially when I sneeze, and I'm not always aware of it. Grandpa was always telling me off, but I swear that sometimes it was him, and he used me as a scapegoat. "Glenda!" he'd say. "Ladies don't fart out loud."'

'Oh Granny, stop!' Holly shook her head.

'What? But why?' Glenda looked surprised, but Holly suspected she knew what she was doing. An occasion like this was bound to be tense. A good laugh would help get rid of any residual tension and make them all far more comfortable.

—

After lunch, Rich and Rex loaded the dishwasher and Holly made coffee, which they took through to the lounge. Rex sat on the sofa cuddling Luke, with Lucinda next to him.

'How about opening some of those baby things?' Lucinda asked.

'Good idea, Mum.' Rich drained his coffee, then got up and went through to the dining room, where they'd piled the boxes before lunch. When he returned, he was carrying two packages, which he set on the floor in front of Holly. 'There you go.'

She looked at Rich, then at his parents, feeling suddenly shy.

'Go on, Holly, please.' Lucinda gestured at the parcels.

'Thank you. You didn't need to do this, but we are grateful, aren't we, Luke?'

Her son was currently patting Rex's chin and humming at him.

She tore the blue paper away to find a bottle sterilizer. 'Oh… thank you.'

'I know you probably have one already, but we thought it's always handy to have a spare,' Lucinda said. 'And it's top of the range.'

Holly nodded. It was the one she'd originally wanted but hadn't bought as she was trying to be careful with money.

Rich handed her the next parcel, which she opened to find a set of bottles and dummies. They were decorated with cartoon polar bears and foxes and were designed for babies of three months and above.

'Again, thank you. These are lovely.'

'Hold on!'

Rich left the room again and returned with two larger boxes. When he placed them next to Holly, she released a breath she hadn't known she'd been holding. This was all proving to be quite emotional. She wasn't used to being the centre of attention either, and she was terrified of not seeming grateful or of appearing not to like the gifts.

'Holly...' Rich put his hand over hers and she met his warm eyes. 'No pressure. We kept the receipts. Anything you don't like or have a double of, we can return and get something else.' He leaned closer and whispered, 'Mum just really wanted to get a few things, and it made her so happy.'

Holly nodded.

The two large boxes contained an expensive highchair with a beautiful giraffe motif, and a battery-powered baby rocker that played lullabies and also had an activity centre for Luke to play with. There was also a baby carrier that Holly – or Rich – could wear like a rucksack. Rich finished off with some softer parcels that contained nappies, vests, pyjamas and little outfits.

'It's like a baby shower,' Holly said as she gazed at the piles of things around her.

'Did you have one of those?' Lucinda asked.

She shook her head.

Rich knelt on the floor next to her chair. 'She was in Exeter... alone.'

'Oh goodness, Holly! With no one to look out for you?' Lucinda pouted. 'If only I'd known. If only I'd not been such a horrid old bag then you might not have left...'

'It's okay, Lucinda.' Holly nodded. 'It's all in the past. We're home now.' Seeing Lucinda's guilt made her sad, and she didn't want to add to it. She suddenly felt claustrophobic in the lounge, in need of some time out.

'Do you fancy getting some fresh air?' Rich asked, as if reading her mind.

'Uh... what about Luke?'

'We can watch him,' Lucinda said, then looked up. 'Us grandparents together.'

'I'd like to get a head start on putting some of these fab baby gadgets together,' Holly's dad said, picking up the box for the rocker.

'As long as you're sure.' Holly stood up, then went and gave Luke a kiss. 'The bottles are in the kitchen. He's due one about—'

'It's okay, Hols.' Bruce held up a hand. 'I know the feeding times now, and how to make up the bottles.'

'I used to make up six and stick them in the fridge,' Lucinda said. 'Then I'd warm them as needed.'

'We're not allowed to do that these days.' Bruce shook his head. 'One at a time only, but Holly has this fab machine that makes them almost instantly. I'll show you how to use it.'

'Looks like you've got the grandparenting thing covered then.' Holly walked to the door. 'Any problems, I've got my mobile and we won't be long, will we, Rich?'

'Not at all. An hour at most.'

Holly went out to the hallway and stuck her feet into her trainers, then located the waxed jacket she'd had since she was sixteen. As she slid her arms into the sleeves, the smell reminded her of the past. The jacket had been stored in the cupboard under the stairs where her granny hung lavender pomanders and mothballs, and the aromas permeated everything they kept in there.

'You ready?' Rich asked.

'Yes. And thank you.'

'What for?'

'For getting me out. It's wonderful having everyone around, but I was starting to feel a bit...'

'It's okay, I understand. I needed a break too.'

'Glad it wasn't just me. Do you have a coat?'

'I threw one into the car just in case. I could see there were some clouds coming in earlier so thought it best to be on the safe side.'

Outside, Holly waited for Rich to get his coat, then he joined her and they headed across the yard and through the gate to the vineyards. They walked in silence, not discussing where they were going, being led by habit and the past. They circled the exterior of the vineyards until they reached the next gate, and the next, then they were in an open field. Holly enjoyed the sensation of the fresh air on her skin, relieved to be outdoors where she always felt that she could breathe properly.

They walked side by side up a slight incline to the hiking path.

'You were right about those clouds.' Holly peered up at the darkening sky. 'Perhaps we should turn back,' she suggested reluctantly.

'We'll be fine, Hols. Can we keep going for a bit?'

'Okay.'

'My parents are absolutely delighted, you know.'

'It's lovely to see them so happy.'

'It means so much to see Mum smile like that. It reminds me of how she looked when I was growing up.'

'She has a sparkle in her eyes, doesn't she?'

He nodded. 'It's because of you.'

'Me?'

'Yes. You brought Luke back.'

'Rich, I came back for Grandpa's funeral.'

'And for no other reason?'

She thought about it as she walked along. When she'd been planning to return for the funeral, had she, on some level, been considering coming home for good? Had she been hoping to see Rich? She certainly hadn't thought Lucinda would apologize to her like that.

'I don't know, to be honest, although I knew that you and Luke needed to meet as soon as possible. Now that I'm here, though, it's so much better than I thought it would be. Everything seems different.'

'Do I seem different?'

'Yes.'

'How so?'

'You don't look so... pained.'

He laughed. 'It's not funny, I know, but did I really look that bad?'

'Before you left, you looked as though you were carrying the weight of the world on your shoulders. The drinking, the late nights, the sadness in your eyes... it was hard to witness. I've tried not to think about all that and it seems like it was years ago, but it was so painful to watch you trying to destroy yourself. I could barely admit to myself that it was happening. I thought that once we had our own home, you'd be happier. I hoped that I could make you happy.'

'I'm so sorry you saw me like that.'

'It wasn't your fault. Not directly, anyway.'

Rich did look so much better now. She hadn't been able to pinpoint what the difference was at first, but now it was clear. He had a glow about him, as if something inside had been repaired and he was getting back to how he always should have been.

She had a feeling that she knew why, though, that it might be linked to Sam, and that knowledge was hard to deal with.

'How far shall we go?' She gazed across the fields. She felt the moisture in the air on her cheeks and her forehead. Rain was definitely on the way.

'A bit further.'

'You want to go... *there?*'

'If that's okay with you.'

She stopped walking. 'I'm not sure. I haven't been there since that day.'

'It'll be okay, Holly. I promise.'

He held out his hand, and she looked at it for a moment before taking it. This probably wasn't wise, but for a while, even just an hour or so, she wanted to feel as though everything between her and Rich was good. He had been her friend, not just her lover, and she had missed him. It had taken being back in his company for her to realize exactly how much.

He was making an effort here, and although she didn't know exactly what he wanted from her, she needed to believe that he wouldn't hurt her again.

In fact, she knew that she wouldn't let him.

Chapter 12

Rich wasn't one hundred per cent sure that he was doing the right thing heading to Plum Tree Cottage, but when they'd decided to go for a walk, he hadn't been able to push the idea from his mind. It might be a big mistake, but something inside him was propelling him forward, encouraging him to try this, to see how Holly responded. To see how he responded himself.

They walked side by side, occasionally brushing against each other as they moved to avoid a rock or a cow pat, and it felt natural to be with Holly again. She'd always been so easy to get along with, not at all high-maintenance like some of the other girls he'd briefly dated at high school. Holly was special.

Back last year, their relationship had reached a point where making a commitment had seemed inevitable. Holly had needed more from Rich and he'd felt in a place to offer that, or at least he'd thought he had. Moving in together had seemed the sensible next step. Until that point, they'd been happy enough flitting between Greenacres and Rich's parents' home, enjoying the freedom of having money in their pockets and being able to save. They'd each had an ISA, having agreed that it would be a good idea to put a deposit away for when they eventually found a property they both liked.

Then Rich had ruined it because his head hadn't been in the right place after all.

He glanced at Holly, and shame crawled over his skin. She was lovely and he'd let her down so badly. If only he'd gone away to Ibiza *before* they'd decided to buy the cottage. She'd had no words for him after that, had cut him from her life completely – except for the child she was carrying.

Pain pierced his heart just as lightning flashed in the sky far out at sea. If she had decided to terminate the pregnancy, he would have had no right to argue with her decision. He hadn't been there for her, so why would she have thought he'd be there for their child? But she hadn't done that. In her usual determined way, she had kept on going, delivered their baby and brought him through his first few months of life. She was incredible.

He'd known he had feelings for Holly, but his issues had prevented him from opening his heart properly. Seeing her now, with his child and his parents, and being able to fully appreciate what a strong woman she was brought everything to the surface.

Whether or not she would ever care about him again as she once had remained to be seen. They reached the end of the field and the hedgerow thickened as they neared the stile. Rich waited for Holly to climb over, then followed her, his new-found knowledge settling in his stomach like a lead weight.

He had lost something very precious when he let Holly go.

They could never go back to how things had been, and it wouldn't be right to want that, but he felt certain that they could move forward and create something different, something new – in whatever form that might be.

–

Holly had known where they were going, but even so, when she climbed over the stile and saw the little cottage, with its stunning sea view and glorious surroundings, her breath caught in her throat.

She hadn't come back here since that day, and hadn't thought she ever would.

But then she hadn't even known if she would return to Greenacres, and look at how that was working out.

Rich joined her again and they waded through the long grass, descending gradually until they reached the point where the land evened out. The gravel road that ran past the cottage clearly hadn't been used in some time, as weeds and grass were reclaiming it, poking up through the stones of various shapes and sizes.

The closer they got, the faster her heart pounded, and the more she wondered if this was a good idea. Surely too many emotions had been played out here: love, hope, passion, sadness, anger and despair. And yet seeing the old stone cottage again brought whispers of hope to her heart. She'd once loved this place so much, adored its fat chimney, blue shutters and small-paned windows set into thick walls. It was so sturdy and strong, a fortress against the elements. It had a dry-stone wall at the front, creating a small square garden that had once boasted beautiful borders full of flowers. As she looked at the borders now, her heart sank to see them choked with weeds and litter, cider cans and cigarette packets – likely left there by teenagers from the village.

The path leading from the wooden gate to the cottage was also strewn with weeds. One of the front windows had three broken panes, and the shutter to the right hung from its hinges at an awkward angle, as if someone had tried to rip it off.

They reached the gate and Holly felt Rich's hand on her shoulder.

'Are you okay?'

She nodded.

'Do you want to go in?'

She turned to him.

'Not really. I don't think so, anyway. What would be the point?'

The air between them fizzed with tension, buzzing with unsaid words, with wasted time.

A crack of thunder overhead made them jump, and Holly screeched. When she realized what had happened, she started to laugh.

'That was really loud.' Rich laughed with her.

Then it came, as it often did so close to the sea.

'Rain!'

Large droplets pelted them as if the heavens had quite literally opened directly above them, and within seconds, they were soaked. Lightning flashed, too close for comfort, and thunder boomed again.

'Come on.' Rich grabbed Holly's hand and led her through the gate and up the path to the front door. He tried the handle, but it was locked, so he gently pushed her further under the porch roof so that her back was against the front door. 'Wait here.'

'Where are you going?'

'I'll be back in a few minutes.' He disappeared around the side of the building.

The rain had come so quickly that Holly hadn't pulled her hood up or zipped her jacket, and now the front of her top was wet, and rain had trickled down her neck and into the back of her jeans. She was cold, and it was a fair walk back to the vineyard. In any case, it wouldn't be a good idea to venture out until the storm had blown over.

Panic rose inside her as she thought about Luke; she'd never been separated from him before, except for the evening she'd gone to Fran's. But no... Luke would be fine; he was with his doting grandparents and had everything he needed, except for her. Irritation niggled as she questioned her decision to walk here with Rich. What had she been thinking?

A noise behind her made her turn to face the door, which opened, revealing Rich.

'How did you...'

'They key was still under the plant pot next to the back door. I'm surprised the local kids haven't been inside, but it looks pretty tidy in there, to be honest.'

Holly entered the hallway and closed the door behind her.

'This feels wrong.'

'Why?'

'Well, it's breaking and entering.'

'No one's lived here in ages.'

'I know, but someone still owns it.'

'Someone who doesn't care that much about it.'

The air in the hallway was stale and damp, as if it hadn't been disturbed in months. It reminded Holly of the old church hall, which smelt that way even thought it was used quite regularly.

To their left and right were two reception rooms, straight ahead was the staircase and beyond that the kitchen. Holly could have found her way around blindfolded; the layout was emblazoned on her mind. She'd walked through the cottage so many times in her imagination, thinking of colour schemes and picturing how happy they would be when it became their home. She'd thought about how she would furnish the reception rooms, the three double bedrooms, the hallway and the kitchen. She'd even been to the DIY superstore and picked out paint. Rich had let her go that far, then torn her dreams to shreds. Anger flickered inside. Why had he been so cruel?

'Come through to the kitchen and I'll see if I can light a fire.'

She nodded, unable to speak, and followed him, watching as he rooted around in the kitchen cupboards for some matches. Eventually he located a box in the cupboard under the sink, then knelt in front of the grate and peered up the chimney.

'I think it's clear enough up there, but we'll soon see.'

'It would have been swept about a year ago, wouldn't it?' She found her voice and tried to unclench her jaw to get the words out clearly. 'I'm sure I recall the estate agent saying something about it having been done before they put the cottage on the market.'

'It might be all right then.'

Rich had already found some old newspapers, and there were logs in the bucket next to the fireplace. While he lit the fire, Holly pulled two chairs over from the table in the corner. The previous owner had left some furniture in the property. Holly had thought it had a certain charm, and suspected some of it might be antique. It would at least have helped to create that eclectic feel that she liked in properties, where things didn't match but rather worked together to create a cosy, homely feel. The table and chairs were solid and built to last, not like some of the flimsy designer furniture she'd seen in shops and online.

Rich came and sat next to her and they gazed at the fire, watching as the flames licked at the dry logs and soon took hold, coaxing the wood into creating heat that spread out into the room.

'We should soon dry off.'

'Not if we go back out in that.' Holly nodded at the window, where the rain was coming down in sheets so thick that the back garden was a complete blur.

'Guess we'd better stay here for a bit, at least until the storm blows over.'

'I could always ring Dad and ask him to come for us.'

'What and disturb his baby-chair building?'

'You're right.' Holly nodded. 'He's probably having a great time.'

'Might be best if they don't know that we came here anyway.' Rich worried his bottom lip.

'Why *did* we come here?' Holly tried to push her anger away. It clouded her judgement and wouldn't help with working out a way for Rich to be Luke's dad.

He stood up and removed his jacket, then hung it over the back of the chair before sitting back down again. He looked around the kitchen and Holly followed his gaze, taking in the cupboard doors that would have looked at home in a wartime drama, the flagstone floor that needed a good sweep and the apron-fronted sink with a big crack in the front. It needed some TLC, and Holly had once thought that she and Rich would be the ones to provide that care and attention.

'Holly… I wanted to bring you here to say sorry.'

'You've already apologized, Rich.'

She was glad that he had said sorry, but she also felt that words would never be able to take away the hurt she had felt. It would be Rich's actions from now on that would matter, and that would take time.

'I have… but I have more to say. Far more, in fact.'

Holly shivered.

'Are you cold?'

'A bit.'

'Take your jacket off and you'll dry quicker.'

She knew he was right, but exposing the bare skin of her arms to the air went against her instinct to hunch over and stay under that extra layer.

'I've seen it on survival programmes, I promise.'

Holly reluctantly removed her coat and hung it over the back of the chair as Rich had done, then shuffled closer to the fire. Rich did the same and reached out to her.

'What're you doing?' She bristled.

'Body heat. It'll help.'

'No… I don't…'

Even as she protested, she knew he was right, and although she didn't think they were in danger of suffering from hypothermia, she was very cold. If she could just push her pain aside for a moment, she could allow Rich close to warm her up.

A voice at the back of her mind screamed that it was foolish, but her chattering teeth silenced it.

Rich couldn't believe he was holding Holly again. His heart was pounding and his mouth had dried up completely. He wanted to tell her again how sorry he was, but he didn't know if he'd be able to speak at all. So for a while he simply held her close, leaning his chin on the top of her head and just enjoying being with her. This was how it should have been; he should have been living here in this cottage with her and Luke now, a happy family under their own pretty little roof.

He'd been such an idiot.

'Holly...' His voice emerged as barely more than a whisper. 'That day last year... your grandpa's birthday. I was wrong to leave.'

She moved away slightly so she could look at him.

'Why did you go?'

'It had been building for a while. I think it was the anniversary looming and the fact that my life was moving on that meant I just lost it.'

Her eyes were filled with pain as they roamed his face. 'I can understand that, of course I can, but I would have helped you if you'd spoken to me. If you'd shared your feelings honestly rather than shutting down.'

He sighed, wishing she'd snuggle into him again, yearning for her to make the sadness vanish for a while as only she could.

'I know I should have spoken to you about it, but I was so wrapped up in my own grief and guilt that I couldn't let go. I couldn't vocalize how I felt.'

'But you can now?'

'I've been learning how to talk about it. I'm not fully comfortable with it, but I'm trying to be more open.'

Holly watched him, her eyes wary.

'When I left, I went to Ibiza thinking I'd have a lads' holiday, that I'd drink and party and forget, but it didn't quite work like that.'

She had stiffened in his arms.

'I met Sam out there and—'

'Oh.' Holly dropped her gaze to the fire and he watched as the glow flickered across her features, highlighting the curves of her cheekbones and making shadowy hollows of her eyes.

'She's been good to me. She's worked with mental health charities and has experience as a counsellor herself, and she seemed to understand what I was going through—'

'And I didn't?' Holly was on her feet now, her arms folded tightly across her chest. 'I was there all the time, Rich, or did you forget that? I saw how it affected you. I thought we had something good… It seems I was wrong.'

He shook his head. 'No, you weren't wrong at all. I cared for you, Holly, but sometimes it was as if we were too close to talk about it.'

'Well you have Sam now, don't you?'

Rich felt his jaw drop. 'No! No… it's not like that. Sam isn't my girlfriend.'

'Oh.'

'You thought she was?'

Holly shrugged. 'I wasn't sure.'

'She's a friend, nothing more.'

'It's none of my business, Rich.' Holly's voice sounded flat, as if she couldn't care one way or the other.

'We knew each other from uni, then we bumped into each other in Ibiza and I stayed at her family's villa. She helped me find a good counsellor, and I started unburdening myself. I couldn't put it all on you, Hols. I felt weak for dealing with things so badly. I was full of self-loathing and it took me some time to come out of that. But now... I'm almost out the other side. I'm still sad, really sad that it happened, but I'm rebuilding, and coming home was the first step in my recovery. I needed a break, to escape Penhallow Sands for a while, but the way I did it was wrong.'

Holly rubbed her eyes.

'Can you forgive me for being such an idiot?'

'It's not just about us now, Rich. We have to think about Luke, and I can't have him hurt or messed around.'

'I won't hurt you... either of you.'

Holly took his hand and stepped towards him.

'I'm not making any promises, Rich.'

'I'm not asking you to. I just want to try to make it up to you in some way. I can't bear to spend the rest of my life knowing that I hurt you and didn't do anything to make it better.'

Rich didn't know what he could do to prove himself, but he knew that he wanted to see Holly and their son happy and settled. He needed to work out how he could make that happen.

Holly walked to the window and peered out at the sky.

'I think the rain has stopped.'

—

Holly slid her arms into her jacket. It wasn't fully dry, but it was better than when they'd arrived at the cottage. Her head was muggy with emotion and she could have lain down on the floor, closed her eyes and slept. As Rich had held her in front of the fire, his strong arms wrapped around her, it would have been so easy to tilt her chin upwards and find his mouth with hers, to undress him slowly and make love to him.

Part of her wished that he'd take over and peel away her clothes, then kiss her as he used to do, but the other part – the sensible, rational part – was screaming at her to walk away and pull herself together. Rich might say that he'd changed – he certainly seemed genuine about it, and he had been through a dreadful experience that would test the strongest of people – but even so… he'd had so many chances to love her the way she wanted and deserved to be loved.

It was her fault too. She'd been a doormat, allowed things to drift without any real, solid commitment. Lots of couples moved in together far earlier than three years into their relationship. Of course, there had been Grandpa to think of, but she had stood up to him on that one, and Granny and Dad had reassured him that she and Rich had been together long enough to make an adult decision. Marriage hadn't been something she'd worried about, but she had wanted to live with Rich and to have their own space where they could be alone together. They'd had the money saved for a deposit and the time had been right.

Then Rich had ruined it all.

Holly had had her own fears and sadness too. Losing her mum had rocked her world, and Rich had been there for her through that. She'd clung to him many times as she cried, and he'd made her mugs of hot chocolate in the early hours when she'd woken in tears, having dreamt that her mum was there before realizing she was gone. Rich had been a friend and a lover; he'd been, in many ways, her rock. But when it came down to it, he just couldn't give her the commitment and stability she craved.

That was why she'd been so confused about him, and about them. He'd said he couldn't commit, but he'd been there. Always.

Until that day.

And now he was asking for a chance to prove himself. He said he'd been working things through, that with Sam's help he'd begun the healing process in Ibiza. It hurt that Sam had been able to do what Holly hadn't, but perhaps he had needed the space to pour his feelings out in different surroundings. Holly was caught in a paradox of emotion. On one hand, she felt jealous that another woman had helped Rich. On the other hand, she was grateful to Sam because Rich had needed support.

And now… He wasn't asking Holly to move in with him or to marry him, or for any type of commitment other than allowing him to be a part of Luke's life.

She would give him the chance to be a father to Luke; it was what they both deserved. As for herself, she didn't know if she'd ever be able to trust Rich with her heart again. He'd said he wanted to make it up to her, that he couldn't bear to know he'd hurt her and not put things right. But she had no idea what to expect from him. She'd thought she'd known him once. She'd been wrong.

She didn't know if she could open herself up enough to love him again.

Chapter 13

The next five days passed in a haze of establishing a new routine for Luke, a routine that involved having more people around in new surroundings. It was wonderful to have helping hands and people to go to for advice, and Holly could see that Luke was enjoying it too. His little face lit up whenever her dad or Granny spoke to him, and when Rich popped round in the evenings after work to see his son, it lifted her heart. Not long ago, she'd wondered if Luke would even know his father, but now he saw him every day. She even found herself looking forward to Rich's visits.

Rich was polite and courteous, kind and attentive. He'd watch Luke so Holly could have a bath or cook dinner, and when Luke had been put to bed – by both of them – he would sit with her and her dad and they'd talk. So far, they'd discussed more ideas for the vineyard, agreeing that some of them were good but discounting others, and Rich had made notes, taking them away with him to work them through. He said he knew some people who might be able to help, and that he'd contact them to see what they suggested. Holly was relieved to see the hope that sparked in her dad's eyes at Rich's words. She had also been working on the website, wanting it to be ready before she shared it with them both.

They didn't involve Granny in their discussions, because they didn't want to worry her, so they talked after she'd retired for the night. Her grief made her tired, so she went to bed early and rose later and later. Holly had worried that it could be depression, but when she'd tentatively broached the subject, Glenda had laughed it off and reassured Holly that she was simply old and tired and missing her husband. Sleep was healing, she'd said, and Holly had to agree with that.

It was already Friday. Rich was coming around later and her dad had suggested that they have a barbecue. Holly was looking forward to the evening more than she cared to admit to herself.

–

Holly carried the tray of paper plates, napkins and cutlery outside to the long picnic table her father had brought out from one of the barns. They'd used it over the years for outdoors celebrations, and after a good wipe-down with a damp cloth, it had been fit for use. It was set with glasses and bottles of wine and soft drinks.

Following a lovely sunny day, the evening was mild, and Holly hadn't bothered with a cardigan over her black cotton shirt dress, which she had paired with white lace-up pumps. She'd washed her hair and put on some new moisturizer that she'd picked up at the supermarket. It was meant to give her skin a light glow, and in the bathroom mirror it had seemed to do as it promised. With a slick of lip gloss and a coat of mascara, she felt presentable. Granted, her legs and arms were white, but she wasn't into fake tan and hadn't spent enough time outdoors to tan naturally since she'd had Luke. She was terrified he'd get too hot, or that his soft white skin would be exposed to harmful rays, so she always kept to the shade. Of course, Luke hadn't yet experienced a hot summer, and that was something she knew she'd worry about too.

How would she manage when he got older and she couldn't protect him all the time?

'What're you daydreaming about?' her dad asked as he passed her on his way to the old gas barbecue. He'd dragged it out of the barn earlier that day and scrubbed it until it shone. Holly could see how pleased he was with his efforts. He had bought the barbecue years ago, for Holly's twenty-first birthday celebrations, but after the first few summers, it hadn't had much use. Holly had thought that was a shame; her dad loved cooking outdoors because he said it reminded him of his youth.

'I was just thinking about Luke and how much I worry about him.'

'It's exactly the same for me, you know, Holly.' He opened the lid of the barbecue and steam rose into the air. 'It doesn't stop because your child becomes an adult with a child of her own.'

Holly joined him at the barbecue and slid her arm around his waist.

'Do you still worry about me a lot then?'

'Every moment of every day.'

'Aw, Dad.' She squeezed him tight. 'I love you.'

'I love you too.' He kissed her head. 'Now, what do you think about the food? Should I do the vegetable skewers first? Before the meat?'

'Well, Rich did say that Sam's a veggie, so I doubt she'll want meat juices over her vegetables.'

'Can't understand it myself.' Her dad shook his head. 'Why miss out on the nutrients?'

'Dad, lots of people don't eat meat these days. I've even considered giving it up myself.'

'You need the iron, what with having a young baby.'

'That's a myth, Dad.' She rolled her eyes, then laughed. 'I can get iron from lots of other sources.'

'But you'd miss out on burgers and steak!'

She shook her head at him. 'There are bean burgers and veggie sausages there too, Dad. Once they're cooked, you can put them to the side to keep warm. I'll go and grab the rolls and sauces.'

She headed back indoors, checking the baby monitor as she went. She could hear Luke's steady breathing, and Granny's radio along the landing. She'd been worried that Luke would struggle to nap while Granny was playing her music, but it seemed to comfort him, the sounds of a busy household playing out as he lay in his cot. It was a good job really, because she'd been thinking over their future and was finding herself increasingly drawn to the idea of moving home.

She piled up the packets of rolls on another tray, then got the condiments from the fridge and added them too. She'd been trying not to think about the fact that Rich had asked if he could bring Sam, and another woman called Nicole, to the barbecue. He'd told her it was because with Nicole's experience in PR, she'd be good to speak to about the vineyard. Holly was grateful for any extra advice, and she knew her dad would be too.

The thought of sharing the website with anyone other than Rich and her dad did make her feel a bit nervous. She had done plenty of research into website design and watched several YouTube videos, and she thought that what she'd done was good, but to an experienced eye, it might appear amateurish. However, it was lovely to be here with her dad – who was clearly pleased to have company – and she was looking forward to seeing Rich again too. His text messages, phone calls and visits all made her stomach flutter, and she knew she'd miss him now if he wasn't around. He was a part of this world, part of Greenacres. She'd been able to temporarily put him from her mind in Exeter, but here it would have been much harder because she saw him everywhere she looked; her memories of their time together haunted the vineyard, the house and the village.

'What do you think?' Granny swanned into the kitchen, dragging Holly from her thoughts. She was wearing a long flowery skirt and pink blouse under a white linen jacket. She'd found a pair of pink court shoes to match, and her lipstick was the same shade.

'Wow!' Holly clapped her hands. 'You look fabulous, Granny.'

'Why thank you.' Granny pouted and twirled slowly.

'Where are you going again?'

'Only for a pub meal, but a girl has to make an effort.'

'What time are you being picked up?'

Granny peered at her gold watch. 'In ten minutes.' She patted her bobbed white hair. 'I do love my hair now. It's so easy to wash and dry.'

'It looks lovely.'

'Is that a car?' Granny went to the window. 'Ooh! It's Rich.' She turned to Holly and smiled. 'How are you two getting along?'

'We're… getting to know each other again.'

'Very wise. Don't want to rush anything, do you?'

'We're not… Nothing like that is going to happen, Granny. I just want him to be a father to Luke.'

Glenda cocked an eyebrow, then nodded slowly.

'I'll believe you, Holly, but do you believe yourself?'

'What?' Holly frowned, but her granny had walked to the door and was peering outside. 'Holly, don't look now, but there are two women with Rich.'

'It's okay, Granny. He works with one of them and the other is her friend. They've come for supper.'

Glenda turned back to her. 'That's all right then. Don't want him falling for another woman, do we?'

'Well… I don't know about that. It's none of my business really.'

Granny pursed her lips. 'We'll see. Time will tell, I guess. And you're a sensible young woman, so I'm sure you'll make the right decision.'

Holly bit her lip, picked up the tray and took it out into the garden. She'd heard a lot over the years about how her mother *wasn't* sensible and how she could be a bit wild, but she thought most of it came down to her grandpa's opinion – something that her granny still repeated as if it was fact. The mother Holly had known was kind and sweet, loving and optimistic, and not the woman her grandparents had sometimes described to her. But perhaps that was a generational thing: parents were bound to view their children as wild or reckless, while children were compelled to rebel against their parents whatever their upbringing was like.

She placed the tray on the table outside, then plastered on her best smile before going to greet Rich, Sam and Nicole. She would be a good hostess to Rich and his friends, and hopefully they would have a productive evening. She liked seeing her dad look so positive and relaxed, and if they could find a way to improve the financial future of the vineyard, then he might look that way more often.

—

Rich forced his mouth to close as he walked towards Holly. She looked incredible in a silky black dress with her blonde hair shining, her skin glowing and her bright green eyes sparkling like rock pools in the summer sun. He had always known she was beautiful, but now she took his breath away. Being near her was like coming home, like finding the place he was meant to be and should have been all along. He'd been such an idiot for not appreciating this incredible woman when he'd had the chance.

'Holly.' He smiled at her. 'I'd like you to meet Sam and Nicole.'

Holly smiled at them, but her eyes were watchful, wary even, as if she was nervous about something. He'd explained that he wanted to bring Sam and Nicole because he thought Nicole in particular could help with some ideas for the vineyard, but Holly's reaction suggested that she might be anxious about involving other people.

'Hello.' The women shook hands, then Holly introduced Bruce, who showed them to the picnic table and asked them what they'd like to drink.

'I'm such an idiot, Holly. I've left the drinks I brought in the car.'

Rich hurried across and opened the boot, lifting out a strong carrier bag and a bouquet of pale pink roses. He'd liked the red ones he'd seen better, but he'd thought that taking Holly red roses might be a bit much. He still wasn't sure if giving them to her was a good idea, but he hated the thought of leaving them in the car to wilt.

'These are for you,' he said when he returned to Holly's side.

She looked at the flowers, then at him.

'You didn't have to do that.'

'I wanted to.'

'Thank you.' She took the bouquet, held it up to her face and sniffed. Her eyes closed and her lips parted slightly. The impact upon Rich was shocking and instant; desire shot through his body, making his heart pound. It hadn't happened to him in a long time, and it took his breath away.

He quickly composed himself, then cleared his throat. 'I also brought these.' He opened the bag and showed Holly some soft drinks and two boxes of chocolates.

'Thanks, Rich.' She took the bag from him. 'I'll put the flowers in some water.'

She turned and walked towards the house, and Rich watched her go, unable to tear his eyes away.

–

Holly arranged the roses in a vase, then set it on the windowsill. They were very pretty and they smelt so good. Her mother had loved roses and had grown them in the garden, training them to climb around the front door and up the trellis of the front gate. They were still there, but tangled and in need of pruning, something else that would need some attention at some point.

Outside, she could see her dad chatting to Rich and the two women. Sam was just as beautiful as Holly remembered, with her sleek waist-length black hair and a supermodel physique. In a light blue playsuit with matching headband and knee-high brown boots, she reminded Holly of Wonder Woman.

'I like her outfit,' Granny said as she joined Holly at the sink.

'Oh! Don't sneak up on me like that!'

'I didn't sneak, dear, I'm just stealthy.'

'No you're not.' Holly laughed, even though she was still waiting for her heart to stop pounding.

'I am, Holly. In fact, sometimes I'm so stealthy that I don't even know I'm there.'

Holly shook her head. Sometimes she couldn't tell if Granny was teasing or if it was just her age.

'Ooh, that woman's got her arm around the other one's waist.'

Holly peered through the glass.

'Yes, she has.' She shrugged. 'Perhaps they're close friends.'

'Now she's got her chin on her shoulder.'

Holly nodded. 'They must be very close. But Granny, what is this? A running commentary on our guests' behaviour?'

Glenda smiled knowingly.

'Actually, Holly, I think they're lovers.'

'What?' Holly turned to her. 'Why'd you say that?'

'I can tell. In this day and age, it's absolutely acceptable for women to love women and men to love men. It always should have been, you know, but when I was growing up, it was frowned on. I had friends who were secret lovers, so it's wonderful to see people free to love who their heart chooses.'

'I agree.' Holly hugged her.

'What was that for?'

'Because you're amazing. Just when I think I know you, you manage to surprise me.'

Her granny chuckled. 'Do I? How wonderful! Your grandpa wasn't so accepting of lesbeens, of course, what with him being so traditional, but I've always said that the heart wants what it wants. Love is love is love. You know what? I'd love to go on one of those gay pride marches.'

'Really?'

'Yes. I'll add it to my bucket list.'

'Okay…'

'We could get one of those gorgeous colourful flags and drape it over Luke's pram. We'd have a grand old day.'

'You're so cool, Granny.'

'So are you, my darling.' Granny cupped Holly's cheek then planted a kiss there.

'Now, I need to finish getting ready, so you go and be sociable.'

Holly nodded, then went back out into the garden, still smiling at the conversation they'd just had.

–

'That was amazing, Bruce, thank you!' Nicole dabbed at her mouth with a napkin.

'It really was.' Sam set her cutlery down on her plate. 'I won't need to eat for a week.'

'That's not going to happen.' Rich laughed. 'You eat like a horse.'

'I do not!' Sam frowned at him, but her eyes were laughing.

Holly looked from one to the other, admiring their easy friendship.

'She does, you know, Holly.' Nicole caught her attention. 'My Sam is a greedy girl.' She wrapped her arm around Sam's shoulder, then kissed her cheek.

'Oh you!' Sam kissed Nicole full on the mouth. 'Always teasing me and encouraging Rich to do the same. They're as bad as each other, Holly.'

Holly smiled and sipped her wine. So they were definitely together then…

'I should check on Luke.' She stood up and climbed over the bench.

'Okay if I come with you?' Rich asked.

Holly nodded.

'When you come back, I'd love to have a tour,' Sam said. 'Greenacres seems like an amazing place.'

'It is,' Holly agreed. 'We have some ideas about how we can develop the business and I have something to show you all.' Her stomach clenched at the thought of sharing her website, but it had to be done.

'We'll wait for you to come back, then we can all go together.' Bruce picked up a wine bottle. 'Ladies, fancy another?'

As her dad poured more wine, Holly and Rich went to the house. She'd left the back door open and the baby monitor had been on the table between her and Rich. She'd checked on Luke regularly, but she could tell from the steady breathing over the monitor that he was still sleeping.

Outside her room, she paused.

'So… Sam and Nicole…'

'They've been together about two and a half years, apparently. You'd think it was six months with how lovey-dovey they are.'

'They are very affectionate.'

'They're good together.'

He held her gaze and her stomach somersaulted. He was close enough to touch, close enough to hold, and her eyes kept flitting to his lips.

She stepped closer, knowing she shouldn't, yet wanting to be held. Perhaps the wine and the good food had relaxed her too much and she'd let her guard slip. But Rich had been so kind and attentive to her all evening, had included her in the conversation and filled her in whenever she'd come back from checking on Luke. He'd also checked on Luke himself, and Holly could feel some of the anxiety about being solely responsible for her child lifting. Whatever happened between her and Rich, she was starting to believe that he would be the father she wanted for her son.

And that was why she shouldn't confuse things by letting her feelings for him grow. There was too much at stake here to allow desire to cloud her judgement. Holly had to stay rational and to focus on what was important: Luke and the future of Greenacres.

–

When they returned to the yard, it was decided that Bruce would remain at the house in case Luke woke, while Holly and Rich would take Sam and Nicole on a tour of the vineyard. Holly had grabbed a cardigan from her bedroom, suspecting that she'd need it as the evening wore on.

They began by showing the women the best views of Greenacres. The vineyard always looked particularly beautiful at twilight, the low sun washing the vines with a golden glow. Holly's grandpa used to tell her that the land was made of gold, and as a little girl, she'd believed him. Now she knew he'd meant that the soil was rich and fertile and that it was as valuable as gold. Not just because of the money it could make them but because of how it produced such fine grapes and, in turn, such delicious wines.

Next they strolled back along the front of the yard, passing the garden area behind Greenacres, where Bruce had set up the barbecue, then along to the winery building and the barn that was used to store machinery, barrels and bottles. The large stone winery had been extended and updated over the years and now housed some high-tech equipment, very different from the machinery Holly's grandpa had started out with. Attached to the main building was another, smaller building, where the wine was stored.

'This is a fantastic place, Holly,' Sam said as they walked. 'What's in the barn at the far side of the yard?'

'That one isn't used for much at all,' Holly said. 'It's been more of a storage facility over the years than anything else. That's why I was thinking that we could clear it out and use it for events.'

'Ooh, yes! What sort of events were you thinking?' Nicole asked as she gazed across the yard at the second barn.

Holly took a deep breath, suddenly a bit nervous about sharing her ideas in case the women thought she was being too ambitious.

'Tell them, Holly,' Rich said at her side, his hand resting gently on her elbow.

'I thought we could have tours of the vineyard followed by wine-tasting.'

'That's a great idea.' Nicole smiled.

'And we could also hold events such as wedding receptions and barn dances.'

'Barn dances?' Nicole raised an eyebrow. 'Tourists love things like that. In fact, I bet some of the locals would too.'

Holly looked at Rich, and he smiled. He'd told her that Nicole knew her job, and that she would make some helpful suggestions, but it seemed that Holly's own ideas were good enough.

'What's along that side road?' Sam asked, pointing at the old track overgrown with weeds and shrubbery.

'That leads to two stone cottages. They were here when my grandpa bought the land and he initially leased them to employees, but in more recent years they've been empty and neglected.'

'Can we have a look?' Sam asked.

Holly nodded, then led the way across the yard and along the narrow road.

'Watch out for the stinging nettles!' she called.

It was dark and quiet along the track because of the way the trees arched overhead like a leafy canopy. On either side the pale blue heads of thousands of bluebells released their sweet, heady fragrance into the air. Beneath the scent lay the richer aromas of earth and vegetation. It was the beautiful smell of Greenacres.

They reached the end of the road and Rich opened the gate that led into an open field with the two stone cottages at the far end. Holly's heart sank – the buildings really did look very sorry for themselves, with broken window panes and missing roof tiles – but Sam gasped and hurried through the long grass towards them.

'These are amazing!' She clapped her hands.

'I was hoping you'd think so,' Holly said.

Her grandpa had seen the cottages as more of a burden than anything else, annoyed that they'd require maintenance and effort if he wanted to do anything with them. He preferred to focus on the vineyard itself and the big old house. Holly had never given it much thought before, assuming that he had known what was right for the business, but now she saw it through fresh eyes. If he hadn't been so stubborn and set in his ways, they could have done so much more here. It must also have been tough for her father, who had clearly seen the potential for diversification but had been unable to take it forward because Grandpa had ruled with an iron fist and wouldn't allow him to make any changes.

Her dad could easily have left the vineyard and taken Holly with him, but he had stayed and bitten his tongue. She knew that he'd done it for her, so that she would inherit the place. At least her granny trusted him to do the right thing. Since Grandpa had passed, Granny had assigned sole management of the vineyard to her son-in-law, and Holly knew it was a lot to deal with. She wanted to help him as much as she could.

'They're beautiful, Holly. There's so much potential here.'

'My dad and I think we could renovate them and use them as holiday rentals.' Holly gazed at the cottages.

'You'd need an architect and some builders' quotes to find out what's possible and to get the best prices, but you certainly could rent them out. For a lot of money in peak season.' Nicole ran her hand over the stone facade of the nearer building, then tried the door. It was locked.

'Grandpa kept them locked even though they're in such a state,' Holly explained. 'I can run back and get the keys if you want to go inside.'

'No, it's fine. I can see though the window.' Nicole peered through the glass. 'It's a bit weathered in there, where the elements have clearly got in, but with some work, it could be lovely. And these views!' She turned and gestured towards the land that spread out before the cottages – fields to the right and vines to the left, then beyond that the dark expanse of the sea.

'Holly also thought that we could do something off-peak,' Rich said, his face etched with pride as he winked at her. 'She had a great idea about offering romantic couples' getaways in late autumn and winter, and possibly writers' retreats for those needing somewhere to hide away while they race towards a deadline or plod through edits.'

'Wonderful ideas! Your accountant will be pleased with them.' Sam smiled. 'Are you still with Mr… what did you say his name was again, Rich?'

'Mr Seymour,' Holly replied. 'Grandpa wouldn't dream of having anyone else doing the accounts, but Dad and I agree that we have to be forward-thinking. We were going to speak to Rich about it this evening actually… We'd like your firm to take over the accounts for Greenacres. With Rich being our contact, of course.'

She glanced at him, suddenly shy about making the request, but when he met her eyes, he was grinning broadly.

'I'd be honoured,' he said.

'We'd love to take on your accounts,' Sam added.

'But Dad needs to speak to Mr Seymour first, to make it all official. We think he carried on doing the accounts out of loyalty to Grandpa, and Dad reckons he'll be glad to let them go.'

'That all sounds fabulous.' Sam clapped her hands together. 'Rich, you'll be a junior partner too before long if you keep finding us more clients like this!'

Excitement fizzed inside Holly. Nicole and Sam thought she had some great ideas and agreed that there was much that could be done here. It would take hard work and money, but Holly knew enough about business to understand that investment was often required to see a profit, and she felt sure that they could find a way to make this work. After seeing the two women's enthusiasm first-hand, she also felt ready to show them the website.

As they walked back to the big house, she listened as Sam and Nicole gave their professional suggestions about how to start the whole process, including obtaining the relevant permissions from the council, and Rich explained what he'd found out about the financial invest-ment required to make the changes. The numbers made her stomach roll, and goose bumps covered her arms, but Rich squeezed her shoulder more than once to reassure her.

There were things to discuss with Rich and her father, and now that she knew more about it, they would have to speak to Granny too. Holly hoped that the old lady wouldn't be averse to making some changes, but she had a gut feeling that she wouldn't mind at all.

She also had a feeling that Rich would be there every step of the way, supporting, advising and helping as much as he could. And that thought warmed her heart.

When they reached the house, Holly went inside to get the laptop. She stood in the kitchen for a moment, gazing out of the window at the vineyard. She had nursed a secret doubt for a long time, a doubt that she had much to offer the world. She'd run the vineyard shop after deciding not to go to university, and although she'd done a good job of it, making a pleasing profit, she'd wondered if she had anything else to contribute. Now, though, even though she was sad that Greenacres had reached a point of instability, she also felt invigorated. She had a good business head on her shoulders, and she possessed a certain creative flair, as well as enthusiasm and a solid work ethic. Along with her dad and Rich, she would strive to make Greenacres great again, and she was excited about what that meant for them all.

Chapter 14

Four weeks had passed, and spring had given way to summer. So much had changed already. Although Holly had found out that planning permission often took up to eight weeks, and sometimes longer depending on what was required, Rich's father had been able to pull a few strings at the council. The plans for the use of the second barn and the stone cottages had been processed, and things were moving quickly. Bruce had been surprised at the amount of money required up front, but he admitted to Holly that it wouldn't be a problem as he'd been saving for years. He also had some money put away that he'd inherited from his parents in Australia – grandparents Holly had never met because they'd died before she was born – and that he'd had been keeping for a rainy day. He told Holly that he'd be happy to invest in the vineyard because essentially it was an investment for her and for Luke.

So the ball was well and truly rolling. There were builders at the cottages and in the second barn, and the work was due to be completed by late July, when they'd be ready to hold a grand opening. The thought made Holly's stomach flip. Her dad had been keen to project-manage everything, and Nicole, whom they'd employed to oversee the PR, had turned out to be extremely efficient and competent. As she had told Holly and Bruce, they had great wine, beautiful views and the right attitude; all they needed was the right advertising and for their reputation to grow. She'd already arranged for a few taster weekends at the cottages for a variety of bloggers and journalists, who would, of course, be given the full Greenacres vineyard tour experience.

Holly's website had won everyone's approval and it was now live, with teasers about the cottages and the events that could be held at the barn already attracting attention. They'd even secured some bookings for the cottages in August and September, as well as some enquiries about renting them over the winter months. It had been agreed that Holly would run the shop and website, answer emails and take bookings, while her dad would continue to see to the running of the vineyard and the winery. Rich would do the vineyard's accounts, now that Mr Seymour had been thanked for his long service and gently retired, and Nicole would head up the PR. Holly was excited about her new role and about taking Greenacres forward, and although it was a lot to juggle alongside caring for Luke, it was work that she could do while being there for him. She knew that as he grew and started toddling, it would be harder to manage, but there was a lovely nursery in Penhallow Sands and Lucinda had already offered her childcare services. Holly knew that she would manage, just as other working mothers did, but she also knew how lucky she was to have a family around her supporting her.

Every day after work, Rich came to visit Luke and to help however he could. He'd been a source of support in more ways than one, and Holly had to try hard not to allow herself to get too close to him. But it was so difficult. He really had changed and was demonstrating it in every way possible, by being a wonderful father and a good friend.

This evening, he was babysitting while Holly went out with Fran. For an actual night out. She'd changed three times already, feeling uncomfortable in the fitted summery dresses she'd tried on, still convinced that even though she'd given birth almost five months ago, her belly was still too soft and rounded. She'd settled instead on a pair of stretchy indigo skinny jeans with hidden tummy support, and a sleeveless white tunic top that fell to mid thigh. With a pair of low wedges, she felt comfortable but smart enough to hit the town.

When she went downstairs just after seven, Rich was in the lounge with Glenda. The TV flickered with some chat show, but the volume was down and Rich and her granny were both talking to Luke.

Her son was lying on his play mat in front of the sofa where Granny sat, with Rich at his side. Rich's long denim-clad legs were stretched out in front of him and he was tickling Luke's tummy, causing the baby to chuckle with glee.

'Evening.' Holly stood in the doorway, feeling like an awkward teenager and wishing she was spending the evening at home.

Rich looked up and his mouth formed a perfect O.

'Wow, Holly! You look fabulous.'

She bit her lip. 'Seriously? It's only jeans and a tunic.'

'Your hair and make-up are divine, darling.' Granny nodded in approval. 'And you have such a lovely figure. Isn't that right, Rich?' She nudged him and he smiled.

'Perfect.' His cheeks flushed but he kept his eyes on Holly.

Holly went over to Luke and knelt next to him to give him a kiss.

'Be good for Daddy and Granny, won't you?' She looked up. 'Where's Dad? Don't tell me he's still working?'

'He's out at the cottages, I think. Speaking to one of the carpenters.'

Holly smiled. Her dad was spending a lot of time out there, ensuring that everything was done properly. He was so enthusiastic about the developments, and it was wonderful to see.

'I'd better go and say goodbye before I leave.'

'I'll tell him you've gone,' Rich said. 'No need for you to traipse all the way out there.'

'Okay, you're probably right. I'd struggle in these wedges, even though the road has been evened out now.' She stood up.

'I'll grab my bag and jacket and wait outside for Fran.'

'Cup of tea, Glenda?' Rich asked.

'I'd love one.'

'Coming right up.'

He followed Holly out into the hallway, then went through to the kitchen, while Holly chose a lightweight blazer from the cupboard under the stairs and fetched her bag from where she'd hooked it over the banister. He was leaning against the worktop when she walked into the kitchen.

'You do look amazing, Hols. Be careful tonight, won't you?'

'I'll be fine. I'm thirty-one now, and a mother. There'll be no dancing on tables or around poles or anything.'

'Gosh, I should hope not.' Rich shook his head. 'Sorry… it's none of my business really, but I do… I do worry about you.'

The concern in his warm brown eyes made her heart flutter.

'I'll be sensible, and I'll be with Fran anyway. You know she doesn't take any nonsense.'

'Good old Fran, eh?'

'She'll probably spend the evening trying to persuade me to adopt that puppy.' Holly smiled as she thought about the grey lurcher with his rough coat and waggy tail. She'd been to Fran's a few times over recent weeks and was getting rather fond of him. But adopting him would be a big step, and she wasn't sure she was ready for it. She had so much going on at the moment; surely a puppy would complicate everything further? Even if his training had progressed wonderfully under Fran's careful guidance. Even if his soulful brown eyes did make Holly want to take him home.

'It would be good for Luke if you did adopt it. They'd probably be the best of friends.'

'Perhaps…' She opened her bag and checked that she had her purse – for the tenth time since she'd put it in there – then closed it again. 'Thanks for doing this, Rich.'

'Doing what?'

'Looking after Luke.'

'He's my son. I want to be involved as much as I can be.'

'I know, and I'm so glad that you do. I was worried…'

'You thought I wouldn't want him?'

'No. Well… I didn't know how you'd react, but you're a great dad.'

'I wish… I wonder, I mean… if I could be more to you too.' His eyes widened, and Holly watched as he rubbed his hands over his face. 'Sorry… I shouldn't have said that. I'm trying to be patient, to…'

'To what?'

He didn't reply, so she moved closer and touched his arm.

'Rich? What's wrong?'

He lowered his hands and met her gaze.

'I want to win your trust, Holly. I want to be someone you can rely on.'

She paused for a moment, then made a decision. Sliding her arms around his neck, she hugged him. He was tense at first, but as he relaxed and his strong arms enveloped her, warmth spread through her body and her skin tingled all over.

'Holly,' he murmured into her hair.

The emotion that had risen into her throat was so powerful that she couldn't reply. Rich felt so good, and smelt so good. It was like coming home after a long holiday, and she held on tight, wanting the hug to go on and on.

Everything was going so well right now: Luke had his dad and Holly had Rich's friendship. If they took things further, how would she cope if it all went wrong? She needed some form of commitment from Rich if things were ever going to develop between them. But just at this moment, she couldn't explain that. Although she knew it was wrong on some level to allow her pride to enter into the situation, it did. After the way Rich had behaved last year, the last thing Holly wanted to do was beg him for a sign of his feelings. She wanted him to make that decision himself, to show her of his own volition that he cared. She didn't want to be the one to tell him how he should do that; she wanted him to just *know*.

Silly? Perhaps.

Selfish? Perhaps.

Risky? Probably.

But if he didn't care about her enough to show her, it wouldn't work. Holly had been hurt so badly that she couldn't take the chance of loving Rich again if he didn't love her back: truly, madly, deeply. Even then, she didn't know if she'd be able to take the risk.

A horn beeping from outside dragged her from her thoughts, and she gently slid out of his arms.

'You have fun with Granny and Luke, and don't forget her cup of tea, or she'll never forgive you.'

'You have fun too, Hols.' His voice was husky, his eyes dark with something she recognized as desire.

She touched his cheek, then turned and let herself out of the back door. As she crossed the yard to the gate, she filled her lungs with fresh air, trying to shake away the longing for Rich that had made her head spin.

'What's up with you?' Fran asked when Holly got into the back of the taxi. 'You look like you've seen a ghost.'

'In some ways, I guess I have,' Holly replied as she fastened her seat belt.

She'd seen the ghost of who she once was, the ghost of the love she'd felt for Rich and the ghost of who he used to be. But she'd also seen the ghost of a chance that they could be reunited, if Rich knew how to show her his feelings. She wished she knew what it would take for him to do that, and for her to love him with her whole heart again.

The wine bar in the centre of Newquay was busy, which surprised Holly, because she'd expected it to be relatively empty on a Monday evening. It was one reason why she'd agreed to go out on the town, expecting it to be quieter than it would be at the weekend. However, it seemed that Monday was a popular evening for colleagues to head for after-work drinks and for women to catch up with their friends.

They found a table in the rear corner of the bar, where the dim lighting and dark leather seats created a cosy atmosphere. They were tucked out of the way and Holly was grateful for that. She could see out into the wine bar but hoped that no one would really notice her and Fran.

They ordered two Manhattans, and when they arrived, Holly sipped hers, savouring the sweet, rich taste and the warmth as the alcohol spread through her system. It relaxed her almost instantly, helping to ease the tension she'd felt as they'd entered the bar; in fact, the tension she'd felt since she'd started getting ready to go out.

'Well?' Fran peered at her over her glasses.

'Well what?'

'How are things?'

Holly took another sip of her drink. 'What things?' Holly said playfully.

'I'm desperate to know if I'm going to have my friend home for good. If you've made your final decision about staying here. No pressure though!' Fran widened her eyes then leant closer to Holly, making her giggle.

'No, I can see that. No pressure at all.' Holly rolled her eyes playfully. 'I'm wondering how I ever managed alone, to be honest. It's lovely being back with Granny and Dad. Luke is a very well-behaved baby, but even so, it was lonely in Exeter, and having people around is very... comforting. Besides which, everything is going so well with the plans and I feel like I'm making a big difference. The shop looks much better with your new stock, and the business already feels... renewed. It will take time to build the reputation we want, but I truly believe that this is the beginning of something great for Greenacres.'

Fran nodded. 'I'm so happy for you all. And how are things going with Rich?'

'Well... it is nice having him there. Luke absolutely adores him and he's a natural as a father. It's funny... I never thought he would be, but you should see him with Luke now. They've bonded and it's lovely.'

'Taking Luke away from him would be difficult then.'

'It would.' Holly watched as a young couple entered the wine bar, laughing together. They looked happy and carefree, as if nothing was going to spoil their night. Sometimes Holly wished her life was simpler, then she took a look at Luke and realized she wouldn't change him for the world.

'Do you think you could do it? Leave, I mean.'

'I don't think so... at least not until everything is up and running. And even then... It would mean leaving everyone in the lurch, and to be frank, I want to stay. I'm already making plans for childcare for Luke, and I know Penhallow Sands has a great village school. There are more reasons to stay than to go.'

'But if you stay... what does that mean for you and Rich?'

Holly met Fran's questioning blue eyes. 'I have no idea. I'm trying to take it day by day with him at the moment, because thinking beyond tomorrow is difficult. I know I need to make some firm decisions, but it's also nice to live for now.'

'I agree with you there!' Fran raised her glass. 'To living for today.'

They clinked glasses, then drank.

'Another?' Fran asked.

'Why not?'

Fran went to the bar, and Holly opened her bag and checked her mobile. No texts and no missed calls. That was good. It meant everything was fine at home. Rich was probably putting Luke down for the night, then when he came back downstairs, Granny would try to feed him a scone or three, and no doubt they'd be drinking endless cups of tea.

Fran returned with their drinks.

'Think that barman is cute?' She pointed at a tall bartender who reminded Holly of a young Johnny Depp. His dark hair was artfully messy and his muscular arms were heavily inked. One of the tattoos led up his neck and finished behind his left ear.

'He's hot in that brooding bad-boy way, yes.'

'That's what I thought.'

'Why don't you ask for his number?'

Fran wrinkled her nose.

'What?'

'Ah… can't be bothered.'

'But you said he's hot.'

'Yeah, but men… they're so demanding.' Fran shook her head. 'I have animals to care for and work to do, especially with your orders for landscapes and pottery.' She winked. 'I can't be sexting all the time, can I?'

Holly laughed. 'Sexting?'

'Well, yeah. That's what some guys expect, and I haven't got time for that nonsense.'

'What about enjoying someone's company and spending time together? You don't have to be sexting!'

'One guy I dated recently wanted me to sext him every day. He even sent me some... interesting photos of himself.'

'What? Like... selfies?'

'Kind of.' Fran pulled a face.

'You mean naked ones?'

She sighed. 'Yeah.'

'Were they sexy?'

'No. He was good-looking and had a fit body, but who wants to see what he called "the mighty staff" when they're eating their porridge?'

Holly's shoulders were shaking now. 'The mighty staff?'

'Yeah. He had some sort of warrior fetish.'

'Oh Fran.' Holly got a tissue from her bag and dabbed at her eyes. 'You are so funny.'

Fran cocked an eyebrow. 'It wasn't me! He just had a tendency to think rather highly of himself.'

'In what way?'

'The word *mighty* was deceiving.'

They sniggered then, and Holly waved a hand to indicate that Fran had to stop making her laugh.

'Enough!'

'Excuse me, ladies.'

They looked up to find two men looking down at them. The one who'd spoken was tall and golden, from his hair to his beard to his dazzling smile. His companion was much shorter, with a completely shaved head and strikingly blue eyes above a shy smile.

'We couldn't help noticing that you two are alone, and wondered if you'd like some company.'

'We're not alone.'

He frowned. 'Pardon?'

'We're together. The very fact that there are two of us means that we're not alone. Get it?' Fran's tone was deadpan, her expression neutral as she stared up at the golden one.

'Oh… uh… we only wanted to offer you a drink.' His eyes flickered around, then he swigged from his bottle of beer. Behind him, his shorter friend stepped back as if he was uncomfortable. 'No need to be so spiky.'

'Spiky?' Fran tilted her head to one side. 'I was merely pointing out a fact.'

'Look,' Holly interrupted them, 'we're grateful for the offer, but we don't want company, or any more drinks. Thank you.'

The tall man eyed her, and Holly held her breath.

'Okay… so you don't want company, but how about if you give me your number and we could meet up another time?' He smiled then, but a vein throbbed in his temple, suggesting that he was far from happy at their rejection of his advances.

'I don't think so.' Holly shook her head.

'Nope. Now bugger off.' Fran stood up, pulling herself to her full height and crossing her arms over her chest.

The bald man put a hand on his friend's arm and attempted to pull him away from the table.

'Get off me, Leyton! It's fine, I'm coming.' The tall man drained his beer bottle, then set it on the table in front of Fran. 'Your loss!' He grinned at them before swaggering away.

Fran sank back onto her seat but didn't take her eyes off the two men.

'Shall we go?' Holly asked, nervous about a repeat performance.

'Why?' Fran finally turned to her.

'Well, we don't want any trouble.'

'We won't have any.'

'We just did.'

'He's a knobhead, but his friend won't let him come back.'

'I hope not.'

Fran nodded. 'And that's another reason why I can't be bothered. Macho men like that leave me cold.'

'Me too. Who does he think he is, throwing his weight around like that?' Holly shivered. The man's attitude had made her feel quite vulnerable, but also incensed, and she was glad she was with Fran and that they'd be leaving together. She'd dealt with idiots like that in the past, but now that she had Luke, she felt more exposed than ever before, because if anything happened to her, it would affect him too.

'There will always be arrogant dicks like that, Holly, but they can't stop us living life the way we want to.'

'I know. It was a bit scary, though, wasn't it?'

'It's all bravado with men like that. I just hope the next woman he tries to woo with his charm has the strength to stand up to him.'

They fell silent as they finished their drinks.

'Do you want to go home now?' Fran asked.

Holly had watched the men leave, the one called Leyton clearly irritated by his friend's aggressive attempts at chatting them up. The wine bar was warm and cosy, the music a mixture of eighties and nineties hits and the barman looked as though he could deal with the men should they return. It was nice to be out with Fran, and Holly felt more like her old self again.

'No, let's stay for a bit longer.'

'Are you sure?'

'Yes.' She checked her mobile. 'It's still early and the taxi's not due for another hour and a half. Let's have another drink, shall we?'

'Good plan.'

Holly picked up their glasses.

'Same again?'

'Yes please.'

As Holly walked to the bar, she told herself to relax. Rich was looking after Luke, her dad and granny were around if he needed help, and she was out with her best friend for the first time in a long time. She could let her hair down and enjoy herself.

So that was what she would do.

The evening had also confirmed something else for her, and she wasn't certain if she was entirely happy about it. She wasn't interested in getting to know another man, whoever he was. In fact, the idea of being with anyone else turned her cold. Her heart belonged to one man only, and if she couldn't have him, she'd prefer to stay single.

For Holly, it had always been Rich.

–

Holly closed the back door, then carefully slipped off her shoes. She listened for voices or the sound of the TV, but the house was quiet. It was only just gone ten o'clock, but Granny liked to go to bed quite early, and she suspected that after a full day, her dad would either be snoring in his chair or in bed. That left Rich and Luke.

She headed for the lounge and peered through the semi-darkness, the only light the glow from the muted TV. Rich was lying on the sofa with the baby monitor on his chest. He was fast asleep.

She crept into the room and took the monitor from his hands then took the crocheted blanket off the back of the sofa and draped it over him. His lashes fluttered on his cheeks and he smiled briefly, reminding her of Luke when he was dreaming. They were more alike than she'd realized.

She loved Luke with every fibre of her being. His happiness, his welfare and his future were her main concern, and she believed they always would be. Before she'd given birth, she'd had no idea exactly how much she'd love her child. As he grew inside her, she felt protective of him and wondered what he'd be like and who he'd grow up to be, but she hadn't understood exactly how powerful the maternal instinct was. It had left her breathless when it had hit her full force after Luke's birth. The days and weeks she'd sat next to his crib in the hospital had been agony, even though he hadn't been half as poorly as some of the other premature babies. She'd have given her life for him right then and there if she'd had to.

She knew that Rich loved their son too. It was a bond they shared and always would. But apart from that, was there something more between her and Rich? Luke would grow up and one day leave home. That thought hurt, but of course it would happen eventually. And then what? If she and Rich did try to make a go of things, would they find that it had been only for their son? Was that enough?

She knew it wasn't.

Rich would love Luke now no matter what. That was how it should be, and she'd do her utmost to ensure that they had a good relationship. But as for her and Rich; she didn't yet know. As tempting as it was, it was risky to give her heart to him again, and she wasn't sure she could do it.

She leant forward and pressed her lips to his forehead. It seemed that her feelings for him were still there, just below the surface, and it was possible that they could be revived. Or she could keep them hidden away, suppress them and get on with her life.

It would take something very special indeed for her to believe that Rich loved her as much as she had loved him. And the only way they could ever be together again was if he could prove that he did.

Chapter 15

Rich was exhausted with trying to keep all the balls he was juggling in the air, but he hoped it would be worth it. He was finding his position at the accountancy firm quite enjoyable, and Sam's suggestion that he could end up becoming a junior partner was quite exciting. He had discovered a hunger to get on since he'd returned to Penhallow Sands, and it was a good feeling. When he'd finished at the office, he got changed, then rushed back to work on his secret project – although it was more in the role of an overseer, as he'd hired someone to help with that one. It was going well and he hoped it was the right thing to do. It was part of his plan to do something nice for Holly, because he knew he needed to make a grand gesture.

Later, he'd head up to the vineyard to help Holly with Luke. It was his favourite time of day, when he got to see his son and to help with his bath and bedtime routine. The smile on Luke's face when he arrived and the recognition that was more and more obvious now lifted his heart. Who knew that a surprise baby could make such a difference in a life that had seemed otherwise confusing, and even pointless? He'd once felt worthless, as if those around him would be better off without him, but since Holly's return to Penhallow Sands with Luke, he'd felt that he had a purpose. Now he had a responsibility to provide love and stability for his son, as well as for Holly, even if it was just as a friend and the father of her child.

Things at the vineyard were progressing well; it would soon be ready for the next stage of development. It was another reason why he hoped that his secret project would be a good thing for Holly and for Luke. They might need that space from the hustle and bustle that opening the vineyard to the public could create.

Holly had really blossomed since her return to Greenacres. She had more colour in her cheeks and her face had lost that pinched look. Her eyes were no longer as wary, and although he still sensed that she was guarded at times, as if she was holding back from him in some way, he did feel that she was starting to trust him again.

If only he could go back in time and give himself a good kick up the backside for being such an idiot. But unfortunately for him, he hadn't yet added time traveller to his CV.

—

Holly shifted Luke onto her right hip, then opened the door and headed out into the yard. She'd heard a car approaching and wondered if it might be a delivery for the workmen.

'It's Auntie Fran!' She smiled at her son and he giggled; he was becoming so reactive to speech, especially to familiar words and to changes in Holly's intonation.

Fran climbed out of her blue Escort, and Holly's stomach dropped to her flip-flops at the expression on her friend's face.

'God, Fran, what is it?'

207

Fran pressed her lips together as she approached the gate that opened onto the yard.

'I had a phone call this morning...' She swallowed hard, clearly trying to maintain a hold on her emotions. 'From my mum. Turns out Dad's not well. He...' She blinked, then removed her glasses and rubbed at her eyes impatiently.

'Come on in and have a coffee.'

'I... I can't.'

'Why not?'

'I have the pup in the car.'

'Well bring him in too.'

'Are you sure?'

'Of course I am.'

Fran opened the passenger door and the grey puppy leapt down, then trotted towards Holly. When she opened the gate, he jumped up at her legs, so she rubbed his soft head, being careful to keep Luke out of his reach. Her son squealed with delight as the dog stretched up and sniffed his socks.

'Come on, doggy, let's make a coffee for Fran.'

In the kitchen, Fran sat at the table and made the pup sit in front of her. His tail wagged hard on the floor but he stayed where she'd put him.

'His training's coming along well.' Holly nodded at the dog.

'Yes, he's a good boy and a quick learner.'

'Right then... tell me what's happened.'

Holly carried the mugs to the table one by one with Luke balanced on her hip, then sat opposite Fran. She could see that her friend had been crying, and no wonder.

Even though Fran's parents had moved to Italy, she was still close to them, and she idolized her dad.

'Mum rang about… oh, about an hour ago, I think. It's all been a bit of a blur. Anyway, she said Dad was complaining about heartburn last night but she put it down to overindulging on cannoli, but by the early hours, he was in a lot of pain and nothing seemed to be helping. Then…' she released a slow breath, 'then he got out of bed and collapsed.'

'So is he in hospital?'

Fran nodded.

'What are you going to do?'

'I have to go out there. I can catch a flight later today. I can't not go… just…' She bit her bottom lip and blinked hard.

Holly reached across the table and squeezed her hand. 'I understand. What can I do to help?'

On her lap, Luke bounced up and down and slapped the tabletop with his chubby little hand.

'I didn't know what to do about the animals, but I rang Shell and she said not to worry. She'll look after them and Bella will give her a hand.'

'Can she manage that with running the shack?'

'I know it'll be a stretch, but who else can I ask?'

'I could always go over and stay at yours.'

Fran shook her head. 'No, it's fine. You've got Luke and your granny to think of, plus everything that's going on here. Besides which, it takes ages to feed the animals and clear up after them, and I couldn't expect you to do that. Shell will sort it; she said she's got a new employee who'll help her with the shack, so she reassured me she'll be fine.'

'What about this little chap?'

Fran looked down at the pup.

'He's doing so well with his training, but I'm worried about leaving him. He's such a sweetie, but he hates being without human company, which he would be when Shell has to leave for work. The others are older and more relaxed, but he's still at that needy stage.'

As if he knew they were discussing him, the pup emitted a low whine, then shuffled forward on his bottom and pawed at Holly's legs. She stroked his head and he licked her palm. She didn't know if she'd regret this, but it seemed like the only answer.

'I'll take him.'

'What?'

'Leave him here.'

'I can't ask you to do that, Hols. You've got your plate full.'

'No arguing about it, Fran. He can stay with me.'

'Thank you so much.' Fran rubbed the pup's ears. 'Did you hear that? You're going to live with Holly and Luke.'

'Live?'

'Stay. I meant stay. Holly's going to foster you... for a while.'

The dog gazed up at Holly with his big brown eyes and she knew that she'd made the right decision.

'He still doesn't have a name?'

'I've been calling him doggo and pup, but he does need a name of his own.'

'I'll have a think.'

Fran sipped her coffee. 'Holly, are you absolutely sure about this? The last thing I want to do is add to your workload.'

'I'm sure. How could I resist those eyes? Now, can I do anything else to help?'

'I'm hoping I'll only be gone for a few days. You know my dad… he's strong. He'll pull through.'

'I'm certain he will. Just tell him to stay off the cannoli.'

Fran smiled. 'Bloody greedy pig! Bet he's piled on the weight with all that delicious Italian food.'

—

Holly waved Fran off, making her promise to call if she needed anything else, then returned to the house. All the time, the pup was at her heels, trotting along like a scruffy little shadow. Luke had already taken to him, clapping his hands and laughing when he responded to his noises. Holly had a feeling they'd be great friends. For as long as the pup stayed, that was. Which would be temporary, of course. He was going right back to Fran's when she got home. She wouldn't soften on that decision.

Would she?

Fran had left a harness and lead, a bed and a few toys, along with a bag of dried dog food. Holly knew nothing about feeding dogs, so she'd got Fran to write down instructions, along with when to let him out, how much to exercise him and when to call the vet, although she hoped that last one wouldn't be necessary.

She checked the time and was surprised to find it was gone twelve.

'I guess now could be a good time for a walk. We could take Dad some sandwiches and get some fresh air in the process.'

She strapped Luke into his pram, packed a bag with sandwiches, a flask of coffee and a bottle for Luke, then called the dog to her to put his harness on. He wheeled around excitedly as she tried to slide it over his head, then grabbed the lead off her and raced around the kitchen table.

'Doggo!' She sharpened her tone. 'That's naughty!'

She strode across the kitchen, but he ran the other way, so she turned and caught him by surprise as he made for the back door.

'Come here!' She clipped the lead to his harness. 'Fran failed to tell me that you get overexcited when you hear the word *walk*. I'd better remember that one.'

He bounced up and down, scrabbling at her legs, and she sent out a silent thank you that he was a small dog. A heavier one would've hurt her, but his paws were light as they patted her thighs.

Somehow she manoeuvred the pram out of the door, along with the dog, then slid the strap of the bag over the pram handle. She already felt as though she needed a sit-down; goodness only knew how she'd feel after a walk with these two.

She crossed the yard, holding the lead with one hand and pushing the pram with the other. It was a beautiful day and the sun was high in the sky. The breeze was cool enough for her to keep her cardigan on but not enough to chill her, and it ruffled her hair gently, making her feel relaxed and content.

As she walked along the road towards the cottages, where her dad had said he'd be today, she breathed in the sweet floral aromas that rose to greet her. She had to stop a few times for the pup to water the flowers, but it was fine, as she wasn't in a rush. From up ahead she could hear the noise of a saw, and carpenters calling to one another as they worked on the cottages. Soon there would be two gorgeous self-catering holiday rentals ready to start earning.

As she emerged from the trees, she smiled at the sight that greeted her. The land around the cottages had been tidied up and the gardens restored to their former glory with new plants, neatly trimmed hedges and freshly mown grass. The small-paned windows shone in the sunlight, framed by newly painted shutters. There were workers on the roofs painting the chimneys, and some outside painting the exterior of the cottages. She could picture how they would look when the work had been completed, and it was exciting,

With the beach a short car journey away, along with the pretty fishing village of Penhallow Sands, the rentals would hopefully prove popular, especially if Nicole's media contacts gave them some favourable coverage. Once the work was finished and the new furniture and furnishings Holly had ordered were installed, she would take photographs to post on the website. She felt so proud to be a part of this venture, and it had rekindled her interest in business and business law. It made her want to give something back to the world if she could, though she wasn't quite sure how to do that yet.

As she neared the cottages, she looked around for her dad. She couldn't see him out the front, so she went to the first cottage and knocked on the door. It swung open to reveal a workman in baseball cap, jeans and T-shirt covered in sawdust.

'Hi, Barry, I was wondering if my dad was around.'

Barry frowned, his bushy eyebrows meeting under the rim of his cap.

'He was here earlier. Think he might be around the back, working on the summer houses. You want me to shout for him?'

'No, it's fine. I'll go round myself.'

Holly pushed Luke's pram around the cottage and opened the side gate. She closed it behind her, checked that the garden was clear, then unclipped the dog's lead. It would do him good to have a run around and burn off some of the energy that had made him pull at his lead on the walk. Holly's arm was aching from trying to hold him back. Hopefully he'd get used to walking alongside the pram, or she'd end up with one arm longer than the other.

'Hello!' she called in the direction of the summer houses. They were so newly built that she could smell the timber and the sealant that had been used on the boards. She'd helped her dad pick out furniture, wanting to make the little houses perfect for their guests.

She pushed down the brake on the pram and peered in at Luke. He'd drifted off in the fresh air, so she had a while before he'd want his next feed.

'Hello! Dad?'

The dog raced towards the nearer of the summer houses and disappeared though the open doors. Holly followed him, anxious to find her father. After hearing Fran's news, worry pierced her and she experienced a slight uneasy fluttering under her ribcage. She hoped Bruce was all right. She didn't know how she'd cope if anything happened to him.

'Bloody hell!' A shout came from the summer house and her dad emerged looking red-faced and flustered.

'Where did you come from?' He questioned the dog as if expecting it to answer.

'Hi, Dad. He's with me.'

'Holly?' Her dad frowned.

'Yes, it's me. Everything okay?'

'Yes...' His eyes flickered towards the summer house. 'Fine. Everything's fine.' His Adam's apple bobbed in his throat and the blush in his cheeks deepened. Holly wasn't used to seeing her dad so ruffled.

'Well, Bruce, I think we can safely say that you've checked out my toolkit.' A female voice came from within the summer house and was quickly followed by a tall, broad figure in scruffy jeans, checked shirt and cap. 'And thanks for allowing me to check your hard wood... *floors*, that is!'

Holly's mouth fell open as she looked from the woman to her dad, and the woman's eyes widened.

'Holly... uh... this is Janine.'

'We've met already,' Holly replied. Janine was a senior carpenter and had been at the vineyard for some time.

'Yes, that's right.' Janine nudged Bruce.

'Of course.' He rubbed a hand over his eyes. 'Janine was... uh... checking that the finish in the summer house is...uh... satisfactory.'

'Right.' Holly stared at them, not quite sure what she was feeling, although it was so awkward that she was worried she might start laughing. 'I brought you lunch.' She went to the pram and unhooked the bag, then removed the flask and sandwiches, which she set down on a picnic table in the garden. 'I'll leave you to it.'

'No! Stay, Holly, please.'

'I don't want to… disturb you and Janine.' She knew she shouldn't laugh at her dad's embarrassment, but it was so sweet that he was blushing, and it was clear that there was something going on here.

'You're not disturbing anything.'

'I should be going anyway. I need to get that order processed at the builder's yard.' Janine kicked at a tuft of grass with her work boot, then flattened it down.

'Okay.' Bruce nodded.

'Speak later.' Janine briefly touched his arm, then smiled at Holly. 'Bye, Holly.'

Holly nodded, and the woman walked towards the back door of the cottage.

The pup raced to the picnic table and jumped up, setting his front paws on the bench and sniffing the air.

'He can smell the sandwiches.' Bruce rubbed the animal's ears.

'Fran dropped him off earlier. She's had to go to Italy to see her dad. He collapsed this morning.'

'That's awful.' Bruce shook his head. 'Poor Christopher. Hope he'll be okay.'

'Yes… I really hope so.'

They sat opposite each other and ate the lunch Holly had prepared, washing it down with cups of coffee from the flask. Holly bit back her questions about Janine, believing that her dad would tell her when he was ready – if there was anything to tell, that was. From inside the cottages, the sounds of sawing and drilling drifted into the air, punctuating the silence that hovered between them.

'So how long's this little fellow staying?'

'I don't know yet.'

'Does he have a name?'

Holly shook her head. 'I said I'd try and think of one.'

'Risky, that.'

'Why?'

'If you name him, you might want to keep him.'

'No I won't.' She didn't sound convinced, even to her own ears.

'You'll get attached, Hols.'

'I'll try not to.' She drained her coffee.

'Are you okay, angel?' he asked, his eyes wary as they roamed her face.

'I'm fine. Are you?'

He nodded. 'What you saw then… I mean, what you heard, rather—'

'It's none of my business, Dad.'

'Well it is kind of, because you live here and I'm your dad and… well, we should be honest with each other. I hadn't said anything before now because I wasn't sure there was anything to say.'

'Are you seeing Janine?' Holly gazed at his familiar features, his broad shoulders and his kind eyes. He'd been alone a long time and deserved to be happy. It was just the shock of hearing a woman joke about sexual activity with him that had thrown Holly, making her want to giggle. Her dad had every right to a sex life – even if it was something she'd prefer not to think about.

'I don't know that we're seeing each other. I mean… I like her and I've been enjoying her company while she's been working here. She's sweet, funny and self-deprecating, and I feel comfortable with her. I'm not really an old man yet… well, when I was your age, fifty-five seemed ancient, but I don't feel any different than I did when I was thirty-five. I do creak a bit more in the mornings when I get out of bed, but that's to be expected.'

'You have every right to be happy, Dad. I'm pleased for you. Delighted, in fact. Though she'd better treat you right or she'll have me to deal with.' She scowled at the thought.

'Thank you.' He screwed up the foil that the sand-wiches had been wrapped in. 'We haven't even been on what could be classed as a date yet. We've met for coffee, and we went for a drink one evening, but the lads were there too. But she makes me laugh, and that's something not be sniffed at. I feel relaxed with her, and that I can be myself.'

'That's good, Dad.' Holly smiled, reaching out and covering his hand with hers. 'I want you to be happy. I was simply a bit... surprised to hear what I did when I arrived. I hope it didn't seem as though I was being judgemental.'

'No, of course not.' Bruce lowered his eyes and chuckled as the flush returned to his cheeks. 'Nothing happened, I promise. She's just a bit of a joker.'

It was good that Janine was able to make Bruce smile, and that he felt at ease with her. Life could be lonely, and finding someone who understood you was important. Holly couldn't imagine finding another man she would care about the way she'd cared about Rich. She couldn't, now she really thought about it, visualize herself with anyone else. Whenever she thought about the future – which she'd been trying not to do too much, because it meant making some big decisions – the only man she could picture with her and Luke was Rich...

A murmur came from the pram, and before Holly could get up, the dog had hurried over and started circling the wheels, whimpering.

'Seems like you've got yourself a guard dog.' Bruce stood up and went to the pram, then lifted Luke out. The pup stopped making a noise and followed him back to the table. Bruce sat down with Luke in his arms.

'He's a good dog.' Holly patted the bench next to her, and the pup jumped up and settled down, watching as Luke babbled at his grandad.

'You know, there's a story… I think it's a Welsh legend, about a dog that gave its life for a baby.'

Holly nodded. 'Yes, of course. It had a terribly sad ending, though.'

'It did. But looking at that scruffy grey boy, I think the name would suit him.'

'You mean Gelert?'

They both gazed at the dog, and he tilted his head as he gazed back.

'Do you like that name?' Holly asked him.

Gelert answered with a bark.

Chapter 16

'Who's this little chap?' Rich asked as he received a very enthusiastic greeting from Gelert at the back door.

Holly finished wiping the kitchen table.

'That is Gelert.'

'Hello, Gelert.' He crouched down and rubbed the pup's chin. 'I didn't know you were getting a dog.'

Holly shook her head. 'Neither did I, but Fran needed someone to look after him. She had to leave suddenly yesterday after her father was taken ill.'

She rinsed the cloth in the sink, squeezed the water from it then washed her hands. As she dried them, she stood for a moment gazing out at the yard. It was early Saturday morning and sunshine warmed the kitchen, making her feel relaxed and a bit sleepy. She was still in her pyjamas, with her fleecy dressing gown over the top; she'd had a restless night, getting up to Gelert as he settled into his new surroundings. In the end, she'd taken his bed upstairs and set it on the landing outside her door – which she'd left open a crack – and the pup had finally settled.

'Sorry I couldn't get here last night. I was waiting for a delivery at the… at the office, and by the time it came and I'd sorted the paperwork, it was late.'

'It's okay.' Holly smiled at him. 'I got your text.'

'I know, but I hated not being here. I like saying good-night to Luke properly.'

Rich stood up and approached the reclining highchair, where Luke was chewing on a teething ring, held in safely with a five-point harness designed for smaller babies. Gelert followed him closely, watching what he was doing.

'Good morning, Luke!'

The baby squealed with delight as his dad lifted him from the chair and blew raspberries on his cheeks.

'Do you fancy doing something today?' Rich asked Holly as he bounced his son on his hip.

'Like what?'

'We could take a walk in the village and perhaps grab some lunch.'

Holly glanced down at herself.

'I need to dress first.'

'That's fine.' Rich handed Luke the teething ring from the tray of the highchair. 'I'll watch Luke while you take a nice bath. There's no hurry.'

'That would be wonderful. Are you sure?'

'Of course.'

An hour later, Holly had enjoyed a soak in the tub, dressed and drunk a strong coffee, then got Luke's things together. As Rich strapped the baby into his pram, she located her purse and mobile and popped them into the changing bag.

'Right, I think I've got everything.'

'You going out, dears?' Granny padded into the kitchen in her nightgown and slippers. Her hair was sticking out at the side and she had a crease on one cheek from her pillow.

'Yes, we're going for a walk.' Holly looked at Rich and he nodded. 'Would you like to come too, Granny?'

'Oh no, sweetheart, thank you. I've a list of jobs to do today.'

'Like what?' Holly frowned. Her granny shouldn't be worrying about getting things done; she should be relaxing or going out and enjoying the sunshine.

Granny waved a hand. 'I promised your dad I'd help him look for some furniture for the barn on the internet, and I need to catch up on my... TV.'

'Oh, all right then.'

'To be honest, Holly, I'm exhausted. I've been keeping so busy that I really could do with a day at home resting.' She carried the mug of coffee she'd made to the table and sat down.

'Of course. Well I've got my mobile, so ring if you need me.'

'Is your father out already?' Granny asked.

'Yes. He went out to the winery first thing. He'll probably be back soon for a drink.' Holly turned to Rich. 'Shall we go?'

'Sure.'

As he pushed the pram out of the door, there was a whine from under the table, and Holly looked down to see Gelert gazing at her, his soft brown eyes unblinking.

'What is it?'

He crept closer to her and held up a paw, and realization hit her.

'You want to go for a walk too?'

He jumped up and started circling on the kitchen tiles, his tail wagging furiously and his mouth open as if he were smiling.

Holly grabbed his lead and harness off the hook by the door and knelt down. 'Come on then, boy. I guess this is how we roll while you're staying with us.'

–

Rich pulled into the large car park at the top of the hill that led down into the village. They got Luke and Gelert out of the car and the dog skipped about with excitement.

'I can't believe I didn't think about bringing him,' Holly said as they strolled down the hill.

'Family pets, eh?' Rich laughed. 'He seems to adore you and Luke. When you went for your bath, he didn't take his eyes off me, as if he thought I might steal Luke away.'

'It's good that he's protective.'

'Definitely. I feel better knowing you have an extra bodyguard.'

'An *extra* bodyguard?'

'Well, you know… When I'm with you, I can look out for you and Luke, but when I'm not there, Gelert can do it.'

'I never thought of you as a bodyguard type, Rich.' Holly stared straight ahead as they walked, her eyes fixed on the horizon. Rich wished she would look at him, but had a feeling she was deliberately avoiding doing so.

'There's a lot you don't know about me, and probably vice versa. Perhaps we need to get to know each other all over again.' He held his breath.

'Seeing as how we have a child together, that does sound sensible.'

Sensible? His heart sank. He couldn't tell in what capacity Holly wanted to know him and he was afraid to ask in case he scared her away. In light of his other, grander planned gesture, things could go very wrong if he hoped for too much. The last thing he wanted was to drive her from Greenacres and to lose her and Luke. He needed to tread carefully.

They walked the rest of the way in silence, occasionally pausing for the dog to sniff at lamp posts and grass, and Rich focused on the gentle warmth of the late May sunshine on his face, the sounds his son made in the pram and the way the sea glittered as if filled with millions of tiny diamonds. The air was sweet and fresh, laced with a salty tang, the gulls cawed overhead, the beating of their wings hypnotic and regular as a heartbeat, and out at sea, a ship's horn sounded. He'd been here hundreds of times before, experienced these things hundreds of times, and yet today they were different. It was as if he was experiencing them all for the first time.

And in a way, he was – this was the first time he'd come into the village with Holly and his son. The first time he'd felt the lightening of the burden he'd carried for so long. Holly's presence at his side, the fragrance of her perfume as she accidentally brushed against him, and the ready smile of their baby son all made everything feel so much better. It was as though his eyes were open now, as though he was fully awake, whereas before he'd been sleepwalking through life, waiting for something to wake him up or to make him pay for what had happened to Dean.

He'd felt to blame for so long, for taking his brother out into the water like that and for failing to help him when he'd struggled. The worst thing that could have happened to Rich after losing Dean had actually happened, and it had been his own fault. He had lost Holly. But he had survived and sought help, and being with Holly now was different because *he* was different. It had taken his time away then returning to Penhallow Sands to bring him to this point, as if he'd almost come full circle in his journey. Being away from Holly had enabled him to clear his mind and to accept that he did have deep feelings for her. His guilt and grief had clouded his mind for a long time, but as they eased, helped by Holly's gentle presence and Luke's joyous one, Rich actually felt that he could see a future.

Life could be good. He just needed to release himself from the final threads of his guilt, and he suspected that Holly was the one person who could help him to do that.

As they neared the street where Shell's Shack was located, the aromas of coffee and freshly baked cakes drifted towards them, making Rich's stomach grumble. The wind chimes outside the café tinkled in the breeze, making him think of children's laughter, of the happy, carefree times before his life had changed. Before he'd lost his way, forgotten who he was and who he wanted to be, and sunk into a darkness that he hadn't thought he'd emerge from. It had been Holly who had kept him going then, her sweetness and her strength that had buoyed him up every time he thought he'd disappear completely.

And how had he thanked her?

By breaking her heart.

It was her complete forgiveness that he needed to release those final threads. She'd told him more than once that she did accept his apology, but as his mother had always said, actions spoke louder than words, and Rich knew he needed to see it in Holly's eyes, to feel it in her embrace.

'Do you want to buy some food and we can have a picnic on the beach?' he asked. Holly looked so pretty this morning with her bobbed blonde hair pushed behind her ears and the blue of her eyes brought out by the colours of her nautical striped hoodie. In faded jeans and white laced pumps, she was dressed simply but it was her style. It was perfect.

'As long as I can have cake as well as sandwiches.' She flashed him a smile.

'You can have two cakes if you want.'

They went into the café and ordered food to go, then took their purchases down to the seafront. Rich pushed the pram down the ramp to the sand and they made their way automatically towards the rocks near the craggy cliffs that hugged the bay to the right.

When they reached a sheltered spot that was out of the breeze and offered shade from the sun, Rich set the brake on the pram and Holly crouched down and pulled out a picnic blanket from the basket underneath the car seat.

'You've come prepared.'

'I'm a mum now. I have to carry everything but the kitchen sink.'

Rich helped her to spread the blanket out over the sand, then placed rocks at the corners to hold it in place. He went back to the pram to get Luke out, but the baby was asleep, so he pulled up the hood and tucked the soft blanket around his body. Even though it was sunny, the wind down on the beach was cool and he didn't want Luke getting chilled while he slept.

Holly had settled Gelert on the blanket, and Rich watched as she gave him a drink of water from a small metal bowl, then produced a chew stick that she handed to the dog in exchange for a high-five.

'It seems you did think of everything.' His voice was filled with admiration, and Holly's cheeks flushed.

'I just grabbed them before we left. It'll keep him quiet for a bit. Fran said the chews help keep his teeth clean.'

Holly handed Rich the bag from Shell's Shack, and he spread the contents out in front of them, ensuring that the coffee cups stayed upright by planting them firmly in the sand. Then he unwrapped the toasted cheese paninis they'd ordered, along with the slices of chocolate cake and Bakewell tart.

'Here's to a happy, healthy and successful summer.' He held his cup up, and Holly gently tapped hers against it.

'I hope it is.' She bit her lip, then raised her eyes to meet his. 'Dad has put so much into the vineyard. If it goes wrong...'

'Hey.' He touched her hand. 'It won't go wrong. And don't forget the effort and hard work you've put in too. You've been a major part of the changes. You came up with most of the ideas, and your website is fantastic. Nicole is very positive about promoting Greenacres' grand reopening, as am I. It will be a great success.'

Holly nodded. 'Thanks, Rich. I needed to hear that.'

They ate their paninis gazing out across the beach. Families strolled on the sand and settled in spots near the sea so their children could build sandcastles and paddle in the water. It was warm enough that some would probably venture in for a swim, but the more sensible would wait for a few more weeks. Dogs barked excitedly as they raced around, making the most of their freedom, as come mid

June, they'd be allowed on the beach only on leads until October arrived.

'Are you having cake or tart?' Holly asked when they'd finished their paninis.

'I thought you wanted both.'

She smiled. 'I'm fuller than I thought I'd be; I'll start with cake and see if I have any room left.'

The chocolate cake was shiny with frosting that cracked as Holly pushed her plastic fork into it, and Rich tried not to smile as he watched her enjoying it.

'That was amazing.' She licked her fork, then put it in the cardboard box with her napkin.

Rich laughed.

'What?'

'You have some on your cheek.'

'Where?' She rubbed the wrong side.

'Let me.' He used his napkin to wipe away the chocolate frosting, and when he pulled his hand away, he found Holly's eyes glued to his face, her pupils large and dark.

'Rich... do you ever wonder what things might have been like if...'

'If I hadn't messed up so royally?'

'Yes.'

'I wish with all my heart that I could change the past.' It would be so easy to dwell on that, but it wouldn't get them anywhere, and Rich knew too well the cost of dwelling on what might have been. 'Sadly, all I can do is be a better man from here on and do my best to make the future as good as it can be.'

'I know. I just... I think about it sometimes.' She cleared her throat. 'A lot, actually. Being home and around you so much has made it difficult not to.'

'I think about what it could have been like too, but I try not to beat myself up for making a mess of things.'

'You do?'

He nodded. 'We had some good times, didn't we?'

'The best times of my life. Until Luke arrived, that is.' She glanced at the pram as if to emphasize her point. 'He's the best thing I've ever done.'

'I can't imagine life without him either.' Rich smiled. 'Hey... remember that night when we had a barbecue in the dunes and couldn't find marshmallows anywhere, so Josh tried to use chocolate teacakes instead?'

'Yes, I do! The chocolate melted completely, leaving the inside of the cakes all sticky, and then the jam burnt.'

'It stank.'

'It was all done to impress Fran, you know.'

'Even then she had plenty of admirers.'

'I'm surprised she's never met anyone she could fall for.'

'She's picky. And she's also too busy, I think, with everything else. Mind you, she'll probably fall in love with an Italian hunk and come home married.'

'I guess anything's possible with Fran,' Rich said, and they laughed in agreement. He paused, then said more quietly, 'Sometimes I think anything is possible if you want it enough.'

Holly pushed her hair behind her ears, then met his eyes.

'I think you're right.'

–

Holly and Rich walked along the seafront, making their way towards the bakery. As they entered the small shop, the delicious aromas of cakes, bread and pastries greeted them. It was a mouth-watering and familiar scent, taking Holly back through the years to all the times she'd come in here after they'd been swimming or spent a day at the beach, when they'd wolf down pies, pasties, cakes and freshly baked crusty rolls.

Rich's parents had run the bakery for as long as Holly had known them, and being there again sent a rush of emotions hurtling through her. After Rich's mother had ranted at her last year, Holly had thought she'd lost Lucinda and Rex as well as Rich, and it had been terribly painful. She'd lost her own mum, and Lucinda had stepped into the breach and helped her to cope, so when the older woman had told her she wasn't good enough for her son, it had torn her apart inside. Holly wanted to rebuild their relationship, but she knew it was going to take time. Lucinda had made it clear that she was sorry for what she'd done, and Holly didn't want her to suffer for a moment of anger. People said things in the heat of the moment that they didn't mean and lived to regret them. Could the same be said of their actions too? Rich had done things that he said he regretted, and although it had been a build-up of emotions over a period of time, it had all come to a head that day last year. Sometimes things needed to boil over so they could be seen for what they were and people could move on. Things were moving on here, and Holly wanted to play her part.

Time passed so quickly, and life could change in an instant. When she'd walked away from Penhallow Sands, she'd tried to put her home, her family, Rich and his family from her mind, but they'd always been there, simmering below the surface, reminders of a life she had once treasured.

'Hello, my darlings!' Lucinda smiled from behind the counter. A hairnet was visible underneath her red baseball cap, and her round cheeks were almost the same shade as the cap. She waved a hand in front of her face. 'It's so warm in here today.'

She came around the counter and headed straight for the pram.

'I swear he's growing bigger every day.'

Holly nodded. 'I can't keep up with how quickly he changes.'

'He'll be thirty-four before you can look round.' Lucinda shook her head. 'Like my baby.' She nudged Rich, and he grimaced.

'Mum!'

'What?' She laughed. 'You'll always be my little boy.'

Rich blushed at his mother's teasing.

'Can I get you anything?' she asked. 'Something to eat or drink?'

'I'm fine, thanks,' Rich replied. 'What about you, Holly?'

'No thank you. We haven't long had lunch and I'm stuffed.'

'Actually, Mum, we thought we'd head up to the cottage and have a cuppa with you and Dad when you get home.'

Lucinda's eyes lit up. 'That would be lovely.' She turned to the counter. 'Rex! Come out here.'

Rex came through the doorway from the kitchen.

'Hello, you two! You four, I mean.'

Holly was holding Gelert on a tight leash, but his tail wagged enthusiastically.

'Who's this little chap?' Rex asked.

'I meant to ask that myself, but I was so pleased to see them all.' Lucinda crouched down and rubbed the dog's head. 'He's a cutie, isn't he?'

'This is Gelert. He's Fran's dog but she had to go and see her father, so I'm looking after him,' Holly explained.

'I heard via the village grapevine that her father isn't well. Hope he recovers, love him.'

A pang of concern filled Holly's chest as she thought of her friend. Part of her wished she could have gone to Italy with Fran to support her, but she also knew that her friend was fiercely independent and would probably have refused to allow her to tag along, even if she hadn't got a young baby and the vineyard shop and website to run.

'Right… we'll see you at home then.' Rich opened the door and Holly walked through it with Gelert while Rich pushed the pram out.

'See you soon!' Lucinda waved at them, and as they walked away, Holly heard her say, 'Rex! Let's close early today. I want to spend some time with Holly and our grandson.'

It warmed her right through, deepening her sense of being home, right where she should have been all along. Everything was going to be all right again.

–

Holly was sitting on a patio chair in Lucinda and Rex's back garden, listening to Lucinda reminisce about Rich's childhood while she cuddled her grandson. She'd wrapped him in a shawl she'd crocheted, and he was sucking at his bottle and gazing up at her. Rex had decided to do some puppy training with Gelert on the lawn. The dog was playing along but seemed far more interested in the treats Rex was offering him than in actually getting things right.

The evening was mild and they'd been outside for hours, sitting out there to eat their supper of Rex's home-made carrot and coriander soup accompanied by crusty granary rolls from the bakery. It had been followed by lemon tart with a shortcrust base so light it melted in the mouth and a dollop of Cornish clotted cream. After their picnic as well, Holly felt as if she might pop.

'My Richard was a boy and a half.' Lucinda chuckled. 'He came into the room one time when Rex was watching a nature documentary and asked him, "Why has that octopus got so many testicles?" It sent us into fits of giggles.'

'Of course I meant tentacles,' Rich said from Holly's side. 'But I was only about five.'

'Ah yes, so you were.' Lucinda nodded. 'And there was that time when he was even younger and we'd taken him to the fair. We were waiting in line to go on the baby rides and I was handing him popcorn one bit at a time. There were people in front of us and behind us, and lots of little children eager to get on the ride. All of a sudden Rich shouted out, "Can I have more COCKPORN, Mummy?" I swear I was so embarrassed I thought I'd faint.'

Holly laughed, holding her sides as tears rolled down her face. 'That is so funny, Rich! What a rude thing to say.'

'It wasn't my fault. What was I... about two or three?' Rich was smiling too, clearly enjoying seeing his mum so relaxed.

'Would you like some more wine, Holly?' Lucinda pointed at the bottle on the table.

Holly glanced at Rich. He hadn't touched a drop as he was driving her and Luke home, but Holly had enjoyed a glass with dinner.

'Have another one, Hols, it's fine.' Rich picked up the bottle.

'Go on then, just one more.'

'I guess we have plenty of funny times ahead to enjoy with Luke, don't we?' Holly said.

Rich nodded.

'He'll bring you so much happiness. That's the thing about parenthood.' Lucinda gazed down at Luke, her expression softening as he gripped her thumb in his little fist. 'Your children bring you worry, they bring you a vulnerability you never knew existed, but they bring so much joy and so much love.'

Holly's throat tightened. She knew what Lucinda had been through and wished she could take that pain away. She bit the inside of her cheek to try to stop herself getting emotional. A gentle touch on her shoulder made her turn to meet Rich's reassuring gaze. He knew what she was thinking. Of course he did. She reached out and took his hand, lacing her fingers between his.

There was so much in life to fear, so much to worry about and so much that could go wrong, and yet... there was so much to enjoy and to treasure.

Moments like this, for example.

Chapter 17

'They're perfect, Dad. We're all ready to go.'

Holly stepped into her father's embrace outside the stone cottages. Another two weeks had passed and progress had been amazing.

'I'm really pleased.' Her dad released her, then nodded towards the cottages. 'I wish your grandpa could see them. I mean… I know they needed some work to renovate them, but it wasn't as big a job as Grandpa would've had me believe. The way he described it, we'd need to knock them down and start again.'

'It's probably a good job that he's not here to see them then.' Holly tucked her arm into Bruce's. 'He hated to be wrong about anything.'

'True.'

'This is it then!' She took a deep breath. 'The new beginning for Greenacres.'

Her dad's eyes widened. 'I'm quite nervous.'

'It's going to be fine.'

'Are you sure about giving notice on your place in Exeter?'

'Positive. I've given it a lot of thought and I don't want to go back there… except to collect my things, that is. And I have three months to do that anyway. I brought everything I needed with me, and none of the furnishings are mine, except for the cot, and seeing as how I have one here, I can donate it to a charity shop or see if the landlord wants it left at the flat.'

'I wouldn't have tried to change your mind if you'd wanted to go back, Hols. It's entirely your decision, but the fact that you've decided to come home for good makes me so happy. Granny is delighted too. It will be wonderful to have you around, and to be able to see Luke all the time.'

Holly leant her head on his shoulder. She had thought carefully about what to do, but over the past two weeks her decision had been made for her. The shop had started to get busier, with orders coming in for wine and for Fran's paintings and pottery, as well as lots of emails requesting more information about the cottages and events that could be held at the barn. The website was proving to be particularly popular and getting plenty of hits every day. Holly had suggested the idea of setting up a blog to run alongside it, where they could tell people about their wine-making processes and also host guest bloggers who could write about their lives in Penhallow Sands.

She looked up at her dad.

'I don't want to miss the grand opening or to be away from you and Granny again. Plus, I want Luke to grow up here like I did.'

'What about Rich?' he asked cautiously. 'Does he feature in the equation?' His eyes scanned her face. He wanted the best for her, she knew that, and whatever that was would be fine with him. Holly knew she could have decided to live on the moon and marry an alien, and as long as she was happy, her dad would have supported her.

'I'm not sure yet. I have some very… confusing feelings. It's even more complicated because of Luke.'

'Of course it is. You must take your time. No sense in rushing anything. Are you happy to continue running the shop and the website?'

'Definitely. I love what I'm doing and there's potential for so much more. I really think the blog is a good idea. People love to find out more about how our wine is made, and it will hopefully encourage them to visit and take one of our wine-tasting vineyard tours.'

'There's always work here for you, Holly. But what about Luke?'

'Lucinda has offered to help with childcare, and there are several options in the village too, when I'm ready to leave him. I might even return to college eventually, possibly night school, and get some qualifications. I was thinking that I could do a degree in business law, like I wanted to do all those years ago, or perhaps I'll do something involving website design. There are so many possibilities, but whatever I do decide will be of benefit to Greenacres.'

'When you were growing up, I didn't think you'd stay around, but after your mum died, I thought your dreams had changed and I worried about you. I've always wanted the best for you, Holly.'

'I know. I did have different dreams before we lost Mum, and although I brushed those dreams under the carpet for a while because I couldn't face the idea of leaving, I never completely forgot them. Back then, I thought I'd need to go away to realize my ambitions, but now I know that's not the case at all. Greenacres and Penhallow Sands have everything I need to be fulfilled;

I just needed to see that through different eyes and to be given a new challenge. I want to stay and build something great here, something that we can leave as a legacy for Luke, and even for *his* children.'

Her dad smiled at her, his eyes full of approval.

'Holly, your mum would be so proud.'

'I hope so.'

'No one will ever replace her in my heart. You know that, don't you?' He dropped his gaze to his boots and Holly knew he was thinking about Janine. It was his way of letting her know that if things did become more serious there, he'd always remember her mum.

'I do. But you also have a life to live, and Mum would want you to live it as fully as possible.'

'She would.' He nodded. 'I still feel guilty at times, though.'

'What on earth for?'

'Well, I loved your mum and I thought we'd be together for the rest of our lives. I feel guilty because it's like I'm betraying her.'

'Oh Dad, you're not betraying her. She's been gone a long time and you've been alone since she died. I know how much you loved her, and she did too, but happiness doesn't always present itself to us, so when it does, you have to grab it and hold it tight.'

As they walked back to the big house, arm in arm, with Gelert trotting along next to her, Holly thought about what she'd said to her dad. Happiness *was* hard to find, as was finding someone to connect with. If it happened, it was precious. Despite everything she had gone through with Rich, she did feel connected to him, even more so now that they had a child together.

She'd left Luke at the big house with her grandmother. He had been sleeping, so she'd given Granny instructions to ring her immediately if he woke and she'd hurry back. She knew the old lady could cope with Luke, and that she loved caring for him, but she didn't want to take anything for granted, especially as Granny tired easily and Luke was getting quite heavy. The sea air was doing wonders for his appetite.

When they reached the yard, she was surprised to see Rich's car there.

'I hope everything's all right,' she said as she quickened her pace. 'Rich should be in work on a Friday morning.'

Her dad placed a hand on her arm to stop her.

'Holly… I want you to know that whatever you decide to do is fine.'

'What do you mean?'

He sighed, then took hold of her shoulders.

'Look… I've known about what Rich has been planning, and I didn't like not telling you, but he asked me to keep it secret and I hope you'll forgive me for it.'

'Forgive you? For what? What's going on?' Her chest had tightened and her heart was thrumming.

'It's nothing horrid, I promise. Rich has done something to try to make up for last year. Please give him a chance and listen to what he has to say. Lord knows I wanted to have words with him back then, and a few times before that when I saw how you had been hurt by his behaviour, but I'm fairly certain that things have changed now. He's told me some things about why he acted as he did, and I've told him he'd better not even entertain the idea of messing you around again, but I honestly don't think he will. After his time away, he seems… reformed

239

isn't the right word, but perhaps… fixed?' He shook his head. 'Anyway, I don't want to give the game away as it's meant to be a surprise. Go and talk to him. I'll watch Luke.'

Holly opened and closed her mouth a few times but no words came out, so she decided to take her dad's advice. She had no idea what was going on, but Dad had told her to give Rich a chance.

He deserved that at least.

—

Rich was more terrified than he had ever been in his life – except for when he'd found himself unable to save his brother, but he wouldn't think about that now. He needed all his energy to focus on the here and now, on him and Holly and what he was about to do.

'Are your eyes still closed?' he asked.

'Yes, Rich, but how long will this take? I don't like not being able to see the road.'

'Not long, I promise. In fact, we're nearly there.'

'Okay. But… why can't you tell me what this is about?'

He glanced at her profile in the passenger seat of the car, and his heart leapt. She was so beautiful and so precious to him.

'I want you to see something, and if I give you any clues, it will ruin the surprise.'

He took the next turning and drove along the narrow country lane. Holly exclaimed as the car passed over a large bump. The road would need to be evened out, but he hadn't had a chance to see to that yet.

When he cut the engine, he released his seat belt then undid Holly's.

'Keep your eyes closed until I tell you to look, all right?'

'All right.'

He got out, then went around to her side and opened her door. Taking her hands, he led her around to the front of the vehicle.

'Before you open your eyes, I need to tell you something.'

'I'm listening.'

In the morning light, her cheeks had a soft peachy glow, her hair shone with health, and her fair eyelashes fluttered on her cheeks. Her lips were slightly parted and her chest rose and fell quickly, suggesting that she was nervous or excited or both. He experienced an overwhelming urge to pull her into his arms and kiss her, to carry her inside and make love to her, but that would be too much, too soon. He had to see how she reacted to what he'd done first.

He had come to a realization over recent weeks. It had crept in at first as he'd spent time with Holly and Luke, watching her with their son and observing her hard work at the vineyard. He had known that he still cared for her, that he was sorry for hurting her and would take it back if he could, but it was more than that. More than he could understand, more than he could control, more than he could convey with words. He hoped his actions would do his feelings justice. Telling Holly how he felt wouldn't be enough – he needed to show her.

A wood pigeon cooed in the trees bordering the property and the gentle breeze rustled through the leaves. The air was sweet with the scent of freshly mown grass, making Rich think of summer days gone by, of a time when life was full of potential and freedom from pain. Surely it could be that good again? Better, perhaps. There were possibilities for happiness ahead, if they only chose to take advantage of them.

'Okay... open your eyes.'

He watched as Holly slowly looked around. She blinked at first as her eyes adjusted to the bright light, then a line appeared between her eyebrows. Rich's stomach clenched and he held his breath.

'What are we... Why are we...' Holly shook her head, then met his gaze. 'Is this some kind of joke?

—

Holly didn't understand what was happening. Was Rich being really mean?

'If this is a joke, Rich, it's not funny.'

He took hold of her shoulders and shook his head.

'No, Hols, this is no joke.'

She slid out of his grip and walked closer to Plum Tree Cottage. She had been impressed by the renovations on the cottages up at Greenacres, but this surpassed what she had seen there. The isolated house was more beautiful than she had ever seen it before. It had been given a fresh coat of white paint and the broken windows had been replaced with small panes that sparkled in the sunlight. There were new shutters at the windows, painted duck-egg blue to match the frames and the front door with its V-frame portico. Pink and red roses climbed the trellises either side of the door, and their scent filled the air, heady and sweet, potent with summer.

'Someone has bought the cottage.' It wasn't a question, and Holly felt as though her heart was breaking anew. 'And done all of this.'

'Yes.' Rich pulled something from his pocket and took her hand.

'What?' She looked down to see that he had pressed a key into her palm. 'You?'

He nodded.

'I bought the cottage... just as we should have done last year. I bought it for you and for our son.'

He led her through the gate and along the path towards the door. Everything felt surreal, as if she was dreaming and could wake up at any moment.

She pushed the key into the lock with a trembling hand and the door swung inwards, revealing freshly painted walls. The hallway they'd walked through only weeks before was clean and fresh, the flagstone floor scrubbed clean and the woodwork of the skirting boards and the staircase sanded down and varnished.

It was perfect.

The kitchen had been cleaned, the cupboard doors replaced, the fireplace filled with logs and pine cones waiting to be lit. There was a solid oak table with four chairs, a vase of colourful sweet peas and pure white gypsophila at its centre.

She followed Rich back through the cottage to the hallway. As they climbed the stairs, none of the boards creaked as they had when they'd viewed the house last year, and Holly realized that the whole staircase had been replaced.

On the landing, they turned left and Rich showed her the two bedrooms on this side of the house, both with neutral colour schemes but without furniture, waiting for the occupants to decide what to fill them with. They retraced their steps and Holly looked into a family bathroom with a white roll-top tub, walk-in shower, sink and toilet. Further along, they entered another double room. This one had a cast-iron double bed with the mattress still in its plastic packaging. There were two double wardrobes in limed oak and two chests of drawers. Next to the bed were small side tables with silver lamps with cream shades.

'One more,' Rich said as he went to the next door and opened it then stood back.

Holly entered the room first and sighed. It was beautiful. There were wooden floorboards and a soft cream rug, a pine cot against the far wall with a mobile of farm-yard animals hanging over it. On top of the brand-new mattress was a bundle of bedding. Next to the window was a changing table with wicker baskets underneath it; she could make out a nappy packet sticking out of the top of one of them. There was also a pine chest of drawers and a matching cupboard.

Rich stepped forward and wound the dial on the mobile, and the animals danced in a circle, bobbing and swaying as a familiar lullaby filled the room.

'What do you think?' he asked, and she noted the uncertainty in his face. In her surprise, she hadn't given anything away, and he wanted, needed, to know how she felt.

But she wasn't sure. Not at all.

Everything she'd thought she'd known about Rich and about how things had gone last year had changed. She'd thought they were rebuilding their relationship but hadn't been sure in what way. As parents, yes, but as anything else? She'd wondered, considered, yearned at times for something more, but feared it too. Because with love came vulnerability.

And now he'd done this… created this perfect cottage of her dreams, renovated, renewed and given new life, all ready for her and Luke to move into. It could be their home.

'Don't say anything yet.' Rich held up a hand. 'Come and see outside.'

They made their way down the stairs and through the kitchen to the back door.

'I… *we*… sorted out the garden so Luke can play out here as he gets bigger.'

Rich's smile wobbled and part of Holly wanted to hug him for what he'd done, but another part feared he'd take that as an acceptance of him and the cottage. She didn't know what he wanted from her, so she was hesitant to react in case her reaction was wrong.

The back garden had been cleared of junk, the grass mowed, the flower beds weeded and composted and filled with bedding plants that created a rainbow of flowers. To one side of the path was a wooden swing set, with a baby swing and one for an older child.

Holly walked to the new four-foot wooden fence that separated the garden from the field behind it and peered over the top. The fields stretched away from this secure space, bright with colour. To the right was a summer house that hadn't been there before either. She opened the doors and inhaled the woody smell, admiring the wicker sofa and two chairs with fat lavender cushions and a cream chenille throw that matched the curtains at the small windows. From one window she could see the where the sky brightened as the land gave way to the sea.

The coast was so close, and she knew that when the wind blew the right way, she'd be able to sit in here with the doors open and smell the ocean. It was all so tempting. All so perfect. If Rich had walked into her head and taken a photograph of her dreams, he couldn't have got any closer than this.

Back in the garden, she turned around, trying to take in all the changes, all the improvements. She was dizzy with wonder and something else – hope. Rich had clearly worked very hard since purchasing the property, and it was all ready for a family to move in.

Ready for a family to be happy.

Ready to become a home.

She turned to him and her heart ached for the way he was gnawing at his bottom lip, for the way he was standing so stiffly, his broad shoulders in his blue and white checked shirt tense. He tucked his hands into his jeans pockets, then pulled them out again. He was nervous, worried, doubting himself.

Holly never wanted to see him anything other than happy; she never had wanted anything other than that for him.

She loved him still. She couldn't doubt that any longer. She had tried to deny it to herself, to be rational about her feelings for him, but her heart always won. In spite of everything that had happened last year, she loved him more than ever.

But she had another responsibility: she had a son. A son who deserved her love and her dedication. She had loved Rich completely, but it hadn't been enough for him. Now she couldn't give him as much as she had before because Luke needed her attention. What if she got back with

Rich and he wanted more than she could give? Yes, he had changed – he did seem better prepared to be the man she needed – but it didn't mean that he was completely healed. How could anyone come back from what he'd been through and be whole again? Everyone ended up damaged by life in some way, but Rich had been shattered by the loss of his brother and she'd been unable to fix him.

Her heart was breaking. She wanted to help him rebuild his life, but she would be risking not only her own feelings but those of her child. Holly was a mother first. That much had changed. She couldn't take the risk of ruining the new life they had at Greenacres, of losing what she had begun to create for Luke.

She swallowed hard.

'It's beautiful, Rich. Absolutely perfect.' Her throat tightened and her vision blurred. 'I love it. How I wish—'

'Holly...' He stepped closer. 'Please don't say no. The cottage was your dream. I ruined that before, but now I want to make it up to you. You can accept it without having to accept me too. I just want you and Luke to live here. For him to grow up here. It's so close to your dad and granny and not far from Penhallow Sands. You'll have some privacy from the visitors to the vineyard but you'll also be able to get there quickly whenever you choose.'

'I can't take this from you. It's too much.'

'If you want it, we can sort something out. I need to pay maintenance to support Luke anyway, and I can stay on with Mum and Dad while you and Luke live here.'

'Oh Rich... if only you'd wanted this before. If only things hadn't been so complicated for us back then.'

'I know. I wish with all my heart that I'd been in the right place to give you what you wanted and needed. I wish I'd been ready to give you everything.'

He took her hand and raised it to his lips, then held it there, squeezing her fingers. When she looked up, his eyes were closed.

'I'm so sorry for the past, Holly. I'm so sorry for letting you down.'

She moved closer to him and hugged him tight, her arms encircling his waist as he embraced her. He was warm and strong, his scent fresh and peppery, reminding her of a walk in the woods following a storm. He felt so familiar, so good, and her whole being called out for him.

'I want to give you everything, Holly.' His lips were against her hair, and as he spoke, it tickled, sending delightful shivers down her spine. 'I want to make you happy and to give you your dream home.'

The words dragged her from sensation, from emotion and into reality.

'Exactly,' she said as she pulled away, fighting against her desire to stay close to him. 'That's the problem.'

He frowned, confusion filling his eyes.

'You just said it, Rich… *my* dream home. It was *my* dream to own this cottage, never yours. You went along with it, but your heart wasn't in it the way mine was. I should never have tried to persuade you to buy it with me. We were fine when we lived with our parents and you didn't have to grow up and face adulthood, but when I pushed for us to buy this place, it was too much for you. It was almost like you didn't want to grow up… like you wanted to stay as you were when Dean died.' She covered her mouth as a sob burst out. 'I can't do this, Rich. I'm so sorry.'

The pain in his eyes broke her heart.

She turned and ran from the cottage, along the path towards Greenacres, ignoring his calls for her to come back, to talk, to listen. What he'd done was so wonderful, and she loved him for trying and for caring.

But it was simply too late.

Chapter 18

Rich sank onto the wicker sofa in the summer house and stared at the cottage.

How had he got it so wrong? Not only had he done the wrong thing by buying the cottage, he'd let Holly believe that he didn't share her dream of buying it in the first place.

He was an abysmal human being. He felt as though his world had fallen apart, and he deserved it.

Buying the cottage for Holly and Luke was meant to be a way of making amends, of starting again. He'd spoken to Bruce, who had warned him that it might not be the best approach. But he hadn't wanted to listen, had been convinced that he was doing the right thing by making such a grand gesture. It had been his secret project, and as he'd worked on the cottage and overseen the renovations, he'd smiled at the hope that had filled his heart. Happiness with Holly and Luke had seemed possible at last. Holly had loved the cottage and wanted to start their life together there. He hadn't been as enthusiastic about it as she had been, but it didn't mean that he hadn't wanted to move in with her. He had simply been afraid of not being enough for her, and he'd felt so guilty about living when his brother's life had been cut tragically short. Holly was right in saying that it was as though Rich wanted to stay in the past, as if he didn't want to grow up because Dean never would. That guilt had eaten away at him and prevented him from fully committing to Holly and to their future, but now he could see that and he wanted to show her that he was ready to move forward, to devote himself to her.

But she had just walked out of the cottage and, terrifyingly, quite possibly out of his life.

If she went back to Exeter now, he knew his heart would shatter into a thousand pieces.

He buried his face in his hands and tried to shut out the world around him, but he couldn't push away his pain and fear. They sat on his shoulders like sacks of cement, dragging him down, threatening to suffocate him. He knew he couldn't allow that to happen; if he sank again, he might not come back up. He had to be positive about things; to salvage what he could from the situation.

He loved Holly, he really did, but if she couldn't love him the way she used to, then he would simply have to accept that and carry on. He would be a good dad to his son and would do his best to be a friend to Holly. She was a wonderful person and she deserved that, at least.

He wouldn't wallow in his sadness or feel sorry for himself. He had things to do, a life to live, and he wanted to set a good example to Luke. He had failed his brother and he wouldn't repeat that by failing his son too.

He knew where he needed to go to speak to someone. Just the two of them.

It was time to take the final step in his healing process.

–

Holly reached Greenacres and bent over to try to catch her breath. She'd run most of the way, through the fields and along the gravel paths, and now her lungs were burning and her feet were throbbing, but it was nothing compared to the pain in her heart. She had been unable to outrun that.

Poor Rich! He'd done something wonderful, made a romantic, caring gesture, and Holly had turned her back on him. Fresh tears sprang into her eyes, so she wiped them away and straightened up. She knew why she'd made the decision and it was for the best, but leaving him behind was the most difficult thing she had ever done.

She'd hoped that she'd be able to get up to her room so she could wash her face and calm down before she had to face her dad or Granny, but the back door opened, so she prepared to explain her windswept state and red eyes. When a small grey dog emerged, she realized someone was letting Gelert out. He spotted her immediately and ran to her, bouncing up and down as he sniffed at her legs and hands.

She crouched down to let him say hello properly, and he paused, gazing up at her face, then tilted his head to one side.

'Hello, boy.'

Holly stroked his head and his soft ears, then opened her arms and hugged him. He sniffed at her ear then gave it a lick.

'Hey, Gelert, no ear snogs!' She laughed in spite of her sadness.

He placed his paws on her shoulders and licked her cheeks, cleaning her salty tears away. The sweetness of his gesture made her cry harder, and before she knew it, she was sobbing into his thick fur.

When she finally came up for air, he looked at her knowingly.

'You're such a good boy. You know that?' she asked.

He wagged his tail and gazed right into her eyes, as if he could see down into her soul.

'There's no way I can let you go now, is there,' she whispered, appreciating his reassuring warmth, his willingness to listen without judging. 'I'm glad you came into my life, Gelert, and I promise to be a good dog-mum to you.'

He gave her cheek another lick, then lay down next to her with his chin on his paws.

'Life is full of ups and downs, Gelert, and right now I'm not feeling too good. I had to make a decision and I'm not fully certain that it was the right one.'

He shifted to rest his chin on her leg.

'We have some thinking to do, don't we?'

Holly ran her hand over Gelert's fur, taking comfort from his presence and devotion. Whatever happened with Rich and the cottage, she would manage, she would find a way, especially now she had a little canine friend who'd imprinted his paw print on her heart.

–

Rich parked outside the church and cut the engine. It wasn't as though this was the first time he'd come here since it had happened, but it was the first time he'd come here convinced that he knew how to put things right. As right as they could be, that was.

He got out of the car, then let himself in through the gate, heading along the path around the building to the graveyard beyond. The breeze had picked up and the swishing of the leaves on the trees reminded him of whispering. The sound kept him moving forward. He'd learnt to live in the moment, to listen to his gut and the world around him, and right now everything was telling him that this was what he had to do.

He passed rows of graves, including that of Holly's grandpa. He ran his eyes over the headstones but didn't allow himself to digest the words, not wanting to allow other people's loss into his heart. Everyone lost loved ones, it was part of life, but you had to go on. The alternative was giving up, pretending to live but in reality drifting in a haze of pain. Rich had done that, but not any longer. His self-pity had hurt Holly, but it wouldn't happen again. He would not risk losing his son too.

He stopped at the end of a row, close to the hedge that bordered the graveyard, and lowered his gaze to the grey headstone. How on earth had twenty years passed since his brother had gone? How was it possible that Rich was thirty-four? Time really did wait for no one, and the next twenty years might pass just as quickly, which was why it was important that he used them wisely. In twenty years, his son would be an adult! Dean had not been given the gift of time, so Rich wouldn't waste another second.

He crouched down in front of the headstone and rested his elbows on his knees, then cleared his throat.

'Uh… this is difficult.' A squawk off to his left made him jump, but when he looked up, he saw that it was just a crow taking flight. 'Hi, Dean.'

He paused, as if waiting for a reply, which he knew was ridiculous because his brother was long gone. He wasn't even sure that he could remember how his voice had sounded any more, and that saddened him.

'I… came to say hello. I know it's been a long time since I spoke to you like this, but I couldn't face it back then, when it happened, and then time went by and I felt foolish thinking about coming here alone. I was an idiot, and to be honest, I was worried that I would lose it… break down, you know… so instead I carried on and tried to bury my feelings about you and what happened, but it was so hard to do. And as with everything that we try to bury, that we try to avoid dealing with, there's only so long we can do that before it eats away at us. Losing you ate away at me, Dean. You were my buddy, my little brother, and I let you down. I'm so, so sorry, mate. If I could go back to that day and change how things unfolded, I would do it in a second. I meant to come here sooner after I got back, but I've been so busy with work and the cottage and the work up at Greenacres and… with my son.'

He closed his eyes and pictured his brother, his slightly rounded face still carrying the softness of childhood and his smile so wide it could light up a room. Dean had been only a year younger than him and almost the same height, but he was far more innocent. He saw the good in everyone, whereas Rich was more wary. Perhaps it was the big brother thing, the firstborn child's instinct that meant he'd grown up wanting to protect Dean. But he'd failed at that. Abysmally. He'd let Dean down as badly as it was possible to do.

When he opened his eyes again, a bright red ladybird was crawling along the top of the headstone, going about its business as if it hadn't a care in the world.

'Mum and Dad… they miss you every day. Mum says she feels you around, but Dad pulls a face when she says it, as if he's not convinced. You know Dad… a man of few words. He's like a closed book most of the time, and I know it's how he deals with things. Perhaps you are with us… I don't know; perhaps it's just Mum's way of comforting herself. I do wonder what you'd be like now, Dean, and what you'd be doing. Would you be a vet? You were always so good with animals and had so much patience and compassion.

'You were a much better person than I was. If it had been me who'd… who'd gone… then you would have treated the woman you loved far better than I did, I'm sure of it.' He gave a rueful laugh. 'I can't believe I have a son now. Me! I'm a dad, imagine that, Dean. Holly was pregnant when she left last year and I had no idea. I was always so wrapped up in myself, and now it seems that I've lost her for good. I made a grand gesture… bought the cottage for her and Luke, and she turned it down. I'm not surprised, though. I was such an idiot.' He ran his hands through his hair. 'I think I've always been an idiot.

'Anyway… bloody hell, I come to speak to you and to tell you how sorry I am, and I end up telling you about my life. A life you don't get to live. Dean… I'm so sorry I failed you.'

A tear rolled down his cheek and dropped from his chin. His vision blurred, so he rubbed his eyes with the heels of his hands.

'I don't expect you to forgive me, Dean. I don't know if you'd be able to even if you could. But I wanted you to know that I'm trying to forgive myself, and I hope you're okay with that.'

The ladybird suddenly took off, and he watched as it disappeared over the hedge.

If his mum was here now, she'd be telling him that ladybirds were a sign of good luck, and how he could leave his worries behind because happier times were on the way. He shook his head; his mother did have some funny ideas about things.

He stayed there watching as the clouds sailed through the sky, as the light changed and the crows swooped and soared before settling in the trees. The air turned cooler, and goose bumps rose on his skin, but still he stayed, and talked.

It was hours later when he finally stood up, cold and stiff and emotionally drained. He had shared everything with Dean and believed that if his brother could hear him, then he would understand now, because Rich had opened his heart.

As he said his goodbyes, promising to return to visit again soon, he couldn't help wondering if there was any significance in the ladybird's presence on the headstone. The thought gave him a glimmer of hope, and he realized that even if it was all superstitious nonsense, simply having that hope was comfort in itself.

—

Holly descended the stairs carefully. Her head felt woolly, her heart heavy. Her mouth was dry, her tongue furry and her stomach unsettled. If she'd had too much wine last night, she couldn't have felt worse. She'd got up an hour earlier to make Luke a bottle and change him, and he was still sleeping now, so she hoped to grab a coffee and clear her head before he started to stir again.

The clock in the hallway chimed 6.30. It was still so early. The light in the house was grey, and it was really cold. She wrapped her fluffy dressing gown tighter around her and pushed open the kitchen door, then jumped when she saw that she wasn't alone.

'Granny?' She gently touched the older woman's shoulder.

'Hello, love.'

'Everything all right?'

'Yes.' Her granny turned around in her seat. 'I'm okay, dear. I woke up about half an hour ago and couldn't drop off again. I felt… cold.' She wrapped her hands around her mug, and Holly watched as steam rose into the air.

'I need a coffee too. I didn't sleep very well.'

'I was thinking about going to church today.'

'Oh… right.'

'I know I don't go every Sunday, but I thought I could attend the morning service, then go and see your grandpa.'

Holly carried her coffee to the table and sat down. She gazed out of the window at the morning. The clouds looked like cotton candy as the rising sun caressed them, teasing them with the prospect of a new day.

'Shall I come with you?'

Granny smiled briefly. 'You could do, dear, although I know it's not really your thing.'

'Yes, but I would like to say hello to Grandpa too.'

'Okay then. Shall we take Luke?'

'If Dad's busy, we might have to.'

'What about Rich? Can't he have him?'

Holly's cheeks filled with heat.

'I… I don't know.'

'What's wrong?'

'Sorry?'

'Don't try to pull the wool over my eyes, Holly. I know there's something. Come on… tell your old granny.'

Holly sipped her coffee and winced as the hot liquid burnt her lips and tongue.

'Yesterday, Rich took me somewhere. Dad knew about it, but in all fairness he did try to prepare me without actually telling me exactly what was going on. It was meant to be a good thing – it *was* a good thing – and yet I couldn't accept it.'

'Accept what?'

'You don't know?'

Granny shook her head.

'Well, you know the cottage Rich and I were going to buy…'

'Plum Tree Cottage?'

'Yes. Rich bought it and renovated it and made it into a home. It's exactly how I imagined it would be. It's been painted and repaired and there are roses around the door and in the garden, and there's a nursery and a summer house and… it's just perfect.'

'He did this for you?'

'Yes. And for Luke.'

Granny nodded. 'Sounds like a grand gesture.'

'It was. It is.'

'But the problem is?'

Holly exhaled slowly and tried to tame her chaotic thoughts into some sort of order.

'The problem is that it's not only about me any more, is it? There's Luke to consider too, and as much as I wish I could believe that Rich has changed and that he's certain we're what he wants… I'm too afraid to take the chance.'

Granny pressed her lips together and nodded. 'It's difficult, Holly, I grant you that.'

'It really is.'

'How do you feel about Rich now? I mean, after spending more time together and seeing him with Luke, and how good he's been with… well, with me and your dad?'

'Confused. He's a good man, I know that. I don't think he'd do anything to deliberately hurt our child or me, but last year was awful, Granny. I thought I'd never be able to carry on, then I found out I was expecting and I had to keep going. I'm stronger now… stronger than ever before, and I know that's because of Luke. I have to go on and make a good life for him and for me. I'm a mum and Luke is my priority.'

'You are, but you're also a woman – a human being with needs, hopes and desires. You can't bury yourself in motherhood and forget who you are or what you want.'

'I buried myself in loving Rich for years.'

'Exactly. You are so much more than an addition to someone else. You are you, Holly Dryden – strong, kind, capable, loving, intelligent, brave… I could go on all day.'

'You're biased, Granny.' Holly couldn't help smiling.

'Yes, my darling, I am but I also see the truth. At my age there are no blinkers on these eyes. You can be a darned good mum to Luke, but you need to be you too. What does Holly want for herself?'

'I can't think that way. I have to put Luke first.'

'You're not listening to me. Luke will be happy if his mum is happy. If you're sad and unfulfilled, he'll sense it and respond accordingly. What do you want from life? Think about it.'

Holly picked at a cuticle, crossed and uncrossed her legs and finished her coffee. What *did* she want?

'I always just wanted to be happy.'

'What does happy mean to you?'

'Well… I thought it was being with Rich, loving and being loved in return.'

'And now?'

'I know that being with him could make me happy, but not if it's how it used to be. He didn't love me as much as I wanted and deserved to be loved.'

'Why not?'

Holly rubbed her eyes. That was the question, wasn't it? Rich had given her a form of explanation and plenty of apologies, but when it came down to it, why had he held back, and could he really overcome that now?

'I think it was because of what happened when he was younger.'

'With his brother?'

'Yes. In fact I know it was, but if he couldn't deal with that then… how can I be sure he can do so now?'

Granny reached out and took Holly's hand. Her fingers were gnarled with age, her skin darkened with brown patches, the veins running like snakes beneath the surface. But her grip was strong and reassuring. Granny had lived, she had made sacrifices for her family, she had loved and lost.

'Holly, we can never be one hundred per cent certain that someone won't hurt us, or leave us, or… die on us. I've lost my husband, but I also lost my child. It was an unimaginable pain losing your mother and one that no parent should ever have to face. Rich's parents went through it too, and their son was much younger than my daughter was. Rich's life would have been different because of what his family went through. Your life was different because of what *you* went through. Your loss was enormous… your pain unfathomable. But we go on, because we have to. My husband was old, and he had lived a good life, but even so, I miss him and it feels that he was taken too soon. I suspect that everyone feels that way. This life is far too brief. For some, it is even shorter.

'There are many ways to be fulfilled and you need to consider them all. Like what you want to do career-wise – whether that means running this place or something completely different – where you want to live, what your hopes and dreams are for the future. But you don't have to be in total control; in fact, you can't control everything. It's just not possible.'

'I know. You're right, Granny.'

'Trying to control everything will only lead to unhappiness. If you love Rich and want to give him a chance, then do it. If you let fear hold you back, if you let past mistakes and errors of judgement deter you from allowing love in, then you might well regret that even more than taking a chance. The first option leaves no opportunities to find out, but the second allows you the chance to discover something that might be far more wonderful than you ever imagined. If you believe that Rich is ready now to be the partner you want and need, and the father that Luke deserves, then the rest is up to you.'

Holly raised her granny's hand and kissed it, then got up and walked to the door. She opened it and stepped out into the morning, taking deep breaths of the cool air. The scents of the countryside were strong, the sweet freshness of grass and the deep richness of the fertile earth. Summer was taking hold of the land, awakening colour and life, and with it came the promise of a good harvest.

She padded over to the fence that separated the small family garden from the rest of the vineyard. There was a cobweb between two of the fence panels, and on it, dewdrops sparkled like diamonds. There was such a wealth of joy to be found here, so many things to appreciate. The tiny spider that had spun the web didn't know what was going to happen to its work when it was finished. It was designed to catch food, a beautiful, flawless design, and yet a careless human hand could tear it to shreds in an instant. Such was life, but the spider kept on spinning. Granny was right. No one knew what was around the corner; no one knew what could happen tomorrow, let alone next week. But if you didn't take a chance on love, on living the life you yearned for, then it would be no life at all.

Holly wanted more than to simply exist, more than to spend her life wondering *what if?*

She wanted the life she could have if she truly followed her heart.

Chapter 19

Holly looked around the barn and gasped in awe.

'It's perfect, Dad.'

'Thanks to you.' His smile lit up his face.

'I can't take all the credit. It was a combined effort from the builders and carpenters, some tips from Nicole and, of course, help from you and… and Rich. Seeing it like this… it's magical.'

She walked across the wooden floorboards, which had been polished to a high sheen, then turned around. Benches ran all the way around the sides of the barn, decked with white and gold ribbons. In front of the benches were rectangular oak tables, and tucked under them were chairs with elaborately carved backs, also featuring ribbons to match those on the benches.

At the far end of the barn was a small platform where a band, DJ or entertainment could be set up, and if the licence came through, where weddings could be performed. At the moment, a local band was getting ready for this evening's barn dance.

Holly peered upwards at the ceiling and her mouth fell open. The beams were draped with thousands of fairy lights that twinkled like stars in the night sky. They also ran down the supporting vertical beams, where they had been entwined with fresh summer flowers that delicately fragranced the air.

Her dad slid an arm around her shoulders. 'How are you feeling, angel?'

'I'm okay, Dad.'

'Are you sure? I know it's been a rough week.'

Holly looked up at him and her heart filled with love. She'd told him what had happened when Rich took her to the cottage the previous week, and how she felt about everything. She'd told him she needed time to think and to decide what it was she really wanted, and during that time, as she'd walked the fields and among the vines, as she'd breathed in the country air and taken Luke down to the bay and sat with him on the sand, things had started to slot into place. Her granny had spoken a lot of sense, as had her dad, and Holly felt that she was in a better place now. She was stronger than ever and would be able to cope with whatever came her way.

'Nothing's easy, Dad, but I have much to be grateful for. I feel at peace now. It's being home with my family and even seeing Rich regularly.'

Things had been a bit strange with Rich since that day at the cottage. When he had come for Luke's bedtime routine, their conversation had been stilted. Holly's heart had thrummed against her ribcage every time he'd been close, but she'd tried not to get into any deep conversations, wanting to take the time to think without pressure. Rich had been kind and polite and a loving dad to Luke. As parents, they would have to have contact with each other – whatever happened between them – for Luke's sake. Holly had hoped that Rich wasn't hurting, that he was focused on his son and his job and not weighed down by what might have been.

What still could be…

She bit her lip hard. Not now. Not yet. There were things to do.

'As long as you're okay, Holly, then I'm happy.'

She lifted her chin. She was learning how to run the vineyard now, not just the shop, and it only added to her devotion to the place. Her dad had shown her the books, and with Rich's help, they'd worked out pricing for bulk buys and set up two newsletters – one for businesses purchasing from Greenacres and one for individuals buying for personal use. It fascinated her how they had seen a rise in sales already; Rich had said that a lot of it had to do with getting the message out there. These days, there was a lot of competition, so vineyards needed to be visible. Hopefully, tonight would also give the business a boost. Whatever happened in Holly's personal life, the work at Greenacres had to go on.

'Right… back to business. Let's prove to all those lovely visitors to the website that Greenacres really does have a lot to offer. We can take plenty of photos tonight and post them on the website and the blog.'

'Sounds perfect, Holly.'

'The caterers will be here at five to set up the hog roast and the vegetarian options, and the waiting staff will be here at five thirty,' she reminded him

'The wine will be brought over shortly.'

'Red and white?'

'Of course, and some of our finest vintages.'

'That's what I like to hear.'

'You know… there's some of your grandpa in you with your business head, but also a lot of your mum.'

'In what way?'

'She loved the vineyard too and would have been delighted to try something new here. She'd be so excited about this.'

'I wish she was here.'

'Me too.' His Adam's apple bobbed and he blinked rapidly.

'She'd be so proud of you, Dad.'

'And of you, my angel. And so would Grandpa. For all his… stubbornness, he adored you.'

Holly smiled. It would be very different if her mum and grandpa were here today. It would have been a battle to get Grandpa to even entertain the idea of change, but perhaps he'd have come round to it eventually. If her mum had lived, Grandpa might have been different, mellower. Grief often changed people and led them to become set in their ways as a form of coping with the pain and deep sense of loss.

'Is Janine coming tonight?' Holly asked.

'Oh…' Bruce cleared his throat. 'Uh… I don't know.' His eyebrows did a strange dance that made Holly giggle.

'Dad! Don't be shy. She's very welcome, and I know you'd like her to come.'

'I didn't like to invite her in case it was the wrong thing to do.'

'Text her immediately.'

'Really?'

'Yes, of course!'

While Bruce sent a message to his lady friend, Holly crossed to the band and whispered something to the singer. The woman nodded, then spoke to her band mates.

'All sorted?' Holly asked her dad.

'Yes. She replied immediately.'

'See! She wanted to come.'

'She did. I felt bad not asking her, as she's done so much around here and at… at Plum Tree Cottage.'

'She did some of the work for Rich?'

He nodded. 'She insisted. She overheard Rich telling me his plans and said she was happy to help.'

'She sounds like a good person with a generous heart.'

Her dad's cheeks turned pink. 'She is,' he mumbled.

'Okay, Dad, before everything really gets going and we have no more time to talk, there's something I'd like to do.'

Holly walked into the centre of the barn and gave a small bow, then held out her hands.

'Holly?' Bruce frowned. 'What's going on?'

'Come here.'

His eyes widened, but he approached her, then the music began and she took his hands. As Bruce Springsteen's 'When You Need Me' filled the barn, the two of them moved around the dance floor. Holly watched as a range of emotions flickered over her dad's face. Her mum had liked Bruce Springsteen, said his name had something to do with it, and this song had been one that she'd often sung to her husband. She said it encapsulated the man that Bruce was as both husband and father: reliable, caring and devoted. As a teenager, Holly had thought they were foolish romantics, and cringed at her parents' lovey-dovey behaviour, but as an adult, she could see it for what it was: true love.

'You know, Dad, any man who comes into my life has a lot to live up to.'

He shook his head. 'Any man in your life needs to give you what you deserve, Hols.'

'So we're agreed that no man stands a chance then?' She smiled and he laughed.

'What are we like?'

'Each other?'

They giggled then and lost their rhythm, leading Bruce to step on Holly's toes.

'Ouch!'

'Sorry!'

He doubled over, and Holly joined him.

'Everything's going to be okay now, Holly,' he said when he'd regained his composure.

'I know.' She nodded. 'Life is what you make it, right?'

'So let's make it a good one.' He held out his hand and she took it. 'And we can start by getting in some dance practice ahead of tonight.'

'Sounds like a good plan to me.'

–

'Doesn't he look divine!' Granny exclaimed as she clapped her hands together.

Holly nodded. 'I can't believe how big he's getting.'

She had dressed Luke in jeans and a grey shirt that she'd found in an online baby boutique. He did look very smart, and very cute. He was currently gurgling away at the plush elephant rattle that Lucinda had bought for him, complete with teething ring.

'You look pretty amazing too, Granny.'

Granny fluttered the false eyelashes that she'd asked Holly to get for her, then gently patted her bobbed hair. She'd had it coloured and blow-dried that morning at the local salon, and the bright silver streaks the hairdresser had added made it seem thicker and fuller. The front was swept up from her face and held in place with a diamanté clip. With her warm-toned foundation, blusher and the excitement in her eyes, she looked twenty years younger. Her outfit of tailored navy trousers and matching silk blouse was smart and sophisticated.

'Thank you, dearie. Shall I watch Luke while you dress?'

'If you don't mind.'

'It would be a pleasure.'

When her granny and Luke had been settled in the lounge, Holly went upstairs and sank onto her bed. She'd had a lovely afternoon with her dad before coming back to the house to feed, bathe and dress Luke ready for the evening. Rich wasn't here to help because he was coming to the barn dance later. Holly intended on taking Luke along too and bringing him back when he needed to go to bed. She couldn't bear the thought of leaving him with a babysitter and didn't want to ask anyone she knew to miss the dance, so bringing him home when he tired was the best option. Besides which, she wanted him there so he could be a part of the celebrations.

Now she needed to get ready.

She opened her wardrobe and found the dress she'd ordered for the occasion along with a pair of bright red cowboy boots. Looking at the dress now, she did wonder if it had been the right choice, as it was more flamboyant than she'd usually wear, but then tonight was all about celebrating the new start for the vineyard, so she'd wear it proudly.

Once she'd dressed and unpinned the clips that Granny had put in earlier to give her bobbed hair a gentle wave, she slicked on some mascara and pale pink lip gloss, then added a few squirts of perfume.

'Ready or not,' she said as she opened her bedroom door and headed down the stairs. But she knew she was ready.

—

'Will you look at this!' Lucinda exclaimed as they entered the barn. She held on to the red and white polka-dot scarf tied around her head as she peered up at the rafters. 'There must be hundreds of thousands of lights up there.'

'I doubt it's that many, Lucy,' Rex said as he rolled his eyes at Rich.

'Close enough,' Rich said, winking at his dad.

His parents had gone full Western for the barn dance, even though he'd explained that it wasn't necessarily a Western theme. They were both clad in denim jeans and shirts, making their physical differences more apparent than ever. Rex was tall and lanky, Lucinda curvy and diminutive. But they fitted, they always had, and even after everything they'd been through, they were still close. It gave Rich hope.

As his parents wandered off and mingled with locals from Penhallow Sands, Rich looked around. He couldn't see Holly; she must still be at the house. It was early, but his parents hadn't wanted to arrive with the rush, although it did seem as though everyone else had had the same plan.

The barn was already bustling with people, some of whom Rich recognized and some he didn't.

'Howdy!' A slap to his back made him start.

'Bloody hell, Fran, I nearly bit my tongue off.'

'Shouldn't have it hanging out of your mouth then, should you?' She waggled her eyebrows above her glasses. 'Who were you staring at?' She looked around. 'Ah… was it that sexy singer with the Cher vibe?'

'Cher?' He frowned.

'Yeah… older woman but hot as hell.'

'No!' He shook his head. 'Absolutely not. She's…' He looked at the singer in her faux-leather cat suit, long black hair hanging down to her shapely thighs. 'She's attractive, I guess, but I hadn't even noticed her.'

Fran sniffed. 'Only one woman for you?'

He was about to deny it, then nodded. 'What can I say?'

'How are things?'

'I should be asking you that question. When did you get back?'

'Early afternoon. I told Holly I might be a bit late tonight because the journey was hellish, what with flight delays, traffic jams and so on. But I'm here now and on time, it seems.'

'How's your dad?'

'Okay. Better. He has to tone down a few things in his lifestyle, like drinking, cigars and fatty foods, but the doctors said that he should be fine. It was pretty scary seeing him so poorly, but he's learnt the hard way that smoking and huge plates of pasta are not a healthy combination. It was great to see him, Mum and Nonna too. In fact, if I can, I'm going back again in a few months. I just need to ensure that someone will watch everything back here for me.'

'Well I think you have one less responsibility to worry about.'

'What do you mean?'

'I think you've homed Gelert.'

'Gelert?'

'The grey lurcher. Holly loves him to bits.'

Fran's smile stretched from ear to ear.

'Ha! My cunning plan worked.'

'He follows her everywhere and guards Luke from just about everything – including the postman. Hence the name.'

'That's lovely. I'm so happy for him, and for Holly and Luke. And… for you?' Her eyebrows rose slowly.

'Me?'

'Well, yes. Won't he be your dog too?'

'Haven't you spoken to Holly?'

'Only briefly, because I was busy and she was busy, and we didn't have time for an in-depth conversation. I was kind of hoping that during my absence you two might have rediscovered each other.'

'Me too.'

'Oh Rich.' She rubbed his upper arm. 'Perhaps it's not meant to be, or perhaps it has yet to work itself out.'

He nodded. 'Perhaps. Anyway, I think I'd better go and see if she needs help with Luke.'

As he turned, the doors to the bar opened and his breath caught in his throat, because Holly had arrived, and he knew in that moment that he had never seen anything so beautiful in his whole life.

The early evening light framed her from behind with a golden glow, making her hair shine and outlining her figure. Rich registered that her granny was next to her, pushing Luke in his pram, but his eyes were glued to Holly. As she walked into the barn, he could see that her hair was gently curled, her face softly rounded and glowing with health, her eyes bright as they scanned the barn, and when they landed on him, her pink lips parted slightly.

She raised a hand in greeting and time seemed to stand still.

The dress she was wearing was made of some soft, floaty material that skimmed her knees. The sleeves capped her shoulders and the neckline was cut to show a hint of the swell of her smooth creamy skin. But the colour of the material was what made the dress so dramatic: red, orange, pink, fawn and cream in a pattern that accentuated her curves and made her skin luminous. Her knee-high red cowboy boots with a low heel and pointed toe matched the dress perfectly.

Holly was beautiful, but Rich knew that it wasn't only physical; she had an essence that was pure, honest and good. She was warm, funny and sincere, strong and determined. His heart raced as she walked towards him.

When she reached his side, vanilla and jasmine notes washed over him and he tried to breathe her in deeper, as if he could hold her scent there, remember it for ever.

'Holly.' His voice croaked on her name, barely more than a whisper and full of his need. He coughed, then tried again. 'You look incredible.'

She gazed at him for a moment, then her smile lit up her face.

'Thank you, Rich. Hi, Fran.'

As the two women hugged, Rich realized that he'd forgotten that Fran was standing next to him; he'd lost all sense of anyone else in the room. He had lost his heart to Holly and he had no idea what he was going to do about it. After all, she had rejected him and the cottage he'd offered her. He was consumed with his feelings for her but condemned to knowing that she didn't love him in return.

And yet... when she looked at him again, there was something in her eyes that called out to him, something simmering below the surface that he wished he could read. It could be his own wishful thinking, but he hoped it was something more.

Chapter 20

Holly hugged Fran, then leant back to look at her.

'You okay?'

'Yeah, I'm fine. Dad's much better now, so I just have to hope that he's sensible with his diet and quits the cigars.'

'He will. He has your mum and grandma there to keep him in line.'

'And they are so bossy!' Fran smiled at her. 'You look gorgeous, Holly.'

'You do.' Rich was gazing at her in a way that made her stomach clench. His eyes were so dark she could see her own reflection in them. She felt as if the two of them were on the cusp of something new, something that would rescue them from uncertainty and hesitation and catapult them into the future.

'Thanks, both of you.' She shook her head. 'You're too kind. Anyway... you look pretty good yourselves.'

And they did, Fran in indigo skinny jeans, purple cowboy boots and matching silk tunic and Rich in jeans, boots and a black shirt.

'It's quite busy, isn't it?' Fran said as she looked around. More people were arriving by the second; soon the barn would be full to capacity and the evening could begin. Waiters in black trousers and white shirts circulated with trays of wine, soft drinks and canapés. 'Ooh! I've just spotted the pup with your granny. Doesn't he look sweet?'

'I brought him along to say hello, but I won't keep him here all evening. It's going to be a bit busy, I think.'

'It'll do him good to get used to having people around, though, seeing as how the vineyard will be busier than ever.'

'True.'

'Looks like he doesn't want to leave Luke's side.' Rich gestured at the corner of the bar, where Granny had taken a seat, parking the pram next to her. Gelert sat in front of it, still as a statue, guarding his precious charge.

Bruce came over to them.

'I think we're ready to make a start.'

'Are you going to officially welcome everyone, Dad?'

He nodded. 'I'm a bit nervous, to be honest.'

'You'll be great.' Holly looked around. 'Is Janine here yet?'

His face broke into a smile. 'She's with some of the other workers who did the renovations.'

'Who's Janine?' Fran asked, frowning at Holly.

'Dad's... friend.' Holly winked.

'Ah, I see.' Fran nodded. 'One of *those* friends.'

'Cut it out, ladies!' Bruce shook his head. 'It's *very* early days. We're enjoying each other's company... for now.'

'She's very nice.' Holly touched her dad's arm.

'Yes. Right. Let's do this.' He sucked in a deep breath, squared his shoulders and set off across the barn to the small stage.

'He's really nervous, isn't he?' Fran said.

'Extremely. But he will be wonderful. He should be very proud of himself and what he's achieved here.'

Silence fell in the barn as Bruce stepped onto the stage and held up his hands.

'Hello, and welcome. We're delighted you could make it here this evening to help us celebrate a new beginning for Greenacres.'

As her dad continued his speech, talking about the vineyard's history and about the changes they had made, Holly was conscious of Rich standing at her side, and of how every so often he'd glance over at Luke to check on him. The way he was so protective of his son reached down inside her and brought a host of emotions to the surface. Rich loved Luke and would do what he could to ensure that he was happy and had a good upbringing. Since they'd returned to the area, he had shown himself to be a changed man. He was caring, supportive and attentive; he was there day and night, whenever he was needed. Holly had only to ask for something and he'd do what he could to provide it, whether it was a shoulder to cry on or a sounding board to work through an issue. In the past, it had been Holly's love for Rich that had bound them together. Yes, he had cared for her, she knew that, but not enough for her to be fulfilled. But something had changed within him and she could see it, feel it and, she hoped, trust in it.

He caught her looking at him and smiled, and she smiled back.

'And so it is with hearts full of love and respect that I would like to dedicate this barn and the changes we have made here to two very special people.'

Holly's breath caught in her throat. She hadn't known anything about this.

'Holly?' Her dad held out a hand. 'Could you come up here?'

Rich gently touched her arm. 'Go on. It's okay.'

She nodded, then crossed the barn, her heart pounding with emotion. When she reached the stage, she stepped up and took her dad's proffered hand.

'For those of you who don't know, this is my daughter, Holly. She has been my inspiration through all of this – my inspiration and motivation throughout life, in fact.'

Holly could see how hard her dad was struggling to maintain his composure. She squeezed his hand tighter, letting him know that she was with him, that she would help him.

'Holly... your granny and I planned this as a surprise for you.'

He led her to the side of the stage, and she spotted a red curtain hanging halfway down the wall. When had that been put there?

'Will you do the honours?' Bruce asked, pointing at the cord to the side of the curtain.

'Of course.'

She took hold of the cord and pulled it.

Nothing happened.

She tried again.

'It's stuck,' she whispered.

Her dad smiled and shook his head, then took the cord from her and gently tugged it to one side. The curtain started moving, so Holly took over from him and pulled until she could see a large wooden plaque. There was a photograph of her grandpa and her mum fixed to it, a photo she knew well, as the original had sat above the fireplace for as long as she could remember. They were both smiling. The photo had been taken at Holly's fifth birthday, a long time before they'd lost anyone they loved; a long time before they'd known what life had in store for them.

Under the photo were their names and a dedication: *For those we have loved and lost, may they live on in our hearts and minds and their memories be wound into our fruitful vines.*

Holly's vision blurred and she had to grit her teeth as she wobbled on the edge of breaking down completely. Her dad slid a strong arm around her shoulders and hugged her.

'It's beautiful, Dad.' She kept her eyes closed, her back to the people in the barn, until the ache in her chest had ebbed away.

'I hoped you'd think so. I wanted you to know that whatever happens in the future, your mum and grandpa will always be remembered, always a part of our lives.'

He pulled her into a big hug then, and a series of *oohs* and *ahs* drifted around the barn. When he released her, Holly turned to the crowd.

'Thank you so much for coming here this evening, and for being a part of this new dawn for our vineyard. Change has been a while in the making, but now is the time to move forward and to embrace all that the future holds. Particular thanks must go to my granny, Glenda Morton, who has been a part of the vineyard's success since the beginning, who supported my grandfather through their early days here and who never complained about hard work or Grandpa's inability to sit still for more than ten minutes.'

All heads turned to the corner where Granny was sitting, holding on to the handle of the pram, pushing it gently back and forth. She raised her free hand and nodded, then her face crumpled and she covered her eyes.

'Granny!'

Holly dashed across the barn and knelt in front of her grandmother, holding her tightly.

'I'm sorry. I didn't mean to make you cry.'

'It's all right, Holly. I'm just so proud of you and Bruce.'

Holly's dad had joined them, and he gave Granny a hug then turned back to the barn.

'I don't think there's much more to do now other than to have a good time! There's plenty of wine, plenty of food – the hog roast will be served in the yard at eight o'clock, with vegetarian and vegan options available – and plenty of dancing to be done. I hope you all enjoy yourselves; if you do, please spread the word about what we offer here – excuse the hard sell, but here I go: accommodation in the recently renovated stone cottages, the wine-tasting tours, the events we can cater for here in the barn, our lovely little shop and... well... just tell everyone how nice we are! All the information you need is on our wonderful website. Welcome to Greenacres!'

As applause spread through the crowd, Holly's heart was filled with love and hope. Everything was going to be okay.

–

Two hours later, her head was spinning from talking, dancing and wine. She'd only had one glass, but the excitement and emotion of the evening had sent it straight to her head.

Gelert was trying to snooze next to the pram, but failing, because every time someone came close, he'd sit up and watch their movements like a hawk. Holly had told Fran she wanted to adopt him, and Fran had been delighted. In fact, she'd said there was no way she could take him back now when he clearly loved his new family so much.

Holly exchanged numbers with a blogger she'd been speaking to about the cottages, then excused herself and went to her granny.

'Are you all right, Granny? Ready to mingle?'

'I'm having a ball right here, Holly. People keep coming over to me and bringing me drinks, and a gentleman from the bowls club brought me a pork and apple sauce roll from the hog roast.'

'Perhaps I should take Luke and Gelert back to the house now.'

'It's okay, my darling, you stay here. I'll go.'

Holly took in the excitement in her granny's eyes and the glow in her cheeks.

'Absolutely not! You stay here and party the night away.'

'If you insist.' Granny accepted a glass of wine from an elderly man in a white shirt and jeans held up with a pair of bottle-green braces.

'I do. You have fun.'

Holly took hold of Gelert's lead and lifted the brake on the pram, then made her way to the door. She had hoped to say her goodbyes to Fran and her dad, and Rich too, of course, but she couldn't see them through the bodies on the dance floor. She looked around the barn once more, at the happy faces, at the band on the stage playing lively country tunes, at her mum and grandpa smiling out at everyone from the far wall, then at her granny, who was now chatting to the man in braces and laughing like she was sixteen again.

Yes, it had been a successful night indeed, and hopefully the vineyard would reap the rewards over the coming months. It was just the beginning, and a very exciting one indeed.

She opened the barn door and stepped out, then unclipped Gelert's lead.

'Go and have a wee, Gelert!'

Her voice sounded loud now that they were away from the music and the chatter of their guests, and the evening air was cool and refreshing on her heated cheeks. She pushed the pram across the yard, keeping an eye on Gelert, then opened the gate to their garden.

'Holly!'

She looked up to see Lucinda hurrying towards her, waving both hands.

'Lucinda! Are you all right?'

'Yes, yes, sweetheart. I wanted to say goodnight to the little man, though, if that's okay.'

'Sorry, I did look for you all, but it's so busy in the barn.'

'What a fantastic night, though! You're certain to have plenty of positive publicity about the vineyard now.'

'I hope so.'

Lucinda leant towards the pram and peered inside.

'He's just waking up ready for a bottle and a cuddle.' Holly looked down at her son and her heart filled with love.

'I don't suppose...' Lucinda bit her bottom lip. 'Well... you could be over there socializing and building contacts...'

Holly put her out of her misery. 'Lucinda, are you offering to put your grandson to bed?'

'I am, but I don't mean to overstep the mark. I'd never want to be one of those pushy, interfering grandmothers who tell you what you're doing wrong and make you feel rubbish about yourself. Because you're an amazing mother and I think you're doing an amazing job.' She offered a shy smile, and Holly smiled back.

'Thank you, Lucinda. I missed your friendship, you know.'

'Holly, darling, I missed you too. I've been so afraid recently about saying or doing something else that would hurt you. I just want you to know that I have always seen you as part of my family.'

'I always felt like I was too. Until... Well, it's all in the past now.'

Lucinda smiled sadly. 'You know, my own mother-in-law was an absolute monster when I had Rich and Dean. She criticized everything and always had a better way of doing it. It made life very difficult at times, and of course, I always doubted myself. You know what Rex is like... a man of few words. He asked her quietly a few times to stop being so critical, but he never really stood up to her for fear of offending her. When Dean... when we lost him, I dreaded her finding a way of making it my fault, but surprisingly, she didn't. She was so devastated herself that she barely said a word about it to me. I suspect that losing her grandson probably contributed to her decline in many ways.'

'I'm sorry.'

'Don't you be sorry. You've nothing to apologize for.' Lucinda sighed. 'There is one thing I wanted to mention, though. Again, I don't want to overstep the mark here, but… you and Rich. Is there any chance that you might… you know… want to reconcile?'

A shout over by the barn caught Holly's attention, but it was just a reveller calling to a friend who'd wandered outside for some air. She watched as they wandered across the yard to see if there was any of the hog roast remaining.

'Oh Lucinda, that's something I can't answer at the moment. I mean… you know how much I loved Rich. I still do in many ways, but…'

'Say no more. It's only because I want to see you both happy. I know he loves you, Holly. He hasn't said a lot, but I see it in his eyes, in the way his expression softens when he speaks to you on the phone or replies to your texts. He's a good boy and he has a big heart. He's been much more open since he returned from Ibiza; he's come a long way. Between you and me, it's like I've finally got my son back. Please think about giving him a chance if you still love him. You two could be so good together, especially now you have this little one.'

Holly hugged Lucinda, then checked on Luke again. He gazed up and smiled before blowing raspberries at her.

'Are you sure you're happy to look after him?' Holly wanted to return to the barn to help with the evening, but she would have been equally happy to feed her son and cuddle him then put him to bed. Those times were so precious and she loved being his mum. She was aware that Lucinda loved him too, however, and that having the time with him would mean a lot to her.

'Of course I am. And I'll watch this cutie pie too.' Lucinda patted Gelert's head and the dog wagged his tail.

Holly helped Lucinda get the pram inside, then stepped back into the evening. Dusk was falling and stars had appeared in the sky, twinkling against the pinky-purple streaks on the horizon. She let herself out of the garden and fastened the gate, then turned to cross the yard.

She froze when her eyes landed on him. Standing there with his hands in his pockets, watching her. Waiting for her. His eyes full of her.

'Rich.' His name drifted from her lips at the same moment as she realized that this was it. Tonight was different from all the other evenings since she'd come home.

Tonight, things would change for ever.

Chapter 21

'Are you going back inside?' Rich asked. They were standing so close they were almost touching.

'Into the barn?'

He nodded.

'I am. Your mum offered to give Luke his bottle and put him to bed.'

She smiled as she thought of how delighted Lucinda had been to get some time alone with her grandson.

'You'll have made her year.' Rich laughed. 'But poor Luke...'

'Why?'

'I bet she's singing him a lullaby.'

'What's wrong with that?'

'My mother can't sing.'

'Isn't she in the village choir?'

'Yup.'

'Oh...'

'I know. I think they put her at the back and try to drown her out.'

'No they don't!'

'Look... much as I'd love to discuss my mum all night, I really would like to talk to you.'

'About us?'

'Yes.'

'I'd like to talk to you too.'

'Shall we walk?'

She nodded.

They turned away from the barn, where music and laughter spilled out into the air through the open doors, and passed the hog roast, then made their way down the path that led to the vineyard. Rows of vines spread out before them, dark sentries heavy with grapes that would be ready for harvesting within weeks. The beautiful aromas of honey and fruit were abundant in the evening air, signalling the ripening of the fruit, and Holly's mouth watered at the familiar scent.

They strolled side by side, not talking, not discussing their destination. But when they reached the far end of the second field, they turned and headed for the big old oak tree in the far corner.

'Here okay?' Rich asked, finally breaking the silence.

Holly nodded.

They sat down, leaning against the wide trunk, and gazed up towards the house. Dusk had fallen now and the full moon cast a silvery glow over the land, highlighting the lumps and bumps and peaks and troughs of the vineyard.

The windows of Greenacres glowed with light, warm and inviting. The house had seen love and laughter, tears and pain. But it was still there, solid and enduring. It had been there long before Holly was born, long before Grandpa was born, and would be there long after they had all gone. There was comfort in that fact, even as there was sadness, because she hoped it would absorb something from all of them, and in that way they would continue through time, never completely ceasing to exist.

'It's magnificent, isn't it?' She glanced at Rich. 'I love this place so much.'

'Me too, Holly.'

He touched the back of her hand and she turned it over so that he could hold it. His hand was warm, his long fingers easily cradling hers. Her breathing quickened at his touch, at his proximity and at what she felt for him. Love welled in her heart.

'What are we going to do, Rich? I thought I knew what I wanted, or at least what I should do, but I'm not certain it's the right path to take.'

He turned to face her and held her with his dark eyes. In the moonlight she could see his expression clearly, read the emotion in the depths of his gaze.

'I need to tell you something, Holly. It's something I've only ever told three people: a counsellor in Ibiza, and my parents, and I only told them everything this past week. It was just too awful to share and I feared what people would think of me if I did, but now... now I know that I need to share it with you, because otherwise you'll never fully understand why I was such an idiot for so long.'

She waited, not wanting to interrupt him in case he changed his mind.

He turned her hand over and traced the forefinger of his free hand around her palm then along each finger in turn. It made goose bumps rise on her arms and her nape and instantly relaxed her. Rich's caress had always had such a dramatic effect on her, able to send her into a state of utter relaxation or high arousal.

'That day when Dean and I went swimming... when it all went wrong... I blamed myself for his death.'

'How could it have been your fault?' Holly couldn't help jumping in, because she couldn't bear for Rich to blame himself. 'It was an accident.'

'I can accept that now, but I didn't then, or for a long time afterwards. I spent my teenage years and my twenties blaming myself for his death. He was younger than me—'

'By just a year!'

He shook his head. 'I took my responsibility as his older brother very seriously. I suggested we go swimming that day even though I knew there was a risk of the water being too cold, and you know what Dean was like...'

'He always wanted to be with you. I remember from school and from when we were kids. He followed you everywhere from the minute he could walk. Rich, you were a good brother to him and he loved you so much.'

He covered his face with his hands. 'And that is why I felt... feel... so bad that I didn't save him. If only I hadn't decided to go out in the water that day. If only we'd taken a different route. If only I'd been a stronger swimmer, I could have saved him.'

'How, Rich? The inquest found that the rip current was so strong that a grown man − even an Olympic swimmer − would've struggled. Add to that the cold and—'

'I survived.'

'By chance. By pulling yourself back into the boat.'

She reached out and put a hand on his shoulder, desperate to comfort him. She knew that he had carried an enormous burden of pain and guilt... no wonder he'd been weighed down.

'Rich, you can't let this dominate your life any more.'

He looked up. 'I know. That's what I've wanted to tell you since you came back, but it was so hard to explain. My inability to share, to confess how guilty I felt made me look inward and hate myself. How could I love you and give you all of me when I was so full of self-loathing?'

She shook her head, unable to speak now because of the ache in her chest. Her eyes were burning with tears and she felt so fragile that a feather could snap her in two. It wasn't just Rich wanting to live in the past, to avoid growing up, but a fear of doing so. He had feared letting go.

'The water was so cold when we dived in off the dinghy, and Dean went into shock. I tried to help him, but he gulped down loads of water and panicked. I told him to stop... to relax and float, but he couldn't hear me. Then we got caught in the swell and he was dragged away from me. I managed to grab the rope on the dinghy and pull myself in, but he was carried away so quickly. Holly, I saw the fear in his eyes and I swear I'll carry it with me until the day I die.'

A tear escaped and ran down his cheek, catching the moonlight and leaving a trail that glowed on his skin. Holly wiped it gently away and moved closer to him.

'You said that speaking to the counsellor helped?'

He sniffed, then nodded.

'It did. Until then, I'd been a ticking time bomb. I drank, I partied hard and did everything I could to avoid actually thinking about Dean and what had happened. That's why I wasn't able to commit to you, to open up to you, and why I never gave you what you deserved. And believe me, I did know deep down that you deserved far more. But I also thought that if I pushed you away, you'd find someone better than me. And yet you were so kind, so loving, and I did find comfort in being with you because you're an amazing person. The most amazing person I've ever met.'

Now the tears in Holly's eyes brimmed over and she leant her head on his shoulder, holding on to his arm as if she'd drift away if she didn't ground herself. He lifted his arm and wrapped it around her shoulders, pulling her closer, their mutual need binding them together.

'I think I knew all along that something was holding you back. You were wounded, damaged, and I recognized that because so was I. Losing my mum when I did, when I needed her, broke my heart, but I found comfort in you too.'

'I've said it before, Hols, but I'm saying it again now… I love you and I am so sorry for hurting you. It was unforgivable.' He took a deep breath. 'I felt that you needed a rock, someone to protect you, to love you, and I tried to be that person, but then my demons would take hold and I'd struggle to be the man I thought you deserved. It was then that I felt most guilty, that my dark thoughts were too powerful to fight. Drinking to excess, behaving recklessly helped me to forget. But it always came back.'

'You need to deal with pain and guilt like that or you'll never be able to enjoy life.'

'That's exactly what the counsellor said. In Ibiza, I was able to find myself, to free myself by speaking to someone who didn't know me and who I knew wouldn't judge me. When I was younger, I baulked at the idea of counselling, thinking it was for the weak, but it did me so much good. The counsellor made me dig deep and see that I had to stop running away from my feelings. I faced up to my pain, poured out my guilt and self-hatred, and then… I began the healing process. Perhaps I wouldn't have been able to work through it before that point in my life and it all had to come to a head as it did. But it took me coming home and seeing you again, being with you and with Luke, to fully heal.'

'You're so brave.'

He gave a wry laugh. 'Brave?'

'Not everyone can do what you did. And I see that you've changed.'

'Telling my mum and dad was so hard. I was worried they'd judge me, because when it happened… I didn't tell them everything. I was afraid to tell them that I believed it was my fault in case they did too, and it ate me up inside. But now they know the full story and they don't blame me at all.'

'I bet they said you were just a boy and that it wasn't your fault.'

'Spot on. They confessed to blaming themselves for being so busy with the bakery and not stopping us going out that day. Mum said she thought she'd been too lenient with us, but then Penhallow Sands has always been such a safe place. We've never had any trouble here and Dean and I could swim almost before we could walk. We knew the rules about going out in the dinghy, and yet we didn't follow them that day. One day changed everything.'

'That's how life works.'

'But now, Holly… I've been able to deal with my past and to accept that I was a child. It's difficult to let go of the guilt, but when I'm with you and Luke, I feel I can do it.'

'It really wasn't your fault.'

'But treating you as I did was. Last summer, after we'd agreed to buy the cottage, then I backed out, that was my fault.'

Pain lurched through Holly's chest and she held him tighter.

'It hurt so much, Rich. I'd thought we were finally ready to make a proper commitment.'

'I would take it back in an instant if I could.'

'I know that now.'

And she did. Because she could finally fully understand what had been holding him back all that time, why he'd felt he couldn't commit. How could he have explained it all to her then if he didn't understand it himself? He'd been lost in his grief and his guilt for such a long time, but now he'd come back from it and for that she was so grateful.

'It was the twenty-year anniversary that pushed me over the edge. I couldn't believe that Dean had been gone that long. There I was, about to commit to the woman I loved, and I realized that he would never have that. He'd never have a girlfriend or boyfriend, never fall in love, never buy a home of his own, never get married, never have children. It snapped something inside me and I couldn't come to the solicitor's office to sign the documents. It was as though making the purchase official would show me for the hard-hearted bastard I thought I was, living my life while Dean couldn't live his, so instead of letting you know, I ran. Then you found me at the cottage and I said such awful things… things that weren't true about not loving you enough.'

'I can't pretend that it didn't hurt me, Rich, but I understand now why you did run.'

'Holly… I need you to know something else.'

She met his eyes and he took a deep breath.

'I have always loved you, but I was afraid something would go wrong and the universe would take you from me too.' His eyes widened. 'Until you came back, I hadn't really understood myself fully. The words had been in my mind as a concept, but they'd been so hazy, hard to pin down. Being with you has helped me to form them into coherent thoughts.'

He leant back and met her gaze, and she could see his distress in the depths of his eyes and etched upon his face. She had never loved him more.

'Rich… what do you want now? I can't take the risk of trusting you with my heart again if you can't give me what I need. Our son needs stability and so do I. If you feel any hesitation or suspect that your guilt will rear its head again and send you running, then please be honest. For Luke's sake.'

He shook his head, then cupped her chin with his hands.

'I can't promise that I won't be sad sometimes. I can't promise that I won't struggle with myself at times, that the darkness won't shadow some of my days. I loved Dean and I'll always be sad that he's not around, living his life and making Mum and Dad proud. But what I can promise is that I know how to deal with my emotions now. I know that burying my pain is self-destructive, and I won't ever do that again. I want to be the best dad to Luke that I can be, and if you want to be with me, I promise I'll be the best version of me that I can offer to you. I swear to you, Holly Dryden, that if you give me another chance, you won't regret it. I'll spend the rest of my days doing everything within my power to make you happy.'

She sighed with relief as the fear she'd been carrying around finally released her and drifted away.

'I want that too, Rich.'

'May I kiss you now?'

'Please do.'

She slid her arms around his neck and he pulled her closer. His kisses were gentle at first, his mouth soft and coaxing, but soon they grew more passionate, and the pain, sadness and confusion of the past year fell away.

Then they lay down together under the oak tree, and Rich showed Holly exactly how much he loved her, and she knew that this time it was for keeps.

Epilogue

Holly unlocked the barn doors and pushed them open to let the warm July air in. The scent of wood and lavender greeted her, and she smiled as she walked inside and flicked the light switch. Even though it was a beautiful bright morning, the large barn could be dark without electric lighting. She walked around the space, checking that every table had one of Fran's candle holders at the centre, then she dropped a vanilla-scented votive candle into each. The barn had been reserved for a fortieth birthday party that evening, so there was a lot to do.

Four weeks had passed since the grand opening at Greenacres, and things were going better than Holly could have hoped. The vineyard shop was thriving, with Fran's latest landscape paintings in such high demand due to their appearance on the website that she had orders for more taking her right up to Christmas. Her pottery was also selling well, her range of goblets and olive bowls proving particularly popular. Holly was enjoying seeing her friend on a daily basis; they had certainly made up for lost time and were closer than ever. They had even signed up to an Open University course in web design together, starting in the autumn. Holly was so busy at the vineyard that she didn't want to attempt to take too many courses at once, but this was a start. She might go on to further studies once Luke was a bit older, but for now she wanted to learn more about how to make the website the best it could be.

The vineyard itself was running three wine-tasting tours a week, and they were planning to take on more staff to get them through the summer months – not just pickers this year, but people who could help with the tours too. Holly was still running the website and the blog, and Rich helped her out in the evenings and at weekends. The rental cottages were booked up until the following spring, and Holly's idea of advertising them as writing retreats had led to one local best-selling author booking the barn for a week in the autumn to hold writing workshops there.

Bruce was walking around with a smile on his face and a spring in his step, and Holly was delighted to see him so happy. Janine had come to dinner every Sunday since the barn dance; it was clear that they were very fond of each other. Lucinda and Rex also joined them on Sundays, and it was wonderful to see how everyone doted on Luke. Holly's heart was full of joy because her little boy had so many people to love him.

As for Rich, he'd been at Holly's side since the night of the grand opening – except for when he had to go to work. They'd talked a lot more about what had happened to Dean and how it had affected Rich, and although it was hard to go over it all again, it also helped them both find a place where they could accept and move on. Dean would never be forgotten and he would always be a part of Rich's life, but Rich no longer blamed himself.

Holly had told Rich that she loved what he'd done to Plum Tree Cottage and thought that it could be a potential future home for them, but for now, she wanted to stay at Greenacres. Bruce was busy with the vineyard and Janine, and Holly wanted to spend as much time with her granny as possible. She still wished she had been there to see her grandpa before he passed away, and she didn't want to make the same mistake with Granny. So rather than Holly and Luke moving to Plum Tree Cottage, Rich had moved into Greenacres, and it was all working rather well. He had slotted back in as a member of the family, and he was so attentive and loving that Holly didn't want for anything. They had put Plum Tree Cottage on the rental market, and within two days, Rich had received a phone call to say that he had a potential tenant: a single man in his thirties who was looking for a quiet location to rent for six months to a year. His references had checked out and he was taking up the tenancy in August.

Holly walked to the rear of the barn and looked up at the photograph of her mum and grandpa. They might be gone, but they would never be forgotten. Their legacy lived on and she felt certain that somehow they were watching over Greenacres and would be happy to see how well things were going.

A noise behind her startled her, and she turned to see Gelert in the doorway wagging his tail. He dropped a tennis ball on the floor and Holly smiled.

'It's that time is it, Gelert?'

He barked, then picked up the ball and ran out to the yard. Holly followed him, knowing that he wanted to play.

She'd thrown the ball around eight times, and Gelert had chased it and brought it back to her, expecting a repeat performance, when Rich called to her from the garden.

'Holly, there's a cold drink here for you.'

'Come on, Gelert, let's have a drink and cool down a bit.'

She walked back up to the garden and let Gelert in through the gate. He ran straight to his water bowl by the back door. Holly accepted a glass of lemonade from Rich and pressed it to her hot cheeks in turn.

'He'd play fetch all day if I had the energy.'

'He certainly would.'

'Where's Luke?'

'In the lounge with Glenda. They've got the fan on and she's reading him a story.'

'He'll have a wonderful vocabulary by the time he's one at this rate.' Holly giggled.

'Your granny loves spending time with him.'

'I know. That's why we had to stay here. Every day as a family is precious.'

Rich took her glass from her and placed it on the table, then opened his arms and she stepped into his embrace.

'I would be happy living anywhere with you, Holly.'

She gazed into his warm brown eyes and smiled. Theirs had been a difficult journey, but they had come through it stronger than ever.

'I love you, Rich.'

'I love you too.'

He kissed her gently, then took her hand and they walked into the house at Greenacres together, happy to be home.

Acknowledgements

My thanks go to:

My husband and children, for your love and support.

My three dogs for keeping me company as I write, edit and write some more.

My warm and wonderful agent, Amanda Preston at LBA, for your support and advice.

The fabulous team at Canelo, in particular my lovely editor Laura McCallen, for helping me to work through the issues in the first draft of this story to make it much stronger, as well as for patiently answering my many questions. Also, special thanks to the real Fran for letting me borrow your name.

Bob Lindo at Camel Valley in Cornwall, for answering my questions about running a vineyard, even when you were in the middle of pressing grapes.

The supporters of Greyhound Rescue Wales for helping me to choose a name for the scruffy little lurcher pup.

My author and blogger friends: thank you for cheer-leading, offering advice and for being there.

The readers who come back for more and who take the time to write reviews and share the book love.

Cornish Hearts

The House at Greenacres
The Cottage at Plum Tree Bay
The Christmas Tea Shop at Rosewood